"I thought…
I thought he had killed you."

Her voice shook with delayed reaction and he heard it with some surprise.

"I am not so easy to kill, my sweet." He hesitated. "Would it have grieved you, then, if he had?"

"Of course it would."

"Gold would buy you another protector."

"I don't want another protector."

Anwyn swayed toward him. Then his mouth was on hers. He felt her arms slide around his neck, her body pressing against his. And then she was kissing him back. His heart seemed to skip several beats. The kiss grew deeper, more intimate. Desire flared.

* * *

The Viking's Touch
Harlequin® Historical #1082—March 2012

Author Note

The birth of Wulfgar at the conclusion to *The Viking's Defiant Bride* not only rounded off the story, but left it on a note of optimism for the future. It also offered the possibility of a sequel. Twenty-seven years after the events in that book, England was a different place. The Danelaw had been established in the north and Alfred had defeated the great Viking leader, Guthrum. However, other Viking raiders still harried the coasts of England and Europe. Among the most notorious was Rollo. He was clever as well as daring, and seemed to be an ideal candidate for a projected partnership with my hero. Of course events don't play out as Wulfgar expects, because on his way to join the pirate force, a storm blows his ship off course. The need for urgent repairs causes him and his men to put in at an apparently deserted bay on the coast of East Anglia. That in turn sets off a chain of unforeseen events and life-changing decisions.

Having lived in Norfolk as a student many years ago, I am familiar with East Anglia. A fascinating area, with a rich and diverse history, it certainly repays exploration. It is also scenically attractive, with gentle green countryside and the huge skies that have proved an inspiration to so many painters. The coast has its own attractions. The big resorts like Great Yarmouth and Hunstanton draw thousands of visitors every year. I have always preferred the more remote, less populated areas, with their rolling dunes, sandy bays and huge expanses of gray-green water. I have drawn on those experiences in this book. When one stands on the edge of the dunes and looks out across the North Sea it isn't hard to visualize a striped sail on the horizon.

the VIKING'S TOUCH

JOANNA FULFORD

Harlequin®

TORONTO NEW YORK LONDON
AMSTERDAM PARIS SYDNEY HAMBURG
STOCKHOLM ATHENS TOKYO MILAN MADRID
PRAGUE WARSAW BUDAPEST AUCKLAND

Recycling programs
for this product may
not exist in your area.

ISBN-13: 978-0-373-29682-8

THE VIKING'S TOUCH

Copyright © 2011 by Joanna Fulford

First North American Publication 2012

JOANNA FULFORD

is a compulsive scribbler, with a passion for literature and history, both of which she has studied to postgraduate level. Other countries and cultures have always exerted a fascination, and she has traveled widely, living and working abroad for many years. However, her roots are in England, and are now firmly established in the Peak District, where she lives with her husband, Brian. When not pressing a hot keyboard she likes to be out on the hills, either walking or on horseback. However, these days equestrian activity is confined to sedate hacking rather than riding at high speed toward solid obstacles.

Novels from JOANNA FULFORD
available in ebook format

The Viking's Defiant Bride #934
The Viking's Touch #1082

In loving memory of Pam Barnard

Prologue

Northumbria—AD 889

Tongues of flames from the roof leaped thirty feet into the night sky and the heat grew so intense that it forced the spectators back. Grim-faced, they watched helplessly as the hall was consumed, beam and rafter and shingle backlit in a blaze of scarlet and orange. Acrid smoke oozed from the timbered walls and poured from the doorway, thickening the eerie glow. No one spoke. The only sounds were of crackling wood and the roar of the fire.

Wulfgar stood unmoving, like a man petrified by fell enchantment, and looked upon the destruction of the place he had once called home, the pyre of those he loved most. The light of the flames dyed his face blood-red and lent his gaze a terrible aspect. All the thoughts behind lay buried, overwhelmed by grief and anger too deep for utterance. His sword companions stood a little way off with the rest, watching in horrified silence from the edges of a vast darkness.

Time lost all meaning. Oblivious to fatigue and chill, Wulfgar remained there until grey dawn stole through the trees. Its pallid light revealed a black and smoking ruin. He did not notice the soft thud of hoof falls on turf or the creak of saddle leather as the rider dismounted. Only when the horseman stood beside him did he look round and, as one emerging from a long sleep, come slowly to consciousness.

The vivid blue gaze that met his might have been the mirror of his own. The face, lined now with age, also bore a striking resemblance to his. However, his father's hair was now more grey than dark. Similar in height to Wulfgar, he bore himself erect and his powerful frame carried yet its familiar aura of power. For the space of several heartbeats the two men surveyed each other in silence. Wulfgar was the first to look away.

'I should have been here,' he said.

Wulfrum shook his head. 'It would have changed nothing.'

'I failed them when they needed me most.'

'You could not have foreseen this.'

'She begged me not to go, but I paid no heed. Tried to convince myself it was for her and the child I was doing it.' Wulfgar's voice shook. 'It was my own selfishness that brought them to this.'

'You could not have saved them, any more than you could have saved all the others who died.'

'I could have tried.'

'Aye, but the result would likely have been the same. The fever makes no distinctions. It kills noble and base-born together.'

'That doesn't help.'

'No, only time will do that.'

'Will it?'

Wulfrum paused. 'What will you do now?'

'I don't know.'

'You could return to Ravenswood for a while.' The words were casually spoken, but underlain with something quite different. 'There will always be a place for you.'

'My place was here,' replied Wulfgar, 'but there is no going back.'

His father pursed his lips and looked away, past the ruin to the trees beyond. 'So, you will rejoin Guthrum then?'

'Guthrum grows old and his days of war are over. It's my belief he'll not live much longer.'

'What then?'

'I don't know. Something else.'

'You don't have to decide now. Take some time, think about it.'

'Ah, what was it you once said? "We are the decisions we make."' Wulfgar's lip curled in self-mockery. 'Well, mine are turned to ashes and I am to blame for that.' He turned to face his father. 'If there is any future for me now, it will not be found here.'

Chapter One

❦

East Anglia—Six years later

Wulfgar stood at the ship's prow, his keen gaze scanning the curve of yellow sand and the rolling dunes beyond, but the small bay was deserted save for the gulls riding currents of air. Heavy cloud scudded across a lowering sky, the remnant of the previous night's storm. The only sounds were the wind and the crash of the surf along the shore where churned sand and a line of bladderwrack and driftwood remained to testify to its passing.

'This will do well enough,' he said. 'We'll bring her in here.'

Beside him Hermund nodded. 'Where do you reckon here is?'

'The Anglian coast probably, although it's hard to be certain.'

'Well, it seems quiet enough, my lord.'

'All the same, we'll send out a party of men to check.'

'Right you are.'

Wulfgar gave the order and a few minutes later the ship's keel ploughed into sand. The crew shipped oars and Wulfgar, with half-a-dozen others, vaulted over the gunwale into the surf and waded ashore. They sprinted up the beach and climbed the dunes. Beyond lay an expanse of heath interspersed with rough turf and clumps of yellow gorse. In the distance were cultivated strips and stands of trees.

'It'll do,' said Wulfgar.

Hermund surveyed the surrounding landscape, his weathered face thoughtful, shrewd grey eyes missing nothing. At three and thirty he was six years older than his companion and a few strands of grey hair showed among the brown, but the quiet deference with which he treated the latter revealed their relative positions in the world.

'Aye, my lord. All the same those fields must belong to someone.'

'We'll post guards.'

'The local inhabitants may be friendly, of course.'

'Perhaps,' replied Wulfgar. 'Although I wasn't planning on staying around long enough to get acquainted. We have an appointment to keep.'

'Rollo won't quibble; he needs warriors and he wants the best.'

'He'll get them, and pay handsomely for the privilege.'

Hermund grinned. 'Naturally.'

They turned and led the way back to the ship where teams of men had already begun to drag her higher up the beach.

'We've done all right in the last six years,' Hermund continued. 'If luck stays with us, we'll be able to retire soon on the proceeds.'

Wulfgar made no reply. His silence was not due to inattention; he had heard the words perfectly well and privately acknowledged their truth. He commanded a body of fighting men whose reputation went ahead of them: they could name their price in the full expectation of it being paid without argument. And luck had certainly been with them in that respect. Some even went so far as to say that their leader bore a charmed life for he emerged unscathed from every conflict. He had no fear of death; for a while he had actively sought it. Yet, perversely, death mocked him, often tantalisingly close in the heat of combat, but remaining always out of reach. He had resigned himself to it now, watching with cynical amusement as his wealth increased.

Unaware of his chief's thoughts, Hermund surveyed the damage to the ship. 'Torn sail, broken yard, cracked rudder... but we got off lightly, all things considered. Only three men hurt, too.'

'Aye, it could have been worse.'

'Several times back there I thought we were food for the fishes.'

'If we don't fix the damage, we soon will be,' said Wulfgar. 'Organise a work detail while I check on the injured.'

Moments later Hermund's voice rang out, 'Thrand! Beorn! Asulf! Get that sail down! Dag and Frodi, help them to free that yard! The rest of you over here...'

As they hastened to obey, the ship became a hive of activity. Wulfgar watched for a few moments, then went over to see the injured men. In the course of the storm one had fallen and concussed himself and a second had a deep and ragged gash along his arm, which was going to require stitching. The third had broken ribs. However, now that they were ashore the injuries could be treated more easily, and Wulfgar offered what reassurance he could.

Having done that, he rejoined the others. Several days' hard labour lay ahead, but he didn't mind it; hard labour meant forgetfulness, his mind focused on the present. Time dulled pain, but not memory. Only work could do that, for a while at least.

It was about an hour later when one of the lookouts recalled his attention. 'Riders approaching, my lord.'

Wulfgar looked up quickly, narrowing his eyes against the wind. He saw the strangers at once: six horsemen reined in on the edge of the bay some hundred yards distant. Their attention was clearly focused on the ship.

'Damn.'

The word was softly spoken, but Hermund caught it all the same. 'What do you want to do?'

'That depends on them. We'll wait and discover their intent. It may just be curiosity.'

'Perhaps.'

Wulfgar surveyed the newcomers. 'We're not looking for trouble. Tell the men to keep their weapons within reach, but no one's to use them without my say so.'

'Will do.' His companion glanced at the riders again. 'At least there are only six of them.'

'That we can see.'

'Point taken.'

The horsemen rode out on to the beach at an easy pace. Now they were closer Wulfgar could see that all of them were armed. However, their hands were conspicuously clear of their sword hilts. He noted it; if there really were only six, they weren't about to stir up trouble, particularly when they didn't know as yet whom they might be dealing with.

The riders halted a few yards clear of the nearest crew members. Their leader, a burly figure in his late thirties perhaps, leaned on the saddle pommel and looked around, stony-faced, impassive, cold eyes taking in the details. Sound died as the crew returned the attention. For several moments both groups weighed each other up.

'Part of somebody's war band or I miss my guess,' murmured Hermund.

Wulfgar nodded almost imperceptibly. 'My thought exactly. The question is, where are the others and how many?'

The leader of the horsemen broke the surrounding silence. 'Who is chief of this rabble crew?'

'That would be me.' Wulfgar strolled forwards. 'Was there something you wanted?'

The stranger's lip curled in a sneer. 'You're trespassing.'

'The shore belongs to no man,' replied Hermund.

'Not this bit of shore.'

'Unfortunately my ship was damaged in the storm last night,' explained Wulfgar. 'We need to carry out repairs.'

'Well, go and do them somewhere else. You're not wanted here, Viking.'

Wulfgar held his temper. 'The work will only take a few days. When it's complete we'll leave.'

'You'll go now if you know what's good for you. Lord Ingvar doesn't like intruders, especially not pirates.'

'That is unfortunate.'

'Unfortunate for you right enough.' He smiled nastily, an expression mirrored in the faces of his five companions.

'That remains to be seen.'

'So you're telling me you're not leaving?'

Wulfgar nodded. 'That's about the size of it.'

For a moment the other met and held his gaze. Then he shrugged and turned his horse's head. 'Don't say you weren't warned.'

With that the mounted group turned and cantered away.

'Nice,' said Hermund. 'I reckon we can expect another visit quite soon, and with reinforcements.'

'They could have been bluffing,' replied Thrand.

Hermund shook his head. 'Not a chance. He'd never have made the threat unless he knew he could back it up.'

'Hermund's right,' said Wulfgar.

Thrand grinned. 'Do we get ready for a fight then, my lord?'

'We do.'

The men around them exchanged anticipatory glances. Thrand's fist closed on the hilt of his dagger.

'I'll look forward to silencing Big Mouth myself.'

'Don't count your chickens,' said Hermund. 'We don't know how many friends Big Mouth has got yet.'

'Just so,' replied Wulfgar, 'which is why we need to be ready for them. Arm yourselves.'

Chapter Two

Anwyn held her mount to a steady walk, her gaze on the horizon where the grey sea formed a darker smudge against the sky. White caps chased across the bay and even from this distance she could hear the roar of surf along the strand. The breeze was cool and smelled of salt and damp earth, a reminder of last night's storm. Even so, it was good to be out of doors again. Good to have the choice.

'The clouds will soon be gone now, my lady.'

She glanced at her maid riding alongside her and smiled faintly. 'I hope so, Jodis.' Privately she wondered if the clouds were not gathering about them rather than dissipating. However, to have said so just then would have been to destroy her companion's cheerful mood.

The girl had accompanied her when, five years earlier, Anwyn had been sent by her father to wed Earl Torstein. In those dark days she had acted more as friend and confidante than personal maid. At twenty Jodis was much of an age with her mistress, too, though taller and more sturdily built. Now she gestured towards the older man and child who rode a little way ahead.

'Eyvind has taken well to horsemanship,' the maid observed.

'Yes, he has.'

'He used to be such a quiet child but he's gained more confidence since—' Jodis broke off and amended hastily, 'gained more confidence now.'

'It's all right. You can say it. He has gained confidence since his father died.' Anwyn's green eyes deepened with contained emotion. 'Of late he has really begun to come out of his shell.'

Jodis nodded. 'That he has.'

'Ina has played a large part in that. He is a good mentor for the child.' Anwyn smiled faintly. 'Eyvind looks up to him. These days almost every sentence starts with "Ina says…"'

'Aye, it does. I think if Ina told him to stand on his head in the midden, Eyvind would do it.'

'That he would. For all his gruff ways, Ina has been more of a father-figure than Torstein ever was.'

'You are both free now, my lady. Torstein cannot hurt you more.'

'*He* cannot.'

Jodis heard the inflection and understood at once. 'But Lord Ingvar could.'

'His reputation is well known.'

Jodis shuddered. 'And well earned, too, as we have proof.'

'No solid proof; he's too clever for that. The loss of livestock or the burning of a rick might easily be attributed to other causes.'

'That's a lot of unexplained mishaps.'

'Too many, and yet I dare not openly accuse him. In any case it is his men who carry out these deeds, not he himself. Thus he can pretend innocence. By keeping up the pressure he thinks that I'll give in eventually.'

'How does he dare to face you?'

'Pretence comes naturally to him. The man is a predator. One only needs to be in his company for ten minutes to know it.'

The maid looked up quickly. 'He has not taken liberties, my lady?'

'No, he's not that stupid. He hides cruelty behind a smooth manner and honeyed words. I will never deliver myself or my son into his clutches, nor my people, neither.'

'No-one could blame you for that. All the same, he grows more importunate.'

Anwyn sighed. 'Don't I know it?'

Lord Ingvar's face loomed large in her mind; with its almost aristocratic lines framed by pale gold hair some might have considered it handsome, but for the thin-lipped mouth and the slanting gold-brown eyes that reminded her of a hunting cat. A little above the average height, he also had the lean form of a cat. The words of their last conversation were etched on her memory…

'Think about it, Anwyn. Beranhold lands adjoin yours. What could be more practical or more sensible than to merge our two estates? My war band is strong. Put yourself under my protection.'

'I thank you, my lord, but I have protection enough.'

'Ah, yes. Torstein guarded you well, did he not? I don't blame him for that; I would do exactly the same.'

A sudden chill raised gooseflesh along her arms. 'I am quite sure of it.'

His voice grew softer, almost tender. 'Would you not prefer to let a man shoulder the burdens for you?'

'I can shoulder my own burdens well enough.'

'That you are courageous is not in doubt. However, widowhood is a sad condition and a lonely one, especially for so lovely a woman.' One hand reached out and lightly touched the edge of her braid. 'Do you not long for a man to share your bed again—especially a man who appreciates beauty and knows how to please a woman?'

Her gut tightened. 'I am not ready to marry again.'

'You say so now, but I know how to be patient.'

'Do not hold out hopes of me, my lord.'

'When I set my heart on something I use every means at my disposal to get it.'

Anwyn suppressed a shiver at the memory. 'I refused his suit long since,' she continued, 'yet barely a week goes by without his calls on some pretext or other.'

'He is much smitten.'

'Smitten with lands and wealth more like.'

Jodis shook her head. 'A woman alone is vulnerable. You won't be able to hold him off for ever, unless...'

'Unless what?'

'Unless you were to find another husband.'

'I have no desire to marry again.'

'If you do not, your father will choose for you.'

'He has already intimated as much,' replied Anwyn, 'or at least my brother did when last he visited. Torstein had barely been dead three months! Osric takes after Father in his determination to increase our family's wealth and holdings.'

'Both of them are determined, my lady, and they see you as the key to future success.'

'Another marriage for me; another step on the ladder to power for them. A wealthy northern earl, Osric said.' Anwyn grimaced. 'But I will not suffer them to make another match for me.'

'You will likely have no choice, my lady. Your father is powerful and ambitious.'

'He has furthered his ambitions at my expense already.'

'But you remain a desirable marital prize.'

'Maybe so, but the very thought of another marriage is repugnant to me.'

'I did not mean a husband like Earl Torstein,' Jodis replied, 'but a good man, a kind man even.'

'A man who is both good and kind? Now there's a thought.'

Before either of them could say more, the child's voice broke in. 'Mother, can we have a canter now?' He and his mentor had halted their mounts, waiting for her to draw level. The child's green eyes were eager, pleading. 'Ina says I can if you give your permission.'

Anwyn looked over his head at his companion. For all his fifty years the old warrior was still an upright figure whose sturdy frame spoke of compact strength. Grizzled locks and beard belied a shrewd mind and his dark eyes missed very little. He had besides an air of quiet authority. In the days after Torstein's death he had been an invaluable ally, one she had learned to trust.

'Very well, then, just as far as the dunes.' She paused. 'And be sure to take it steady.'

Needing no further encouragement, Eyvind turned the pony's head and clapped his heels to its sides. The sturdy little creature broke into a canter. Beside him, Ina reined back, checking his mount's longer stride to keep pace. Anwyn grinned and looked at Jodis.

'How about it?'

Moments later their horses were cantering after the others. It was perhaps four hundred yards to the dunes, but the swifter pace was exhilarating and Anwyn fought the temptation to let the horse out to a gallop. It felt so good to ride out again without constraint, to feel the wind in her face, to feel almost free.

When at length they pulled up she found herself laughing, her spirit lighter than it had been earlier. She leaned forwards and patted the horse's neck. Eyvind eyed her hopefully.

'Can we ride along the shore, Mother?'

She knew he was thinking of another canter along the strand, but she had not the heart to refuse. Besides, she had no mind to return just yet either. 'Why not?'

They rode single file through the dunes, letting the horses pick their way, and came at last to the bay beyond. Ina and Eyvind stopped abruptly.

'Mother, look!'

Anwyn followed the line of his pointing finger and stared in her turn, her startled gaze taking in the ship drawn up on the beach and before it the massed host of the crew. There had to be seventy of them at least.

'A warship,' said Ina.

Uneasiness replaced her earlier mood. 'But why would it put in here?'

'At a guess it's been damaged. See the sail spread out there?'

She nodded. 'That would certainly explain their presence.'

Looking more closely, she surveyed the crew. Though they were apparently giving their whole attention to the sail and yard that lay on the sand, she noted that all of them were armed with sword or axe and that shields and spears were within easy reach. She wasn't the only one to mark it.

'Professionals definitely,' said Ina.

'But apparently not aggressors,' she replied.

'No. *They're* coming now.' He nodded towards the force that had just appeared on the far side of the bay.

Anwyn frowned. 'Who on earth…?'

'Ingvar's war band, my lady.'

'Are you sure?'

'Quite sure. That's Grymar out in front.'

'But they have no business here. This bay adjoins my lands.'

'Which they must have crossed to reach it,' he replied.

'How dare he?'

'Even Grymar would not have presumed so far unless the action had been sanctioned by someone more powerful.'

'He takes his orders directly from Ingvar.'

'Just so, my lady.'

The implication was disturbing. Under Ina's stewardship her late husband's men patrolled and guarded Drakensburgh, and they had no need of help from Ingvar. The fact that he had taken it upon himself to send an armed force onto her land had ramifications she did not care for. It was as though he were already adopting the mantle of lord protector, a role she had no intention of granting him.

'This bodes ill,' she said.

Ina nodded. 'Where Grymar's concerned it never bodes anything else. That one would slit his grandmother's throat for the fun of it.'

'This must be a show of strength. He cannot seriously intend to fight.' She hesitated. 'Can he?'

'I have a gut feeling that's exactly what he does intend, my lady.'

Wulfgar watched the war band approaching, mentally estimating their number. His jaw tightened. There must be fifty of them. His own force was larger and he had every faith in their prowess, but any confrontation was likely to be bloody and expensive. However, since the ship was effectively crippled there was no real choice. He glanced at Hermund.

'Have the men fall in.'

'Aye, my lord.'

They formed up alongside him, waiting.

'Let them start it if they must,' said Wulfgar, 'but after they have make them regret it.'

The words were greeted with grim smiles as each man there eyed the advancing foe with shrewd, appraising eyes. Fists tightened on shield straps and sword hilts.

Anwyn felt a knot of apprehension form in her stomach. Even from a distance now there was no mistaking what was about to happen. She looked across at Ina.

'I will not have a blood bath on my land though a dozen Ingvars wished it.'

'What are you going to do?'

'Stop it, of course.'

'A laudable aim, my lady, but you will have noticed that together they number well over a hundred while we...'

'Yes, I know. However, this bay abuts onto my land, not theirs.'

'True, but I don't quite see...'

'We have right on our side, Ina.'

'Oh, well, naturally that makes all the difference.'

'Exactly.' Anwyn turned in the saddle. 'Jodis, stay here and look after Eyvind. Ina, come with me.'

With that she nudged her mount forward and cantered away across the sand. Ina stared after her in disbelief. Then, setting his jaw, he rode off in her wake.

Watching the oncoming force, Hermund frowned. 'Have we fetched up at a local rallying point by any chance?'

'Could be.' Wulfgar followed the line of his gaze. 'We do seem to have kicked a hornets' nest, don't we?'

'How in the name of the Nidhoggr could Big Mouth have this many friends?' muttered Thrand.

Beorn shook his head. 'Makes you wonder, doesn't it?'

Wulfgar made no reply, mentally estimating the distance between themselves and the advancing warriors. Seventy yards…fifty yards…forty. He watched as the line of their spears shifted from the vertical to the fore.

'Here we go,' muttered Hermund.

Beside him, Wulfgar drew his sword. 'All right, lads—'

He broke off, seeing a blur of movement from the corner of his eye. The blur became a galloping horse. Moments later the rider reined hard and the animal plunged to a halt between the two opposing forces. Almost simultaneously a woman's voice rang out.

'Stop this at once! All of you!'

The oncoming warriors stopped in their tracks. All eyes turned towards the speaker. Wulfgar mentally registered a slender figure in a deep blue gown. It was partly concealed by a grey mantle over which a thick red-gold braid flowed like a river of fire. Then she turned in his direction and for a moment he forgot to breathe.

'Thor's blood,' muttered Thrand.

Beorn stared. 'Am I really seeing what I think I'm seeing?'

'No, you're dreaming, Brother.'

'Don't wake me then, I beg.'

Wulfgar could understand the thinking, although clearly the woman before him was a living being and not a dream. Before he could pursue the thought she spoke again.

'There will be no bloodshed here!'

Hermund leaned on his spear and his craggy features split in a broad grin. 'Well, Frigg alone knows where we are, but it was worth coming just for this.'

Wulfgar's eyes gleamed and he relaxed the grip on his sword hilt. 'You never said a truer word, my friend.' Even as he answered his mind was buzzing. Who was she? Why had she intervened? What manner of woman would dare to come between two opposing war bands? Not only dare to come between, but do it in the expectation of being obeyed? His curiosity mounted.

Ignoring the collective attention focused on her, Anwyn turned to confront Grymar. 'What do you think you're doing?'

He jerked his head towards the ship's crew some twenty yards distant. 'My men and I were about to get rid of these scurvy intruders, my lady.'

'On whose orders?'

'Those of Lord Ingvar.'

'These are my lands,' she replied. 'Lord Ingvar has no jurisdiction here.'

Grymar reddened. 'He desires that we protect you, my lady.'

'That is most kind of him, but I have my own protection.' She gestured towards Ina. 'Your help is not required.'

'One old man? He couldn't defend an argument.'

'Put the matter to the test, oaf, and we'll see what I can defend,' growled Ina.

'I wouldn't take advantage.'

'You'd be foolish to try,' replied Anwyn, 'especially as there are forty more of my men waiting in the dunes yonder.'

A muscle spasmed Ina's cheek. However, Grymar missed it, darting a glance to the place she had indicated. The dunes were quiet, the only movement the wind in the marram grass. He regarded her suspiciously.

'There's no-one over there.'

Ina raised a grizzled brow. 'Are you calling my lady a liar?'

Grymar reddened further. 'I did not say so. I meant only that I cannot see anyone.'

'That's because they're hidden.'

'Be that as it may, what I *am* saying is that yonder riff-raff are trespassers.'

'So are you,' replied Ina, 'but if you and your men leave now we'll overlook it—this time.'

Grymar's glare was poisonous. 'Lord Ingvar isn't going to like this.'

'Dear me, how awful.'

Anwyn threw Ina a warning glance, knowing she could not afford to make an enemy of Ingvar. He was strong and potentially dangerous. Somehow he had to be kept on side while she made it clear that she would not tolerate this kind of interference in her affairs.

'Lord Ingvar has always been a good neighbour,' she replied. 'He would never have sanctioned such a violation as this.'

Ina nodded. 'You are right, my lady. It's my belief that Grymar has acted on his own initiative in an excess of zeal.'

She saw the chance and seized it. 'Yes, that must be it. His lordship will no doubt be greatly angered when he discovers what has happened.'

Grymar scowled. He knew enough about his master's ambitions to realise that he would not be pleased by the creation of an open rift with Lady Anwyn. Moreover, it looked now as if all the blame was shifting his way.

'If I have offended you, my lady, I am sorry for it.'

She favoured him with a haughty stare. 'You have indeed caused me offence. You will take your men and leave.'

He threw a last look of detestation at her escort and at the ship's crew, then turned his horse and barked an order to his men. Moments later the whole horde marched away up the beach. As she watched them depart, Anwyn let out the breath she had been holding.

'Good riddance.'

Ina grimaced. 'Good riddance indeed, as far as that goes.'

'They won't be back'

'No,' he replied, 'they won't, but *that lot* are still very much here.' He jerked his head towards the watching crewmen. 'And now we have their undivided attention.'

Chapter Three

Anwyn darted a glance at the silent warrior band and felt her heartbeat quicken. For a brief instant she wondered if she had not made a terrible mistake: visions of capture and slavery loomed large. Then resolution reasserted itself. She had come too far to back down now.

Turning her horse, she rode the last few yards towards them. They let her come. What she saw left her in no doubt that Ina was right: they were professionals, bearing themselves with the quiet confidence of men who have nothing to prove. Far from showing any expression of hostility, their faces revealed a very different range of emotions. These covered everything from rapt interest to amusement and frank enjoyment. For some reason it was far more disconcerting than warlike intent could ever have been. Anwyn lifted her chin and took a deep breath. Then, under the gauntlet of their eyes, she sought out the man who led them.

'Which one of you is chief here?'

From the van of their ranks a man stepped forward. 'I am.'

For the space of a few heartbeats they surveyed each other in silence. Her gaze took in a lithe and powerful figure clad in a mail shirt worn over leather tunic and breeches. One hand held a fine sword, companion no doubt to the dagger that hung from his belt, and on his left arm he carried a linden-wood shield embossed with iron. The upper part of his face was hidden by the guards of a helmet whose crest bore the likeness of a hunting wolf. Below it she could make out the strong lines of his jaw and mouth. Undisturbed by her scrutiny, he turned and handed the shield to one of his men. Then he removed the helmet and tossed that over, too. As he turned back again, Anwyn's breath caught in her throat. The face with its chiselled clean-shaven lines was striking for its good looks. A vivid blue gaze met and held hers. In it she saw the same light of amusement she had detected before in his men. Her chin lifted a little higher.

'Do you have a name?'

'Do you?' he replied.

'I asked first.'

His lips twitched. 'Lord Wulfgar, at your service.'

'I am Anwyn, Lady of Drakensburgh.'

'I beg you will forgive our trespass, my lady. My ship was damaged in the storm yester night and we sought a quiet haven in which to carry out repairs.'

'A quiet haven?' she replied. 'It has hardly been that.'

'No, but matters would have been much worse had you not intervened.' He paused. 'Why did you?'

'Because I would not have blood shed here for no good cause.'

'Your neighbours do not share that view.'

'They had no right to pronounce on the matter.' Anwyn met his gaze. 'Yet their suspicions were perhaps not without foundation.'

'We intend no harm if that is what you mean. We have business elsewhere and once our repairs are complete we will leave.'

'I see. May I ask whither you are bound?'

'We go to join Rollo.'

'Rollo? But he's a notorious pirate.'

'That's right.'

Anwyn paled a little. 'You are mercenaries then.'

'Correct.'

This frank admission was deeply disquieting, and rendered all the more so by her inability to read what lay behind that outwardly courteous manner.

'However,' he continued,' until we can repair our vessel all else is irrelevant.'

'I can see that.'

'Have we your permission to stay and do the necessary work?'

She took a deep breath. 'I think you have no choice since your ship cannot leave without it.'

'We could leave under oars,' he replied, 'but the next large wave we encountered would likely sink us.'

'How long will it take to mend the damage?'

'With luck, a few days only.'

Relief washed in. She nodded. 'Very well. Carry out your repairs if you will.'

'I thank you.' He paused. 'One thing more I would ask.'

'And that is?'

'The use of a forge if you have one—and a carpenter's workshop.'

'That's two things.'

He smiled. 'So it is. But then, as I am a mercenary, it cannot surprise you that I should try to secure the best possible bargain.'

His words drew a reluctant answering smile. Inwardly she wondered if she could trust him or whether this was some kind of trick. All the same, the only way to be free of the problem now was to help him.

'We have both things. Send some men to Drakensburgh tomorrow and we will show them where.' She pointed to the dunes. 'The way is yonder, due west about half a league distant.'

'Again, my thanks, lady.'

Anwyn nodded and turned her horse's head. Then, accompanied by Ina, she rode back to where Jodis and Eyvind were waiting. Wulfgar looked on in some surprise; he had been so preoccupied with events that he not noticed the presence of the other two figures at the edge of the beach. They were too far away for him to make out details, but again his curiosity stirred. Who were they? What was their connection with Lady Anwyn? He watched as they exchanged a few words and then all four rode away through the dunes.

'A mighty pretty woman,' said Hermund, when the last of the riders was gone from view. 'Courageous, too.'

'Aye, she is,' replied Wulfgar.

His companion chuckled softly. 'I thought that Grymar oaf was going to explode. I'd like to be a fly on the wall when he gets back.'

'So would I.'

'His master doesn't sound much better.'

'Ingvar?' said Wulfgar. 'No matter. We're not like to meet him anyway.'

'Small mercies, eh?'

'As you say.'

'Well, now that peace has broken out I guess we can get on with those repairs.'

Wulfgar nodded. Then, divesting himself of weapons and armour, he rejoined his men and set to. However, although his hands were busy, his mind returned to recent events and he smiled to himself. Hermund was right; the woman was courageous. He'd never met anyone quite like her. Anwyn. He wouldn't forget the name or the face, either. No man would. Yet it was the eyes he remembered most clearly; eyes as green as a summer sea and deep enough to drown in...

Unbidden, the memory returned of another pair of eyes, blue this time and bright with welling tears. The face was harder to recall now, though once it had occupied his every waking thought. Freya: golden-haired, gentle, quiet...her beauty had captivated the youth he had been. Captivated for a while, at least. In the final analysis he had been a poor husband to her.

No doubt Lady Anwyn's lord was smart enough to know what he had; a woman of fire with wit allied to beauty and courage. He caught himself then—where *was* her husband? If the lady had found it necessary to deal with the situation herself it argued that her man was away—fighting, no doubt. It was a common enough occurrence. Had he not done the same?

He sighed. It was too late for regret or remorse, though he had experienced both. *We are the decisions we make.* It was true, thought Wulfgar, which was why he found himself wandering the earth with a group of mercenaries: fighting, feasting, living for the day. It wasn't a bad life, take it all in all. Anyway, what else was there now? Eventually, of course, his luck would run out, or the gods would tire of him, and he would meet his end on some field of battle. So long as he died with a sword in his hand and could take his place in Odin's hall, the time and place of his demise mattered little. All that mattered was the readiness.

The afternoon's encounter had also left Anwyn much preoccupied and not a little concerned. It dominated her thoughts even after she had retired. By now Lord Ingvar would have heard the tale and would, no doubt, be greatly displeased. She could almost certainly expect another visit from him in the near future. As if that were not enough a force of trained mercenaries was presently encamped on her land, or as good as. Now that there was leisure to reflect, she wondered if her earlier decision had been the right one. She sighed. It was too late for that. If they chose to take advantage, she would be caught between a rock and a hard place. Yet their leader had not seemed treacherous to her. On the contrary.

Unbidden, his face returned in sharp relief. The memory was

disturbing. She had never met anyone quite like him; he bore all the trappings of the warrior, radiated an aura of strength, but she had not felt personally threatened. He did not make her feel as Ingvar did when in her company; as Torstein had made her feel. Indeed, when she had ridden away the sensation had been quite different, almost as though something had been lost. It was difficult to account for, difficult and perturbing. Unable to sleep, she crept from the bed and, wrapping herself in a mantle against the night air, went silently to the adjoining chamber where her son lay sleeping. For a long time she watched him. He was the one good thing to come from her marriage. His birth had been long and hard, but Eyvind made sense of all the rest; he was the reason she kept on living, the reason she submitted to Torstein's will.

Anwyn shivered and pulled her mantle closer. Torstein was dead. Her son was safe from him. She bent over the child and dropped a kiss on his forehead. He stirred a little, but did not wake. Looking at him lying there, she suddenly felt fiercely protective. As long as she had breath in her body no harm should come to him. She must look after his interests until he grew to manhood. Nothing else mattered now. It would not be easy; her family was ambitious and, as Jodis had said, a woman alone was vulnerable.

Returning to bed, Anwyn curled up, pulling the coverlet close. Tired now, she closed her eyes and let her body relax, pushing the day's events from her mind. Gradually the bed grew warmer and sleep eventually claimed her. However, it came with the same troubling dreams…

Somewhere she heard a door opening, heavy footsteps in the outer chamber, a hand drawing aside the partitioning curtain to reveal her husband's ursine figure silhouetted against the dim light beyond. At forty Torstein was more than twice her age. Though only of average height, his bulk reinforced the impression of bearlike strength. The dome of his head was bald, the remaining fringe of hair worn long and tightly braided into numerous thin plaits that hung past his shoulders like rats' tails. A moustache and bushy, grizzled beard concealed a thin mouth and hid the lower part of a heavily lined face from which small black eyes surveyed the world with quiet cunning. Now they came to rest on her and glinted.

Crossing the intervening space to the bed, he threw aside his cloak and, unfastening his belt, pulled off his tunic and tossed it after the mantle. His shirt followed, revealing the mat of crisp black hair that covered his torso. Anwyn stiffened, feeling the mattress sag beneath his weight. He unfastened his breeches and then reached for her. She tried to turn away, but strong hands dragged her back and a gust of fetid breath hit her in the face. Sickened, she turned her head aside.

'Torstein, it's late and I'm tired.'

'You'll do as you're bid.'

He fumbled for her linen kirtle and dragged it up around her waist so that her lower body was naked. Involuntarily she shuddered. As he leaned closer his hairy paunch scratched her belly, the beefy, leering face within inches of hers.

'I thought I'd schooled you in obedience,' he went on, 'but perhaps I was mistaken.'

She bit back the reply that she wanted to utter, knowing better. 'My lord, you are not mistaken.'

'No? Let's see, shall we?'

Anwyn woke with a start, panting, heart pounding, staring wide-eyed into the furthest corners of the room. Nothing moved. Her gaze came to rest on the bed. The place beside her was empty. She was alone. Slowly she let out a long breath as her mind assimilated the knowledge. Torstein was never coming back. As the minutes passed, horror was replaced by relief so intense it left her trembling. She swallowed hard and lowered herself onto the pillows again, waiting for her heartbeat to quiet a little. Torstein was never coming back. Now Ingvar waited, biding his time.

'Never,' she murmured. 'Not while I have breath.'

To think that once, long ago in another life, she had dreamed of being married, of having a man's love. She smiled wryly. How naïve she had been then to think that the two things went together. All such girlhood fantasies were long gone; if love between husband and wife existed in this world it was for others, not for her.

Chapter Four

The following morning Wulfgar left Hermund in charge of the ship and, accompanied by Thrand, Beorn and Asulf, set off for Drakensburgh. Built on a low hill and surrounded by a deep ditch and a high, spiked wooden pale, it wasn't hard to find.

'Balder's toenails! The place is a fortress,' said Thrand. 'Whoever lives here is a man of some importance.'

'Is this a good idea, my lord?' asked Beorn. 'It could be a trap.'

All three men looked at Wulfgar. He shook his head. 'I don't think so, but keep your wits about you all the same. Come on.'

They reached the wooden bridge that spanned the ditch and, when challenged, identified themselves. It seemed they were expected. There followed sounds of a bar being removed and then the small wicket gate swung open to admit them. From there they were escorted across a large compound in which stood various buildings. Wulfgar noted a barn, storehouses, workshops and small dwellings before at length they came to a large timbered hall. Fantastically carved pillars flanked the great oaken doors. However, the atmosphere within was more sombre. The only light came from the open portal and the hole in the roof above the rectangular hearth pit where the remains of a fire smouldered in a bed of ash. Through the gloom Wulfgar made out smoke-blackened timbers adorned with racks of antlers and wolf masks. Trestle tables and benches were stacked against the walls, but at the far end of the room on a raised platform was a huge oaken chair, carved with the likeness of birds and animals. The air smelled of smoke and ale and stale food.

'Wait here,' said the guard. With that he departed and left them alone. The four looked around.

'A gloomy lair,' muttered Asulf.

Thrand nodded. 'You said it. What manner of man lives here?'

'A powerful one. That chair looks more like a ruddy throne.'

'Let's hope its owner is as gracious as his lady.'

In the event it was Lady Anwyn who came to greet them a short time later. Wulfgar felt a pleasurable sense of recognition. She was accompanied by the old warrior he had seen before: Ina. With them was a young boy—the one on the pony, he assumed. Even if the facial likeness had not been apparent, the red-gold hair and green eyes would have proclaimed him her son. Just for a moment he was reminded of another child and another hall and his throat tightened. Forcing the memory from him, he watched his hostess approach.

When word was brought of the men's arrival Anwyn had wondered if Lord Wulfgar would be one of their number. Indeed, in some part of her mind she had hoped he might. Even so, seeing him there caused her pulse to quicken a little. Last time they met she had been on horseback. She had not realised just how tall he was.

'Good morning, my lady.'

Recollecting herself, she returned the greeting. 'You are come to use the forge.'

'The carpenter's shop, too, if you have no objection.'

'None,' she replied. 'What is it you require?'

'We're going to need a new yard, and there's a crack in the ship's rudder that needs reinforcing. If we can fashion a couple of steel plates, that should do the trick. We could also use some bolts.' He paused. 'Naturally we will pay a fair price for the wood and the iron.'

'Naturally.'

He thought he caught a gleam of something like amusement in her eyes, but it was so quickly gone he couldn't be certain. All the same it intrigued him. He saw that she was wearing a different gown today. The soft mauve colour suited her, enhancing the delicate pink and whiteness in her cheeks and providing a foil for that wonderful hair, confined in a neat braid. He tried to visualise what it looked like unbound, what it felt like to touch.

Aware of his scrutiny but unable to read his thoughts, Anwyn became unwontedly self-conscious and looked away. Mentally chiding herself, she took a deep breath. She was no green girl to be discomposed by a man's casual regard.

'I'll show you the forge,' she said.

Even as she spoke she knew there was not the least need for her to go with them; Ina could have done it. On the other hand they were visitors here and it was a courtesy. She averted her eyes from Wulfgar's. Courtesy had nothing to do with it. The truth was that she did not want to lose this man's company just yet.

They left the hall and set out across the compound. He fell into stride beside her, leaving the others to follow. Despite the decorous space between them every part of her being was aware of him, every part alive to his presence. He made her feel strangely self-conscious, and yet she could not have said why. It was not an unpleasant sensation exactly; rather it was unaccustomed.

For a moment or two neither of them spoke. Then Wulfgar glanced in the child's direction.

'Your son?'

'Yes. Eyvind.'

'A fine boy. His father must be proud of him.'

'His father is dead.'

'I'm sorry.' He paused. 'Recently?'

'Ten months ago.'

'It cannot be easy for a woman alone.'

'I manage well enough.'

'So I infer if yesterday is aught to judge by.'

Something in his tone brought a tinge of colour to her cheeks. Quickly she changed the subject.

'You are not from these parts, Lord Wulfgar.'

'No, I grew up in Northumbria.'

'You have kin there still?'

'Some.'

He didn't qualify that and Anwyn didn't pursue it. After all, it was none of her business.

'And now you live the life of an adventurer.'

'That's right.'

'It must be exciting.'

'It has its moments.'

Before she could reply they reached the forge. The smith looked up from his work and, seeing who it was, made his duty to her.

'My lady?' He glanced from her to her companions, surveying them with open curiosity.

Anwyn smiled. 'Ethelwald, we need your help…'

Having performed the introductions, she briefly outlined the situation. The smith listened attentively. 'It is not a hard task, but I have work on hand that must be completed first. I cannot begin anything new until the morrow.'

'And the job will take how long?' asked Wulfgar.

'A few days, no more,' the smith replied.

'We have other places to be. Can it not be done sooner?'

'No. I must honour the agreements made before you came.'

His men exchanged quizzical glances but, though Wulfgar noted it, he continued to eye the smith steadily.

'Fair enough,' he said. 'A man should keep his word. We'll wait.'

Ethelwald nodded. 'In that case I'll do what I can.'

They left him then and made their way across to the carpenter. Ceadda, too, had a task in hand but, on hearing that the newcomers required only tools and would do the work themselves, he readily agreed to let them use his premises.

'Good. I'll leave you men to talk, then.' Anwyn took hold of Eyvind's hand and then turned to go. Instead she encountered gentle resistance.

'Mother, can I stay and watch? I won't get in the way, I promise.'

Anwyn hesitated. Seeing it, Ina interjected. 'I'll keep an eye on him, my lady.' He glanced at their visitors. 'Make sure he comes to no harm.'

'All right.'

Eyvind's face lit with a smile. 'I promise I'll be good.'

She returned the smile and squeezed his shoulder gently. 'See that you are.'

For a brief moment she looked over his head and her gaze met Lord Wulfgar's. The blue eyes held a gleam of amusement.

'We'll all be good,' he said. 'I promise.'

Anwyn fought the urge to laugh. There was something about that deadpan expression which was both provoking and enigmatic. Unable to think of a suitable reply and all too conscious of that penetrating gaze, she decided that the wisest course lay in dignified retreat.

The men worked steadily, but it was a hot and arduous task. They were not at all sorry when, an hour or so later, a servant appeared with a jug of ale. Wulfgar acknowledged a moment of disappointment that Lady Anwyn had not brought it herself, but then mentally upbraided himself. Why should she? There must be a dozen tasks awaiting her attention within doors. She had kept her word and let them use the workshops; they had no further claim on her time.

The delay with the iron work was a nuisance, but there wasn't much to be done about that. Rollo would just have to wait. If he didn't like it, that was too bad. No doubt they'd make up for lost time with a series of successful raids later. Not that they lacked for wealth. Previous expeditions had proved lucrative enough. *We could retire soon...* Hermund had been right about that. Retirement from adventuring meant putting down roots again, staying in one place. Wulfgar smiled in self-mockery. It wasn't going to happen. He was already seven and twenty, long past the time when he might have remarried. Not that he had ever felt the least inclination to do so. In any case, a mercenary's life was not suited to such responsibilities. His choices now did not hurt innocents. The decisions he made invariably carried a degree of danger but, in the long run, they were likely to benefit his crew. They knew the risks and accepted them. Grown men were not vulnerable in the same ways as women and children, a lesson he had learned too late.

He was drawn from his thoughts by the sensation of being watched. Looking up, he met the child's eyes. Immediately the boy looked away. Wulfgar smiled, but said nothing. Although the lad was curious, he was also shy. Nothing would be gained by trying to force his confidence. How old was he? Four? Five, perhaps? Too young to have started military training yet, at all events. If he lived so long. Life was precarious, especially for the young. Had that not been clearly demonstrated to him?

'You've got a ship, haven't you?'

As the boy's voice recalled him, Wulfgar took a deep breath. 'That's right. She's called the *Sea Wolf.*'

'What's wrong with her?'

'She was damaged in a storm. Her sail and rudder need mending.'

Eyvind listened attentively. 'Is she fast?'

'Very. A warship needs to be.'

'Have you been in lots of battles?'

'Quite a few.'

'Were you scared?'

'Sometimes.'

'Did you kill people?'

'Aye, when they tried to kill me.'

Eyvind nodded slowly. Then he looked past Wulfgar and smiled. His companion turned and, with pleasurable surprise, saw Lady Anwyn standing there.

'I've brought you more ale,' she said, 'and a platter of bread and meat. You must be hungry by now.'

As soon as he saw the food Wulfgar realised he was. His men must be feeling the same. 'Thank you. It is most welcome.'

She set the platter and jug down on a bench and then held out a hand to Eyvind. 'Come.'

He tucked his hand in hers and then looked back at his erstwhile companion. 'Can I come and see your ship?'

'If you wish,' he replied. 'But first you had better ask your mother.'

Eyvind looked up her. 'May I? Please?'

Anwyn hesitated. These men were strangers and, though they had shown no ill intent, she did not know how far they were to be trusted.

Her anxiety did not pass unnoticed. Wulfgar met and held her gaze. 'Perhaps you would like to come too, my lady?' The blue gaze held a distinct gleam. 'With as many of your escort as you wish to bring.'

Rosy warmth bloomed in her cheeks. 'I don't know.'

'What don't you know?' he asked.

'We've barely met and, well, I…'

'You suspect I might hold the boy to ransom, or carry you off, perhaps?' He surveyed her keenly and the gleam intensified. 'Now that I come to think of it, the notion is most pleasing.'

'Pleasing? To whom?'

'To me, certainly.'

'So that you could sell me for a profit later?'

'Oh, I wouldn't sell you,' he replied and was gratified to see her blush deepen. 'However, the situation doesn't arise since I am not in a position to do any such thing. You are therefore quite safe.'

Safe was not the word she would have chosen just then. Nor was she entirely sure how much of what he said had been spoken entirely in jest. The expression in his eyes was sufficient to bring back all her former self-consciousness.

Seeing her indecision, he smiled faintly. 'Should I not receive the benefit of the doubt?'

Anwyn was silent, trying to order her scattered thoughts. He was an avowed mercenary, a pirate. She had known him less than a day. How far could she trust him? Eyvind looked up at her anxiously.

'Please, Mother?'

'I think you're outvoted,' said Wulfgar.

She threw up her hands in a gesture of surrender. 'All right. I give in.'

Eyvind jumped up and down with glee. 'Can we go now?'

'Why not?' replied Wulfgar. 'No time like the present.'

In spite of his suggestion that she might bring a large escort, Anwyn contented herself with Ina and half-a-dozen others. As the ship couldn't go anywhere it seemed unlikely that Wulfgar would do anything untoward. They rode back to the bay, she having lent him a horse for the purpose. When they arrived it was to the sound of hammering and banging. Men swarmed all over the deck and the sand where the striped sail was still spread above the tide line. Eyvind took it all in wide-eyed.

Beside him, Anwyn quietly surveyed the vessel's sleek lines. Built for speed and manoeuvrability, she would descend on an enemy like a hawk on its prey. Resistance would be swiftly

overcome. Her crew were hunters, too, like the man who led
them, the stranger beside her now. The knowledge sent a *frisson* down her spine.

'A fine ship,' she observed.

'Would you care to take a closer look?' he asked.

Eyvind regarded him eagerly. 'Can I go on board?'

'Of course.'

The child looked at his mother, waiting.

'You may go.' She looked at Ina. 'Stay with him.'

The old warrior dismounted and lifted the boy down in his
turn. Wulfgar summoned Hermund.

'Go on ahead and show our guests around.'

'Delighted, I'm sure.' Hermund gestured towards the vessel
and the three of them set off.

Wulfgar turned to Anwyn. 'My lady?'

Seeing little other choice now, Anwyn dismounted. He followed suit and once again she was forcefully reminded how
powerful he was, in every sense of the word. It did little for
her equanimity. Neither did that unfathomable blue gaze.

'Shall we?' He glanced towards the ship.

She inclined her head and they set off together, he shorten-
ing his stride to match hers. Although he made no move to
touch her, his closeness set her skin tingling. Yet what she
felt was not fear. It was a strange mixture of anticipation and
excitement.

'How old is Eyvind?' he asked.

'Five now.'

'It must have been hard for him to lose his father.'

'He has Ina.'

It wasn't what he expected to hear, and the words elicited a
swift sideways glance. However, her attention was apparently
on the three in front.

'A woman alone is vulnerable, too,' he said.

'I have protection.'

'A dozen men?'

'There are plenty more.'

His eyes gleamed. 'Ah, yes, I had forgotten—forty more—hiding in the dunes.'

It drew a rueful smile. 'All right, I fibbed about that part, but there really are more than a dozen men.'

'I'm glad to hear it, given the warlike nature of your neighbours.'

'Grymar was presumptuous.'

'You are charitable.'

'I cannot afford to be at odds with his master.'

'That would be Lord Ingvar?'

'Yes.'

'Is he so powerful, then?'

'Powerful enough to make me want to keep the peace.'

She had spoken matter of factly, but he heard the seriousness beneath and understood it. However, she did not elaborate further.

Anwyn's attention was claimed now by the ship. It was an arresting sight. She guessed the vessel to be roughly seventy feet long and perhaps fifteen or sixteen feet wide. Clinker built, her strakes were formed of solid oak planks fastened with tree nails and iron bolts and caulked with a cord of plaited animal hair. Anwyn's gaze moved on, taking in the wooden planks that comprised the deck; the tall mast; the rowers' benches and wooden storage lockers; the circular rowlocks in the main strake and the great oars—sixteen to a side. However, it was the magnificent prow that seized her imagination; a piece of oak intricately carved in the likeness of a snarling wolf.

'She's beautiful.'

'She's not the largest vessel afloat, but she's swift enough and handles well.'

'How long have you had her?'

'Three years or so. We captured her as a prize of war.'

'Oh.' Looking at that carved prow again, Anwyn was forcefully reminded of the company in which she found herself. 'You must have taken many prizes over the years.'

'Enough,' he replied.

The word was casually spoken, but it sent another tremor through her. In their way these men were every bit as dangerous as Ingvar's war band. Though she said nothing, he sensed her unease.

'What are you afraid of, Anwyn?'

The use of her name brought the warm blood to her cheeks, but she could detect nothing in his manner that suggested over-familiarity. On the contrary, it had sounded natural on his lips.

'I...nothing.'

'Something, I think.' The tone was quiet, inviting confidence. Her confusion mounted.

'I hardly know myself. Perhaps it is because I have never been so close to a warship before.'

'Then let us allay your fear.' He ran lightly up the gangplank that had been erected to allow easier access from the sand. Then he turned back to face her. 'Come.'

The word was both invitation and command. Anwyn took a deep breath and followed. Around them the smell of brine mingled with rope and wood and tar, and the air rang with the sound of male voices, punctuated at intervals by laughter.

Having reached the top of the gangplank, she checked a little, mentally negotiating the step down on to the rowing bench and thence to the deck. Wulfgar saw the hesitation.

'Allow me.'

Strong hands closed round her waist. There followed a brief sensation of absolute weightlessness before she was set down beside him. Just for a moment she breathed the scent of wool from his tunic and beneath it the musky scent of the man. It was unexpectedly arousing, like the warmth of his hands through her clothing.

'Welcome aboard the *Sea Wolf*,' he said.

In the name of self-preservation she took a step away, but

had forgotten the now angled deck and stumbled. A strong arm caught her by the waist and prevented her from falling.

'Oh, I…er, thank you.' Her heart was thumping so hard she was sure he must hear it.

If he was aware of any awkwardness, it was not apparent. 'Take care. I would not have you break an ankle.'

'Yes. No.' Her face reddened. 'I mean I will take care.'

Gently she disengaged herself from his hold and was relieved when he made no attempt to stop her. Rather he spoke about the ship, pointing out various aspects of her design as they went. Anwyn relaxed a little. In front of them she could hear Hermund patiently answering Eyvind's questions. Wulfgar surveyed the pair for a moment.

'The boy has an enquiring mind.'

'Enough for half-a-dozen children.' She smiled fondly at her son. 'He has really come out of his shell.'

'He was not always so forthcoming?'

'No.' She hesitated. 'His father was overly strict with him. It made the child shy and fearful.'

He thought he detected anger beneath the quiet tone and was suddenly curious. 'Some firmness is essential, but a child should not be afraid of its father.'

'My late husband was not a patient man.'

'I see.'

Anwyn had no wish to talk about Torstein. He was a part of her life she wished to forget. Accordingly she changed the subject.

'Do you have sons, my lord?'

He should have been expecting that, but it caught him unawares. 'No.'

'A wife?'

'No.'

He did not elaborate and something about those succinct replies forbade further inquiry. Perhaps the life of a mercenary was incompatible with domestic ties. Such men

took their pleasure where they found it. She shivered a little.
Had he ever taken a woman by force? Almost immediately she
rejected the idea—a man like this would never have a problem
getting women to share his bed. Her experience was limited,
of course, but she guessed that most would not object. That
thought led to others, unexpected and disquieting. Quickly she
looked away lest he should read her face.

'We have trespassed on your time too long, my lord. We
should go.'

'I think it is we who trespass,' he replied. 'All the same I
cannot regret that we did.'

Anwyn smiled. 'Nor does my son.'

'And you, my lady?'

'No, of course not.'

They reached the gangplank and he stepped up ahead of her,
offering his hand once more. Strong fingers closed over hers.
The touch sent a charge along her flesh. When they gained the
beach once more she called to Ina and Eyvind. They rejoined
her and the whole group walked back to the horses. Anwyn
half-expected that Wulfgar would take his leave of them then
and remain. However, it seemed that was not his intention.

'I must find out how work is progressing on the yard,' he
said.

Anwyn nodded. 'Of course. We have kept you away too
long already.'

'It was a pleasant interruption.'

'I am sure that Eyvind will talk of nothing else for days.'

They remounted and rode slowly back to the homestead.
The tension that Anwyn had felt earlier was missing now and
she felt a little ashamed of her suspicions. *You suspect...I might
carry you off?* The idea should have been abhorrent. Pirates
took slaves to sell them on. *I wouldn't sell you.* The implications of those words should have been abhorrent, too, but the
thoughts they engendered were rather different. The realisation sent a flush of warmth through her entire being. Mentally

giving herself a shake, she reflected that Lord Wulfgar had been amusing himself at her expense. Moreover, if he had intended harm he would have done it already. In spite of his avowed profession there was much about him that did not seem to fit the conventional image of a mercenary. It was something of a mystery, like the man himself.

Chapter Five

Her buoyant mood lasted until they reached the pale and she saw the horses waiting outside the hall. Recognising them, her heart sank.

'Ingvar,' she murmured.

She and her companions scarcely had time to dismount before half-a-dozen men emerged from the hall with Lord Ingvar at their head. For a moment he surveyed the little scene and then hurried forwards to meet her.

'Lady Anwyn. I came as soon as I could.'

'Is something wrong, my lord?'

It seemed to throw him for a moment, but he was quick to recover. 'I refer to what happened yesterday. I can only apologise.'

'Grymar has already done so.'

'It is meet he should. He is fully aware of my displeasure.'

Anwyn had no doubt of that. 'I knew he had exceeded his authority.'

'It is deeply to be regretted.' Ingvar paused. 'Of course he meant well. He knows how much care I have for your safety.'

'I was never in danger, my lord.'

'He did not know that at the time. When he saw a warship and her crew he feared the worst.'

'His fears were quite unfounded. The ship was damaged and put in for repairs. When they are completed it will leave.'

His eyes narrowed a little. 'You have given permission for this?'

'That is correct.'

'Was that wise, my lady?'

'I should not have done it if I had thought otherwise.'

'No, of course not.' He paused. 'All the same...'

Wulfgar spoke up. 'Lady Anwyn has nothing to fear from me, or my men.'

Ingvar looked beyond Anwyn's shoulder, apparently noticing him for the first time. There followed a tense and silent mutual appraisal.

'Do I infer, then, that the ship is yours?' asked Ingvar.

'You do.'

Anwyn interjected quickly. 'This is Lord Wulfgar. He and his men are my guests for a few days.'

'Indeed?'

'As you can see, my lord, there is not the least occasion for alarm,' she continued.

'I am relieved to hear it. You know the depth of my concern for you.'

'Yes, I believe I do.'

Ingvar turned to her companion. 'I hope you will forgive the unfortunate incident of yesterday, Lord Wulfgar.'

'No harm was done, my lord.'

'My men were overzealous,' Ingvar continued, 'but that is because they know the extent of my regard for the lady.' He possessed himself of her hand and pressed it to his lips.

A muscle twitched in Wulfgar's jaw. 'Perhaps you should exert tighter control over your men.'

'As I hope you will do over yours.'

'*My* men are not in the habit of interfering where they have no business.' Wulfgar turned to Anwyn. 'Now I beg you will excuse me, my lady. There are matters requiring my attention.'

'Ah, yes,' said Ingvar. 'I'm sure you want to be on your way as soon as possible.'

'We'll leave when we're ready, my lord.'

'Be sure to let me know if there's anything I can do to help you achieve that state.'

Wulfgar met his gaze and held it. 'When I need your help I'll certainly ask for it.' With that he bowed to Anwyn and walked away.

For a moment or two Ingvar watched him go. 'I shall take my leave, too, my lady. I would not wish to impose on your time.' He summoned his escort and remounted his horse. Having done so, he reined in beside her. 'When I return, I shall expect to find Lord Wulfgar gone.'

The subject of their conversation had reached the carpenter's shop as Wulfgar rejoined the other three.

'Everything all right, my lord?' asked Thrand.

Wulfgar nodded. 'Well enough.'

'Are we right in thinking that was Lord Ingvar?'

'You are.'

'What did *he* want?'

'To speed us on our way.'

The three men regarded him incredulously for a moment, then Asulf snorted.

'I'd like to see him try.'

'Maybe he will,' said Thrand.

'There's always hope, eh?'

It elicited a laugh from the rest. Then they turned their attention back to the task in hand. As he worked, Wulfgar let his mind return to that recent encounter. He had learned early to read men and Ingvar presented no difficulty, nor did his ambitions with regard to Anwyn. A woman alone was exposed, especially one who was wealthy and beautiful. It was none of his business, of course. In a day or two he and his men would be on their way. All the same, he had no intention of being hurried towards departure, by Ingvar or anyone else.

Anwyn paced the floor of the bower, her face pale with anger as she recounted to Jodis the details of Lord Ingvar's visit.

'Insufferable man! Who does he think he is?'

'He grows more confident, my lady.'

'He has no right to be confident of me. Drakensburgh is mine now, and I will say who is welcome here and who is not.'

'Perhaps it is as well our visitors do not stay long,' said Jodis. 'All the same, I fear their departure.'

Anwyn sighed and sank down on to a chair. 'So do I.'

She did not want to think about what might happen when their restraining presence was gone. Lord Wulfgar's face drifted into her mind. He, too, unsettled her, but the feelings his company gave rise to could not have been more different. She had known him only a day, but she knew she would never forget him. In that moment she envied him: how would it be to board a ship and sail away from Drakensburgh and never come back? How often she had dreamed of it in times past. Torstein would never so much as permit her to speak with a stranger, never mind go near a ship.

Once she had been naïve enough to think she might escape, to summon the courage to ask for a divorce. It was not uncommon and nor was it a difficult process to arrange. A woman might part from her husband and take her children with her, along with the goods and dowry she had brought to the marriage. That was the usual way of things. However, it hadn't taken her long to realise that her husband would never agree to such a proceeding. The only other alternative would have been to run away but, even had it been practicable, Torstein would have hunted her to the ends of the earth and then exacted a dire retribution.

Perhaps he guessed her thought for escape had been well-nigh impossible. Her freedom was limited to the confines of the pale. On the rare occasions that she was permitted to travel beyond, it was always in his presence and with an armed escort. Though they looked their fill, his men did not address her unless it was absolutely necessary and then only in the briefest and most respectful of terms. It was more than their lives were worth to do other. For the rest, human contact was limited to the women servants. She was, effectively, a prisoner. Anwyn sighed. In many ways she still was. Had it not been for Ina, life would have been much more difficult.

Their friendship had been formed in her first winter at Drakensburgh when he had fallen ill with the ague. By dint of careful nursing and the right medicine he had recovered well. It was a kindness he had not forgotten. In the days immediately following Torstein's death he had been an invaluable aide in helping to establish her authority among the men. Ina had made it quite clear that she had his full support and their respect for him compelled them to listen. Whatever doubts they might have entertained, they did not voice them aloud. However, she was in a precarious position and she knew it. Common sense dictated that the sensible course was to remarry, but to wed a man like Ingvar would be to leap from the cooking pot into the fire.

Revisiting that embarrassing encounter just now, she wondered what Lord Wulfgar had thought. It shouldn't have mattered, but it did. Ingvar's possessive anger had been thinly veiled. That in turn roused her own, as though she were somehow wrong-footed. Having reached peaceful agreement with the visiting force, it was infuriating to have her decision questioned like that, and by one who had no right to pronounce on the matter. Now she felt a need to put things straight again. Leaving Eyvind with Jodis, she left the bower and made for the workshop. She had no idea of what she was going to say when she got there, only knew that some form of words were necessary.

* * *

The sound of sawing and hammering drowned out her foot-steps and for a little while he was unaware of her presence but, on turning to retrieve an adze, looked up and saw her there. His men exchanged knowing glances. Wulfgar paused, his face impassive. Had it been any other woman he might also have wondered at her motive for seeking him out again and, had the case stood as it so often had in the past, he would have followed up the invitation. What red-blooded man would not? However, she was as unlike those others as strong mead was to water. There was nothing remotely flirtatious in her manner; she made no attempt to attract or beguile. Moreover, she seemed to have no idea how successful a stratagem that was, unless of course she played a deeper game. Either way it was intriguing. Leaving his companions, he crossed the workshop to meet her.

'My lady?'

'I must speak with you, my lord.' She hesitated. 'Privately.'

He inclined his head in acquiescence. 'As you wish.'

When they had walked sufficiently far to be out of earshot she turned to face him. He surveyed her speculatively, waiting, his curiosity thoroughly roused.

Anwyn drew a deep breath. 'I wanted to apologise for what happened earlier.'

'Why?' he asked. 'It wasn't your fault.'

'Ingvar should not have spoken as he did.'

'Seemingly he misread the situation.'

'I believe he did.'

Wulfgar eyed her coolly. 'There is an understanding between the two of you?'

'No, nothing like that. At least not on my part.'

'Certainly on his, I would say.'

'That is as may be, but I have given him no reason for encouragement.'

Wulfgar raised an eyebrow. 'Then he takes much upon himself.'

'You saw what happened in the bay.'

'Why do you tell me these things?'

'In truth I don't know, except that I didn't want you to think…'

'What?' he pursued.

'That Ingvar spoke with any tacit support from me.'

'I am honoured by your confidence, my lady, but I don't quite see how all this concerns me.'

A rosy flush crept into her cheeks. 'Forgive me, I did not mean to involve you in my affairs. I merely wished to…to explain.'

He regarded her steadily for a moment. 'You know, of course, that a man like Ingvar will not give up easily?'

'Yes, I know.'

'A widow's life must be lonely. He is strong and could protect you. Perhaps you should consider his offer.'

'Lonely or not, I will never give Ingvar a husband's authority over me.'

The words, spoken with quiet vehemence, elicited a quizzical look. 'Do you object so strongly to a husband's authority, then?'

'I would object to any authority that is based on tyranny. Ingvar is of that kind, and I will never put myself or my son in his power. Nor will I have the people here subjected to the tender mercies of Grymar and his men.'

'I can understand why you might not wish to. However, such men tend to take what they want.'

'He will not take Drakensburgh. I have already given him my reply and I stand by it.'

Wulfgar met her eye and held it. 'When it comes to the crunch, words have no power. Only swords and superior numbers will stop men like Ingvar.'

Anwyn pondered over that conversation later and privately acknowledged the truth of it. That led to other, more worrying thoughts. After her husband's death some of the men had chosen to move on. Their departure left roughly thirty; not enough to stop Ingvar if he decided on the use of strength to achieve his aim. It seemed she was not alone in the thought.

'If only Drakensburgh had a larger force of men under arms,' said Jodis later when the two of them were alone in the women's bower.

'It would make us independent of Grymar and men like him,' replied Anwyn.

The maid laid aside the distaff on which she had been winding wool. Although her expression was hesitant, it was clear she had something to impart.

'What is it, Jodis?'

'Forgive me, my lady, but it seems to me that you have the means to do that now.'

Anwyn stared at her. Then understanding dawned. 'You refer to Lord Wulfgar and his men.'

'Aye, my lady. With their numbers added to ours…'

'We would be safe?'

'Would we not?'

'Perhaps. There's just one difficulty attaching to all this.'

'What is that, my lady?'

'They would never agree to stay.'

'They might…if they were paid enough.'

Anwyn shook her head. 'It's a crazy idea.'

'Maybe so, but it's also a perfect solution to the problem.' Jodis paused. 'Lord Ingvar would be out of your life for good.'

'If only it were so simple.'

'I don't understand.'

'He would not give up so easily,' replied Anwyn.

'He might have no choice if the odds were too great.'

'It might take a long time to convince him of that. Meanwhile, the services of seasoned warriors do not come cheaply.'

'No, but Earl Torstein was rich.'

For a moment Anwyn said nothing, turning over the possibilities in her mind. What her companion said was true; her late husband had gold, though she had never enquired exactly how much. In marrying her he took a wealthy bride, for her dowry had been considerable. To the best of her knowledge the greater part yet remained. It should be more than enough on its own.

'The money could likely be found,' she said, 'but hiring such men brings its own risk.'

'How do you mean, my lady?'

'We do not know if Lord Wulfgar is to be trusted.'

'Has he done anything to make you think he cannot?'

'No, but it is not in his interest to cause trouble here. Drakensburgh is a means to an end for him.'

'So it could be again, but this time for gold—a business arrangement.'

'A business arrangement that would give him great power.'

The maid regarded her sympathetically. 'I understand why you hesitate, my lady, but all men cannot be judged by Earl Torstein's standards, or Lord Ingvar's, either.'

'It may be so. I wouldn't know.' Anwyn sighed. 'However, what's past cannot be amended. I am free of the brute my father chained me to, and I will not exchange him for another.'

Jodis looked hurt. 'My lady, if I thought Lord Wulfgar such another I would never have suggested this idea.'

'I am sure you meant well. It matters not in any case; he'd never agree to such a scheme. He's an adventurer, a man who values his freedom. He'd never saddle himself with this.'

'No, perhaps not.' Jodis sighed and retrieved the distaff, carefully winding on more wool. 'It was just an idea.'

They lapsed into silence after this but, although she tried to dismiss it, Anwyn found that the idea persisted. What if she *were* to hire the services of the mercenary force? How long would they be prepared to remain? More to the point, how long would she be able to pay them? Long enough for Ingvar to give up hope and find another rich wife instead? Or at least to give up hope of Drakensburgh? That would be a desperate gamble. Torstein had been wealthy, but the gold was not inexhaustible. The *Sea Wolf*'s crew would indeed command large sums for their services.

And then there was Lord Wulfgar. He disturbed her more than she cared to admit, though she could not have said precisely why. In him were depths she could not sound. The man was a mass of contradictions. Something about him suggested danger, but not in any familiar sense of the word. His manner was direct and assured but, despite the predatory nickname, it was not that of an obvious aggressor. At the same time she knew instinctively that it would be a serious error to cross him. Only a fool would do that, and then only once. If he agreed to help her, she certainly wouldn't make that mistake. She had no wish to earn his enmity. Besides, if she hired his services he would take orders from her. She smiled in self-mockery. It was ridiculous to let her mind range so far ahead. Only a fool would imagine that such a man would involve himself in the affairs of a woman. And only a coward would avoid sounding him out.

Chapter Six

He heard her out in silence, his face impassive. She had not known what to expect for he was skilled at hiding his thoughts; but at least she was spared any appearance of scorn. Somehow her voice remained level as she outlined the proposal, giving no indication of the thumping heart within her breast. No indication either of how keenly this invited proximity disturbed her equilibrium. Nothing in his manner suggested that this interview was having the least effect on him; he seemed to take it in his stride, like everything else he did.

They were standing in the hall, ordinarily a place she avoided whenever possible for its old associations with Torstein. Yet somehow the presence of this stranger drove the shadows back; he dominated the space and made it his own. While he was there she felt no desire to leave. Besides, as the heart of Drakensburgh, the hall seemed a fit setting for this conversation. She had ordered that the fire be remade, and the warm light did much to lift the gloom from the atmosphere. All the same, it could not dispel her inner trepidation. Would he even consider this scheme?

When at length she finished speaking he said nothing for a moment, only continued to regard her steadily. Her heart sank.

He was going to refuse and now sought a means of letting her down gently.

'Such a decision is not mine to make alone,' he said. 'I would need to put the idea to my men.'

As swiftly as it had sunk her heart leapt. He was not turning this down out of hand. The sudden expression of hope in her eyes had not gone unnoticed.

'I told you that we were on our way to join Rollo before the storm delayed us.'

'Yes.'

'Such an alliance promises to be lucrative.'

'I realise that.'

'Then you will also realise that my crew would need to be sure the reward was sufficient to justify this change of plan,' he continued. 'That would be expensive.'

'I know, but I am not without the means to pay for the services that Drakensburgh needs.'

'They won't consider it for less than ten gold pieces per man.'

Anwyn blinked. It was going to come to an eye-watering total, but worth the cost if it achieved her aim.

'Very well.'

He nodded slowly. 'You also need to understand what it means to start something like this. Ingvar won't bow out gracefully. Things are likely to get unpleasant.'

'I understand that, too.'

'Do you?' The blue gaze locked with hers. 'I wonder.'

'I know what Ingvar is.'

'Good, because I can assure you that all pretence of neighbourliness is going to vanish as though it had never been.'

'I have no wish to play the role of aggressor. What I want is a trained force that will be strong enough to act as a deterrent against aggression.'

'A comfortable ideal,' he replied.

'You think it won't work.'

'I didn't say that, but there's a real risk that such a force would be tested at least once before the enemy understood its strength and backed off.'

'Bloodshed must be a last resort.'

'Of course. Even so, the affair will likely be protracted.'

'That is a chance I am prepared to take.'

'But I am not.'

Her heart sank again. 'Not?'

'The extent of my commitment here would be to train up a force sufficient to the task of protecting Drakensburgh. It might extend to leaving a few of my men here to oversee things, if they were willing to stay.'

'They would be well paid.'

'They would need to be.' He paused. 'Then there is the matter of your late husband's men.'

'What about them?'

'If I stay, they will take their orders from me.'

For a moment Anwyn was silent. 'They may resent that.'

'Nevertheless, that's how it will be. Without a force united under one commander there is no hope of prevailing against the likes of Ingvar and his henchman.' He paused. 'This point is not negotiable.'

Her brow wrinkled a little. To consent to this condition would effectively put Drakensburgh in his power. However, she needed his help and to get it she would have to trust him. 'If I agree to this, I want to be informed of your plans before you carry them out.'

'You have that right.'

'Very well, then—it is agreed. You will command both forces.' She regarded him steadily. 'Ina is greatly respected among the men here. If you would win them over, first begin with him.'

'I shall heed your advice, my lady.'

The sober tone was at distinct variance with the glint in his eye and she wondered now if he were gently mocking her.

'Does it irk you that a woman should offer advice?'

'By no means,' he replied, 'when the advice is good.'

The blue gaze was now closely focused on her face. Her heart thumped harder. Forcing herself to an outward expression of calm, she returned the look, hoping he could not read her confused thoughts just then. He already had too dangerous an advantage.

'Will you speak to your men, then, my lord?'

'I'll speak to them, but I cannot promise that they'll agree.'

'But you are their chief, are you not?'

'Aye, but decisions like this are reached by consensus.'

Privately she owned to surprise. Most commanders did not consult in that way. It gave another insight into his mind and confirmed the thought that he was unlike anyone she had ever met. Her experience in these matters was not great, but she knew that men remained loyal to leaders they respected, and such respect had to be earned. He had not won his reputation for nothing. Once again she had the sense of hidden danger, but it remained undefined.

'I will speak to them later,' he continued. 'When I know their mind I will tell you.'

He left her then and for some time she remained where she was, deep in thought. Were her instincts correct? Could she trust him? Or was she making an error that would cost her dear in every sense of the word?

Wulfgar waited until after the evening meal before broaching the subject with his crew. They had built a fire of driftwood to keep off the evening chill, sitting around it and swapping tales over a cup of ale. They listened attentively while he outlined Anwyn's proposal, though many faces registered surprise. Others registered more knowing looks.

'Well, I can see your reasoning, my lord,' said a wag from the crowd. 'The lady *is* fair.'

'Fair game?' asked another.

That drew guffaws of laughter. Wulfgar smiled wryly. 'The lady is fair,' he agreed, 'and game enough as we have seen, though no game for you, Dag.'

More laughter followed this.

Dag looked mournful. 'The story of my life.'

'Got designs on her yourself, my lord?' asked Thrand.

'It would do me no good if I had,' said Wulfgar. 'The lady is proof against my charms.'

Several ribald comments followed this, chiefly concerning the nature of his charms, but he bore it good-humouredly. When they saw he was proof against their baiting they left off.

'What about Rollo?' asked Beorn.

'We can still join him when the repairs are complete, if you so decide,' replied Wulfgar, 'or we can meet him later.'

'He may not take kindly to the delay, my lord.'

'Rollo's emotions don't enter into it. Our alliance with him was discussed because it would be to our mutual advantage. The day it isn't, the agreement ceases to exist. In the meantime, if we choose to earn ourselves some extra gold, it's none of his affair.'

Murmurs of agreement greeted this.

'How much gold exactly?' asked Beorn.

'Ten pieces for each man, plus food and board, of course.'

They digested this in thoughtful silence. Then Hermund spoke up.

'Why not? One more job makes no odds. Rollo will still be there afterwards, won't he?'

'That's right,' said Thrand. 'Besides, this shouldn't be too hard.'

Hermund met his eye. 'Don't underestimate the enemy. Ingvar's force is not small, as we've seen.'

'Maybe not, but we're more than a match for them. Besides, I'm looking forward to meeting Grymar Big Mouth again. Then we can talk about trespassing.'

His companions muttered agreement. Wulfgar surveyed them keenly.

'All right, let's come to an accord. All those in favour of remaining here a while, raise your hands...'

It was a unanimous vote in favour of remaining. He wasn't surprised. As a business decision it made sense. Such a sum was more than most men would see in a lifetime. All the same, he felt a certain ambivalence about it, which had nothing to do with the nature of the task or with the reward they would receive. It was concerned with his own motives for agreeing to put the scheme to his men in the first place. This was a private matter and therefore none of his affair. So why had he allowed himself to be drawn in?

Recalling the recent jibes from his men, he began to wonder. Surely it wasn't just on account of a beautiful woman, though Anwyn was certainly that. In truth, she was a lot more than that; she was the kind of woman who was capable of making a man forget everything else. When he'd been with her earlier he had schooled his face for fear she should glimpse the thoughts behind. He knew that she was lonely. It was an emotion he recognised, and indeed she had admitted as much. Might she not be willing to take comfort where it was offered, as he had on other occasions, and without any fear of suffering a husband's tyranny? If he'd seen any sign of mutual interest... However, she had given no such sign. Neither would she. Theirs was purely a business arrangement. He smiled wryly. She was probably right; anything else would lead only to the kind of complications that neither of them needed.

The following day he and a dozen men returned to Drakensburgh. Telling them to wait outside, Wulfgar went to the hall and sent a servant to find Anwyn. As the woman hurried off, he looked about him. Though the hall was unchanged in essentials the fire had been lit again and, from the sweeter smell, he thought that new straw had been spread upon the floor. It was a considerable improvement. He let his gaze roam past the fire to the dais and the carved chair that surmounted it. Recalling Asulf's words, Wulfgar smiled to himself. It might not be a throne, but it was a statement of power. What manner of man had its former owner been? Anwyn had said little about her late husband, and those details he had gleaned from their conversations gave him to think that the relationship had not been happy. Perhaps that accounted for her reticence.

The sound of light footsteps carried on the quiet air, and he turned to see the subject of his thoughts. At once everything else went out of his head. Watching her now, he took in the details. The colour of her gown reminded him of forest leaves in summer, a shade that became her exceeding well. Unbidden his imagination removed it to dwell on the shapely form beneath. The result was a surge of warmth in the region of his loins. He drew a deep breath and forced his thoughts into less dangerous channels.

When the courtesies had been observed he came straight to the point. Anwyn listened in a silence that was concerned with surprise and relief and trepidation. Surprise and relief that his men had agreed to stay, but trepidation on account of what she was doing. Something of this showed in her face.

'It's not too late to change your mind,' he said.

'I do not intend to change my mind.'

'Be very sure, Anwyn, because once this begins there will be no going back.'

'I know.'

'Then we have an agreement.'

Her heart thumped, but she met his eye unflinchingly. 'Yes.'

'Very well.'

'What happens now?'

'What happens now is that my men and I move into Drakensburgh.' He smiled faintly. 'However, first I shall heed your advice and speak to Ina.'

'I'll have someone fetch him.' She would have turned aside, but his hand closed round her arm, preventing it.

'Presently. First there is something we must discuss.'

Anwyn remained quite still, trying to ignore his physical proximity and the warmth of his hand through her sleeve. 'My lord?'

'It may be that we shall not agree on every point in the days to come.' He continued, 'but I will keep my undertaking to tell you what is on my mind. In return I want yours that any disagreements will be discussed in private.'

'A united front?'

'Just so.'

She nodded. 'As you will.'

'Good.'

She would have disengaged herself then, but he retained his hold. 'One more thing: I shall expect my men to be well lodged and fed, but while we are here I shall answer for their conduct.'

'The women of Drakensburgh are safe, then.'

The blue eyes glinted. 'If they wish to be.'

The tone was ambiguous; the implication wasn't. Pink colour deepened in her cheeks, a circumstance that did nothing to diminish his admiration or, at that moment, his enjoyment.

'I'm sure they'll be relieved to know,' she replied. 'In the meantime, perhaps you'd like to speak with Ina.'

This time he made no attempt to prevent her going, though in truth he would have liked to. Instead he stood looking on as she crossed the room to the far doorway to summon one of the servants. There followed a few murmured words that he did not catch and then the sound of departing footsteps.

Anwyn took a deep breath, willing herself to composure again. It wasn't so easy when she could still feel the pressure of his hand on her arm; it hadn't hurt, but its strength was alarming. Like his sheer physical presence. Safe from him? Perhaps—but not safe from her own thoughts. He unsettled her too easily. However, that was probably true of most of the women he met. That thought rallied her at once; this was a business arrangement, nothing more. It would be the height of folly to think anything else.

Fortunately for her peace of mind Ina appeared a few moments later. He threw a quizzical look at Wulfgar and then turned his attention to Anwyn.

'You wished to speak with me, my lady.'

'Yes. There are matters of which you must be apprised…'

As she outlined the scheme Ina listened intently, his face impassive. Even his eyes revealed nothing of the thoughts in his mind. However, knowing him well enough by now, she immediately sensed reservation there.

'I need your help,' she said in conclusion. 'The men will listen to you.'

'They listen because you are Lady of Drakensburgh and they owe allegiance to you. To Lord Wulfgar they owe none.'

Wulfgar nodded. 'What you say is true. However, if we are to prevail against Ingvar, I must have their allegiance.'

'It may not be easy to gain.'

'Perhaps not, but I mean to have it all the same.'

His gaze met and held Ina's. Then the older man nodded slowly. 'What do you intend to do?'

'Speak to them. Offer them a choice.'

'Serve you or leave?'

'Something like that.'

'They may defect to Ingvar.'

'It's a risk I'll have to take,' Wulfgar conceded.

Anwyn looked thoughtful. 'There's no love lost between my late husband's men and those whom Grymar leads.'

'It's what I'm counting on,' he replied.

'When do you mean to speak with them?'

'The sooner the better. I need to know exactly where I stand with regard to numbers.'

While Ina departed to muster the Drakensburgh force,

Wulfgar summoned his own men into the hall. He had quite deliberately kept their number small, not wishing to make a difficult situation worse. Then he turned to Anwyn and held out a hand.

'Come.'

Rather tentatively she placed her fingers in his, felt them close on her hand. The touch was warm and strong, oddly reassuring. He led her to the dais on which stood the great carved chair. Anwyn's eyes widened a little.

'You want me to sit there?'

'Aye. These men need to understand who wields authority at Drakensburgh.'

It wasn't at all what she had been expecting, although she could see the point. However, the thought of actually taking Torstein's seat was somewhat daunting. No one had ever sat there save he. No one would have dared. She drew a deep breath; Torstein was dead and could make no objection. Somewhat gingerly she sat down. The great chair seemed even bigger now. Possibly Wulfgar guessed at some of her thoughts for he squeezed her fingers gently.

'Have no fear. It will all be well.'

Then he released his hold and stepped back, standing a few feet off to her left, his men ranged behind. They had no sooner taken their places than Ina returned. His steady gaze took in the scene at once.

'The men are on their way,' he said.

'Good.' Wulfgar gestured to the place at Anwyn's right hand. A ghost of a smile flickered on Ina's lips and then was gone, but he took up his position without question.

As the Drakensburgh retainers began to file in, the buzz of conversation died and each man there turned his gaze to the waiting group. The first few halted at a respectful distance from the dais, their expressions revealing mingled surprise and curiosity. Surveying them from her vantage point, Anwyn understood then exactly what Wulfgar intended. At a stroke he had created an instant and powerful visual image that was all about authority: her authority, underpinned by Ina and himself. A few in the assembled crowd began to exchange glances and murmurs. Then Ina stepped forwards.

'Silence!' The command and the fierce accompanying glare killed off the murmuring at once. 'Lady Anwyn would speak with you.'

All eyes turned her way. Sweat started on the palms of her hands. In all the ten months since Torstein's death she had never addressed these men *en masse,* relying on Ina to convey her instructions. Now in truth she was going to have to adopt the mantle bequeathed her and she could not afford to show fear. Deciding that directness was probably the best course, she came straight to the point.

'Recent hostile actions by Lord Ingvar's war band have suggested a shift in the relationship subsisting between him and my late husband. It amounts to unwarranted interference in Drakensburgh's affairs. This I will not permit.' She paused, letting her gaze sweep round the assembled crowd, meeting their eyes. No one spoke. Nervousness diminished. She was in charge here and they would hear her. She lifted her chin and resumed, her voice firm and clear. 'His lordship has also made known his wish to unite his estate with this one...' that caused some sideways glances and drew faint, knowing smiles '...a wish he intends to fulfil by *any* means in his power.' The smiles faded. 'This also I will not permit.' They were regarding her intently now. 'However, Lord Ingvar's war band is strong and, at present, Drakensburgh's forces, though valiant, are too small to counter them should the need arise. To rectify that situation I have commissioned the services of Lord Wulfgar and his men.' Again a murmur of voices broke out, this time in surprise. 'There is more.' She waited for quiet and then went on. 'To have any hope of defeating Ingvar's forces, there can only be one military commander. That will be Lord Wulfgar.' The murmuring grew louder now and she intercepted a few angry looks among the expressions of surprise. 'Ina will be his second-in-command.'

A man stepped forwards, big, burly, swarthy skinned. She recognised Thorkil for he had ever been one of her husband's most loyal adherents. 'Why should we take orders from Lord Wulfgar? We have sworn no oath of fealty to him.'

A chorus of agreement greeted this. Anwyn let it die down. 'No, but you do owe fealty to me.' She paused. 'It is my will that he be invested with the authority to command the combined force.'

'Only Ina has that right,' replied Thorkil.

Anwyn fixed him with a cool and level stare. 'It is I who have the right to decide what happens at Drakensburgh—no one else.'

Thorkil's bushy eyebrows knit together, but before he could say more Ina spoke out. 'Lady Anwyn speaks true—her word is law here.' He paused. 'Do not dispute it again.'

Thorkil glowered, but remained silent, exchanging eloquent looks with his immediate neighbours, Sigurd and Gorm. Anwyn drew in another deep breath and then turned to look at the man to her left.

'Perhaps Lord Wulfgar can clarify the situation.'

He inclined his head in acquiescence and strolled forwards to the edge of the dais, looking round at the assembled group.

'I can well understand why some might find this situation hard to accept. Change is not always welcome. Some men see it as a threat.' He looked at Thorkil for a moment. 'However, I am not the threat confronting Drakensburgh: Ingvar is. Only a united force has any hope of prevailing against him and, as any warrior knows, a force can have but one leader.' He paused. 'I will not compel any man to pledge allegiance to me. Those who have no wish to do so may leave, and with no ill feeling. However, those who choose to remain will acknowledge the authority that Lady Anwyn has seen fit to give me.'

He fell silent then, waiting. The silence stretched out, but no one moved or spoke. Wulfgar nodded.

'Then I take it we are all agreed.'

Again none disputed his words. Anwyn let out the breath she had been holding, even as she acknowledged the skill of the performance she had just witnessed. It seemed to call for a gesture from her.

'Tomorrow night our two forces shall feast together in friendship. Until then, go in peace.'

Immediately a loud buzz of conversation ensued, but she was relieved to note only a few creased brows among the crowd. Most of them seemed to have accepted the new state of affairs. However, they had a vested interest in doing so since it was a lot easier and more convenient than trying to find a new place elsewhere. Of course, Lord Wulfgar had known that and calculated accordingly. Glancing round, she met his eye and saw him nod in quiet approval.

'Well done. You were magnificent.'

His praise caused a real sense of pleasure. 'Thank you. You weren't so bad yourself.'

He smiled. 'Between us, I think we convinced them, my lady—the majority, anyway.'

'Yes, I believe we did.' She grew serious for a moment. 'But Thorkil will bear watching.'

'Ah, the dissenter.'

She nodded. 'It's my thought he may stir trouble if he can.'

'I'll keep an eye on him,' said Ina.

'Do that,' she replied. 'We cannot afford internal quarrels now.'

Ina bowed then and left them. Anwyn rose from her seat, by no means sorry to vacate it, and glanced around. Wulfgar's men were talking quietly among themselves, but their chief was looking at her. In that brief keen regard she surprised a look of warmth that she had not seen there before. It both gladdened and perturbed.

'What will you do now?' she asked.

'Forge a united fighting force,' he replied.

'Quite a challenge.'

'I've always enjoyed those—in whatever guise they might appear.'

'I find it hard to believe that even you could enjoy a challenge that came in the guise of Grymar.'

'He's the exception that proves the rule.' He grinned. 'A truly ugly challenge.'

Anwyn laughed. 'A cruel but accurate description.'

Wulfgar had not seen her laugh; it lit her face and made her eyes sparkle, enhancing beauty and rendering it stunning. Her lips might have been formed for a man's kisses; almost invited them. Moreover, now that he was standing closer, he caught a hint of floral scent from the folds of her gown. It was light but sensual as well and unexpectedly arousing, like the soft curve between her neck and shoulder, a warm hollow just made for a man's lips. If they'd been alone he might have put that theory to the test... He pulled imagination up short. They weren't alone and he had no business thinking in those terms. His business was war, a mistress who suffered no rivals.

'My lord?' The green eyes met his, their expression puzzled now. 'Is something wrong?'

'Er, no. Forgive me, I was thinking about military matters.'

'Of course. It is I who should apologise for detaining you.' She smiled. 'If you will excuse me, I have a feast to arrange.'

With that she left him. Wulfgar let out a long breath. Then, having regained his customary composure, he turned and rejoined his men.

Chapter Seven

Jodis regarded her wide-eyed. 'You've really done it, my lady?'

'Yes. I can only pray that it was the right decision, though in truth I think I had no other choice.'

'Lord Ingvar isn't going to like it.' The maid paused. 'Lord Wulfgar's very handsome, isn't he?'

'Yes, he is.'

'A pity he were not Lord of Drakensburgh.'

Anwyn stared at her. The maid reddened.

'Beg pardon, my lady. I meant no offence, I'm sure. I was thinking aloud.'

'A bad habit, Jodis.'

In fact, the remark had not caused offence; rather it led Anwyn's thoughts in an entirely different direction. If Wulfgar had been Lord of Drakensburgh... Just for a moment she indulged the thought. The result was a strange fluttering sensation in the pit of her stomach. How would it be to share *his* bed? To surrender to *his* will? The notion did not engender the feeling of instant antipathy that it should have. What she felt was more like wistfulness. She drew a deep breath. Such thoughts were foolish and irresponsible. She had no wish to be a whore, and she had found out the hard way what it meant to be a wife; she would not give a man such power over her again.

Anwyn turned her mind to the matter of the forthcoming feast. It was short notice, but Drakensburgh was well supplied and she was sure that something creditable could be achieved. Accordingly she spent the rest of the forenoon speaking to the servants. If all went according to plan, then it might bring both sides together in amity. Perhaps even Thorkil and his friends might come round after a few mugs of ale.

Wulfgar and Ina took it upon themselves to organise the seating at the feast, arranging matters in such a way that the company was mixed, giving both sides the chance to meet and talk. If they were going to work together, it was an important requirement. Anwyn had made no demur, letting them have complete freedom in this. Her contribution to conviviality was to ensure substantial amounts of food and drink. To this Wulfgar had contributed several casks of mead from the ship's store. It seemed to be working, too, for the flow of conversation was more or less continuous, and punctuated at intervals by good-natured laughter. It pleased him to hear it. If things went as he hoped, then it would smooth the way for what was to come.

A movement in the doorway caught his eye and he glanced in that direction. Then he was quite still, forgetting even to breathe, his gaze fixed on the woman who stood there. Nor was he alone in this; more than a few covert glances went that way and then lingered. Anwyn seemed not to notice. He saw her glance around the hall and then, apparently satisfied that all was well, she made her way towards him. He took a breath then and found his feet, rising to greet her.

To do honour to the occasion she had dressed with more than usual care that evening. The blue gown was one of her finest, richly embroidered at the neck and sleeves with a pattern of leaves and flowers picked out in green and gold. Matching blue ribbons adorned her hair. It was, she knew, a most becoming outfit, an effort justified by the need to do honour to Drakensburgh's new allies. However, as soon as she entered the hall she knew there was only one man present whose opinion mattered.

He had risen to meet her and her heartbeat quickened as she crossed the space between them, aware that she had his full attention now. His eyes appraised every detail of her appearance and the blue depths warmed. She saw him bow.

Wulfgar, too, had changed his habitual garb and was now clad in a fine shirt and a tunic of deep blue wool worn over dark leggings. His shoes were of good leather, and a tooled-leather belt rode his waist from which hung his magnificently wrought dagger. The costume was at once simple and elegant, a perfect foil for his warm colouring and dark hair. Looking at him now, Anwyn could only conclude that Jodis was right. He was a very handsome man, dangerously so.

He met her eye and held it. 'You look like a queen.'

His expression was demonstration enough that the praise was sincere, and the result was to create a real sense of pleasure. He took her hand, guiding her to the chair beside his. The touch burned. To cover her confusion she feigned to look around the room, though in truth she was aware only of the man beside her. A servant approached to fill her cup. With apparent casualness she took a sip. The mead was sweet and mellow and it steadied her.

'The mood seems convivial enough,' she said then.

'That it does. It was a good idea to bring everyone together thus.'

The words were mildly spoken, but they warmed her anyway, like the apparently casual regard he bent on her now.

'I hope it may create a bond of friendship between us,' she replied.

'I also hope for a closer bond between us.'

The words carried an unmistakable nuance and all at once the spectre of temptation reared its head. A temptation she couldn't afford. This man was a mercenary and she was paying

for his strength and his sword. She mustn't allow herself to
forget that if she hoped to remain in control of their relationship.

Fortunately the servants brought in the food just then and
diverted attention away from what might have become a difficult conversation. Although she was faced with a succes-
sion of savoury dishes, Anwyn ate sparingly. For some reason
her appetite was less than usual so she contented herself with
watching others and sipping from her cup. The men around
them ate with apparent enjoyment, a sight which pleased her
greatly. At least they could have no doubts of her ability to run
her household well and would be more reconciled to staying
awhile.

Her gaze flicked to Wulfgar. He seemed quite at ease, occu-
pying his place as though he had been born to it. In truth,
he might have been the Lord of Drakensburgh. She sighed
inwardly. If it had been he and not Torstein, she might have
been more easily reconciled to her situation. As it was, their
lives were destined to touch only briefly. The knowledge
brought an unexpected sense of sadness.

Unaware of her thoughts, Wulfgar leaned across his chair
towards her. 'An excellent meal. You are to be congratulated,
my lady.'

She rallied and returned his smile. 'I thank you. The effort
has proved worthwhile.'

'Indeed it has. If this is a foretaste of things to come, my
men will never want to leave.'

Her pulse quickened; while they stayed so would he. 'If so,
then the way to men's hearts really is through their stomachs.'

'Do you doubt it?'

'In my experience men have no hearts.'

His eyes narrowed a little, regarding her more closely. 'Not
even your husband?'

Every sign of amusement vanished. 'Especially not him.'

'Forgive me, I did not mean to pry.'

'It doesn't matter.' She met his eye squarely. 'Our match was arranged by my father because it suited his purpose. I had no say in it.'

'I see.'

'Do you?'

He could hardly miss the sarcastic edge to the question but, though he knew he ought to let the matter drop, he was curious. 'How old were you?'

'Fifteen. Torstein was forty.'

'Hardly an ideal combination, and yet with good will on both sides it might work well enough. Such things are not unknown.'

'It may be as you say. I have no idea.'

'I'm sorry to hear it.'

'I was sorry, too,' she replied. 'Every day I was with him.' The tone was unwontedly bitter, quite unlike her usual manner. Then she collected herself and smiled. 'But let us not speak of unpleasant subjects. This is supposed to be a celebration after all.'

Wulfgar took the hint and the conversation moved into other channels. All the same, her words had given him plenty of food for thought. They also explained her earlier comment about a husband's tyranny. Again he couldn't help but wonder what kind of man Earl Torstein had been that he would so crassly alienate a lovely woman. Most men would give their eye teeth to possess such a jewel and, possessing her, treat her well. It occurred to him then that he was hardly in a position to criticise. Had he not once possessed a fair wife and treated her ill? He winced inwardly. It seemed he might have more in common with Torstein than was comfortable.

Anwyn drained her cup, annoyed with herself for blurting out the details of her marriage thus. She didn't know why she had done it. Now he knew even more about her while she knew next to nothing about him. What had his life been like before?

He had given her a few small details, but otherwise seemed unwilling to speak of the past. Perhaps in that he was right; there was no point in dwelling on what was done.

'Do you not find it lonely to be on your own?' he asked.

'I have enough to keep me occupied.'

'Work doesn't take up the whole day, though.'

'No, it doesn't. Sometimes I sleep, too.'

'Only sometimes?'

'In the first months after Torstein's death I found it hard,' she replied.

'And now?'

'Less so, now I know that he isn't coming back.'

He surveyed her steadily. 'Did you never think of finding a more congenial bedmate?'

'I have no wish to remarry.'

'I wasn't suggesting that you should.'

Anwyn's gaze locked with his, her eyes a dangerous shade of emerald. 'Nor do I have any intention of taking a lover, my lord.'

'What a pity.'

For a moment or two she was speechless, hardly able to credit the blatant boldness of that remark. Yet she could see no sign of contrition in his face; on the contrary, the gleam in his eyes suggested keen inner enjoyment.

'Do you have any idea how provoking you can be?' she demanded.

'I have the feeling that you want to tell me.'

'Had we been alone I would already have done so.'

'Well, my luck really is out, isn't it?'

'It's no use. I shall not rise to the bait.'

'Worse and worse—I must try harder.'

'It seems to me that you are trying enough, my lord.'

Wulfgar laughed. It wasn't what she expected, nor was the way in which it transformed his face, like the expression in his eyes now. Unable to withstand their scrutiny, she lowered her own lest he should read too accurately the thoughts she tried to hide.

As the evening wore on and the men continued to drink, the jokes became lewder and the sound of ribald laughter increased. The heat mounted with it and the room became stifling, reeking of roast meat and ale and male sweat. Anwyn began to feel the effects of the mead she had drunk. It was sweet and smooth on the tongue but, evidently, much stronger than she'd thought, even taken with food, and she'd had several cups. Any more would be a mistake. She had played her part tonight and to all intents and purposes the occasion had gone well enough. Perhaps better than expected. It was time to leave them to it.

As she rose, the room lurched. She checked, holding on to the arm of the chair, waiting for it to stop. When she opened her eyes she saw that Wulfgar had risen, too.

'I will escort you as far as the women's bower, my lady.'

'I…it's all right. There's no need.'

He glanced at her and then towards the company. 'I think there is.'

She didn't bother to argue further. He had clearly made up his mind, and the men *were* fairly drunk. His presence would ensure their behaviour remained within bounds.

Walking with exaggerated care, Anwyn made for the nearest exit, a smaller side door. He opened it and stood aside to let her pass. The night air hit her like a slap, but after the heat and fug of the hall it was blessedly cool. It was full dark now and the breeze tossed the flames in the lighted cressets nearby, sending dancing shadows across the timbered wall and the ground beyond. In the flickering light she could just make out the dark shape of the women's bower. She turned to her companion.

'There is no need for you to come further, my lord. It is but a short walk from here.'

She took a step away from him, but the path tilted

under her feet. A powerful arm caught hold of her waist and steadied her.

'The mead is strong, isn't it?' he said.

She shook her head. 'I'm fine, really.'

The arm remained round her waist. He was so close she could feel the heat from his body through her gown and, though his face was lost in shadow, she felt the intensity of the gaze bent on her face. Her heart missed a beat. Another arm slid around her shoulders, drawing her against him, and then his lips brushed hers. The pressure increased a little, encountered resistance, became more gently insistent until her mouth opened beneath his. She shivered, but not with cold. His mouth tasted of mead, sweet and strong, as heady as the brew she had drunk earlier. It sent flaring warmth the length of her body as though, deep within, a dormant fire had been kindled. The kiss grew deeper, more intense, seeking her response. As of its own volition her body relaxed against him and yielded itself up to his embrace.

In some part of her mind she could hear a distant faint alarm. This was madness. It was dangerous. She tensed, drew back, turning her head aside, panting. The stars spun crazily overhead.

'Please…'

'What would you have, Anwyn?'

His lips grazed her cheek and nibbled gently at her earlobe. The touch sent a delicious tremor to the core of her being. In that moment she wanted to surrender, to let this run its course, and give herself up to the demands of that inner fire. Yet still she could hear the faint warning bell at the back of her mind. She shook her head.

'I cannot…'

She tried to draw away, but her legs would not support her properly. Without his arm she would have fallen. Moments later another slipped under her knees and then heaven and earth tilted and swayed together as he carried her the remaining yards to the bower. He shoved the door open with his shoulder and followed the passage within, coming at last to the room he took to be her chamber.

Someone had lit a lamp and the room was bathed in a soft glow. Wulfgar laid his burden on the bed. For a moment or two he remained still, looking down into her face. The green eyes were wide, their colour deeper now, her lips slightly parted. Recalling that stolen kiss, he knew an almost overmastering temptation to follow it up, to pursue this to its conclusion. He wanted her as he had not wanted a woman for a long time. He wanted to unfasten her hair and remove her clothing, piece by piece, until she was naked; wanted to join her there and make love to her through the night and let the fire consume him. It would be easy. She would not resist: she was lonely and she needed the temporary solace he could give her—solace offered with gentleness. Her whole being cried out for it. The defences she had erected were down now and she was more than ready for him; the mead had seen to that.

He closed his eyes and drew in several deep breaths, wrestling for self-control. He wanted her all right, but not under the influence of mead when she was scarcely aware of what she did. When he took her—and he meant to—it was going to be with her full knowledge and consent. When he took her he wanted her to remember every part of it and to leave her craving more. Her kiss had let him glimpse the passion of which she would be capable, and he knew that nothing else would do.

He bent and drew off her shoes, setting them down beside the bed. Then he pulled the coverlet over her and dropped a kiss on her forehead.

'Good night, Anwyn.'

She smiled, half-asleep now, and murmured something he didn't catch. Wulfgar sighed and retreated to the outer door, closing it softly behind him.

When Anwyn woke her mouth was dry and her head pounding. Squinting against the light, she realised that the sun was already high. However much had she drunk last night? Slowly she eased herself onto one elbow and looked around. It was then that she became aware that she was still fully dressed. She had no recollection of how she had got to bed.

Gingerly she swung her legs over the side and stood up. The thumping in her head intensified a little. Crossing to the far side of the room, she reached for the ewer and poured cold water into a horn cup and gulped the contents down. Then she poured some more into the bowl and plunged her face in. The shock revived her a little and she repeated the exercise several times.

By then her head had cleared somewhat and fragments of the previous evening began to return. As they did her brow creased. She could recall leaving the hall now, but she had not been alone. All at once other details reasserted themselves into the missing areas of the picture. Anwyn paled. She had left the hall with Wulfgar and he had walked her back to the bower. Except that they hadn't walked straight back. Her heart began to thump in her breast. He had taken her in his arms and kissed her and she had let him. Her cheeks went a shade paler. Goodness alone knew what he had intended. She swallowed hard. She knew exactly what he had intended. In a sudden leap of intuition she knew who had carried her to her chamber and who had put her to bed.

Crimson colour replaced the pallor in her face. Had he... had they? She took a breath, trying to calm herself, trying to remember. They had kissed and then he had carried her. What had happened after that, she had no idea. Except that she was still wearing her clothes. She removed her gown and the linen kirtle beneath it and scrutinised the flesh beneath, but her body bore no indications whatever of any sexual intimacy. Feeling weak with relief, she pulled the kirtle back on and sank down on the edge of the chest nearby.

What a fool she had been, albeit unwittingly. He might so easily have taken advantage of the situation. She shivered, feel-

ing suddenly cold. For a moment Torstein's face returned and
Anwyn was sickened; her late husband wouldn't have hesitated.
He'd have stripped her without a qualm and used her at his will.
Yet seemingly Wulfgar had not followed up his advantage.
Relief mingled with shame. What must he think of her? How
was she going to face him again after this? Yet face him she
must, somehow.

When she had donned a fresh gown and tidied her hair,
she went to find Eyvind. The child was with Ina, watching
the farrier shoe a horse. For a moment the old warrior met
her gaze over the child's head and he smiled faintly. For one
awful moment she wondered if he knew what had occurred
last evening. Then common sense returned and she told herself
not to be so stupid.

'I'll look after him, my lady, if you have business elsewhere.'

She thanked him and, breathing a sigh of relief, left them
there. A glance around revealed plenty of the *Sea Wolf*'s crew,
but no sign of her captain. Recognising Hermund, she decided
to ask.

'He's gone to the ship with some of the men, my lady.'

She did not know whether to be relieved or disappointed.
'I see. Well, no matter, I'll speak to him later.'

'I'll tell him you were looking for him, shall I?'

'Don't trouble yourself. I'm sure to meet up with him eventually.'

She began to retrace her steps, when she caught the sound
of hoofbeats. She heard an exchange of greetings and then
the gates swung open to reveal half-a-dozen riders. As she
recognised the foremost of them her heart leapt towards her
throat. Ingvar!

Caught unawares, Anwyn stopped in her tracks, trying to
force her mind to lucid thought. The horsemen pulled up outside the hall and she saw Ingvar take a comprehensive look
around. Then he said something to his escort and they dismounted. With a sigh she bent her steps that way.

He saw her coming and, as she drew nigh, offered a courteous greeting. However, his customary smile was absent and the gold-brown eyes were speculative. This interview wasn't going to be easy. To play for time she invited him and his escort into the hall.

'Perhaps you would care for a little refreshment after your ride, my lord?'

'Thank you, no. I would speak with you, my lady. Alone.'

The tone was sharper than usual, almost a command, and Anwyn felt the first stirrings of annoyance. Nevertheless, she nodded.

'As you will.'

She led the way to the hall and then, when they were out of earshot of anyone else, she turned to face him, waiting. His gaze burned into hers.

'Would you care to tell me what is happening here, my lady?'

'What is happening?'

'With the repairs to the ship.'

'Oh. They are progressing well, I believe.'

A little of the tension went out of him. 'I'm glad to hear it. How much longer is it going to take?'

'Not long—a day or so at most.'

'I'm sure you will be glad to see the back of the mercenary force.'

'On the contrary,' she replied, 'I have nothing to complain of.'

'Been minding their manners, have they?'

'Yes, a good deal better than others have done.'

He did not pretend to misunderstand. 'Grymar will not make the same mistake again. You have my word on it.'

'The lady will have a lot more than that,' said a voice from behind them.

Anwyn's heart leapt towards her throat and she turned quickly to see Wulfgar. She had not heard him approach and had no idea how long he had been there. Spots of warm colour leapt into her cheeks and for a moment they surveyed each other in silence. However, his expression was enigmatic.

'What do you mean?' demanded Ingvar.

'I mean that Drakensburgh will have additional protection from now on.'

'You speak in riddles.'

'Plainly, then—my men and I will be providing that protection.'

Ingvar's face became a mask of cold fury. 'Drakensburgh has no need of your services.'

'The lady thinks it does,' replied Wulfgar. 'From what I saw the other day I'm inclined to agree with her.'

'That was an unfortunate misunderstanding.'

'It was certainly unfortunate, but I don't think there could be any misunderstanding.'

'You meddle in matters that do not concern you.'

'But they do concern me—now.'

Ingvar glared at him and then turned to Anwyn. 'You cannot seriously intend to allow these pirates to remain?'

'Pirates, no,' she replied. 'But I do intend to let Lord Wulfgar and his men remain.'

For a moment he surveyed her in chilling silence. 'I am sorry to hear it. I thought you had better sense.'

'My sense is unimpaired.'

'I think you have made a foolish decision that you will come to regret very soon, my lady.'

'I will stand by my decision nevertheless.'

'I see.'

'Let's hope you do,' replied Wulfgar.

The two men faced each other in silence for a moment. All pretence of goodwill was stripped from Ingvar's expression now to reveal naked hatred.

'I will not permit any man to meddle in my affairs, or to steal what belongs to me.'

At this Anwyn felt her anger flare. She controlled it. 'There is nothing here that belongs to you, my lord. Nor ever will.'

'You're wrong, Anwyn. All you are doing is to postpone the inevitable. I always get what I want, one way or another.'

Wulfgar's hand rested casually on the hilt of his sword. 'You would be well advised to forget all thoughts of Drakensburgh, and its lady.'

'So you intend to take them for yourself then, Viking?'

'If I did, it would still be no business of yours.' He intercepted a look of sparkling indignation from Anwyn and ignored it, continuing, 'You have nothing more to do here, my lord, except to leave.'

Ingvar threw him a savage glare. 'I'll leave—for now.' With that he turned on his heel and strode away.

Anwyn let out a long breath. 'We have not heard the last of him.'

'Of course not.'

'Doesn't that bother you?'

'Why should it? I have his measure.'

'And if he opens hostilities?'

'Not if…when.'

'You think it inevitable?'

'It is inevitable, and when he does I shall kill him.'

Anwyn's eyes flashed indignation. 'That was not what we agreed. I said I wanted no bloodshed.'

'We don't always get what we want.'

'We made a bargain, Wulfgar.'

'So we did.' He surveyed her steadily. 'But, if it comes down to a choice between my death or his?'

'It won't.'

'It might.'

Indignation dissolved to be replaced by something quite different. She knew then that, were there ever to be a choice between the two of them, Ingvar would lose hands down.

'Then you would have to kill him,' she replied.

'Just so.'

She experienced an inner qualm as the true implications of her plan came home. 'So it begins.'

'Aye, it begins, but you knew it would.'

'I suppose I'd hoped to have more time.'

'Better this way; everyone knows where he stands.'

She nodded. 'I suppose so.' Then, recalling a detail of the recent conversation, continued, 'What did you mean by that remark to Ingvar just now?'

'Which one?'

'You know which one.'

'No, enlighten me.'

She reddened slightly and the green eyes took on a militant sparkle. 'When you said it was none of Ingvar's business if you *did* take Drakensburgh for your own.'

'Ah, that one,' he replied.

'What did you mean by it?'

'Exactly what I said.'

Her colour deepened. 'You had no right to say any such thing unless…'

'Unless what?'

'You were being deliberately provoking.'

'Of course it was deliberately provoking. The man was almost rampant with jealousy.'

'He has nothing to be jealous of.'

Wulfgar raised an eyebrow. 'No? Well, what the eye doesn't see…and he wasn't here last night, was he?'

Anwyn's cheeks went scarlet. He grinned appreciatively and took a step closer.

'Is it coming back to you now, Anwyn?'

She glared at him. 'It came back long since, you rogue. Did you think I would be unaware that you had taken advantage of me?'

'What I took was a kiss, lady, though the rest would have been simple enough.'

'Why, you utter…'

'When I take a woman to bed I prefer her to be sober, you see.'

Anwyn's eyes blazed scorn. 'So that she will remember?'

'The pleasure is all one-sided else.'

'The pleasure is all one-sided anyway,' she retorted.

Wulfgar regarded her curiously. 'If so, you were in bed with the wrong man.'

'It was not my choice to be in his bed at all.'

'The man would be careless indeed who, having once taken you to his bed, could not persuade you to return there willingly and often.'

Something in his expression set her heart to beating as fast as it had erewhile, and all at once the memory of that stolen kiss returned with force. Unable to bear his scrutiny, she looked away.

'I have no idea what you're talking about and it is irrelevant anyway.'

'Irrelevant is not the word I would use. On the contrary, it seems highly pertinent.'

'I drank too much.'

'*In vino veritas*—in wine is truth.'

'Only a loss of inhibition, which I now regret.'

'Do you?' He paused, waiting. 'Look at me, Anwyn.'

Heart pounding, she forced herself to face him. 'What happened last night was unfortunate and it will not be repeated.'

'I'm sorry to hear it.'

'And I am sorry that my actions gave you to think that I… that we—' She broke off, floundering.

'I do think so. That kiss was no pretended passion and we both know it.'

'Even if it wasn't, the matter can go no further. Surely you see that.'

'Clearly our views differ on this point.' He smiled wryly. 'But you're probably right.'

'You know I'm right. We must forget it ever happened.'

'Some things are not so soon forgotten.'

'This is a business arrangement, my lord, nothing more.' She paused. 'I regret that I should have given you reason to think otherwise. It was most unwittingly done.'

'So, what now?'

'Can we let things go back to being as they were before?'

'If that is what you want.'

She nodded. 'Thank you. And once again, I'm truly sorry about what happened last night.'

'I wish I could say the same,' he murmured, as she walked away.

Chapter Eight

In the days that followed, Wulfgar made it his business to find out as much as he could about Drakensburgh. A more detailed exploration of its defences confirmed his first thought that the place would be easy enough to hold. It was a good start. What he needed to do next was to forge two disparate groups of men into one cohesive fighting force. To that end he organised a series of training sessions that would bring everyone together and allow him to gauge the mettle of the Drakensburgh contingent. In this, too, he was pleasantly surprised. Whatever else he might have been, it seemed Earl Torstein had known how to choose able fighters.

He had seen little of Anwyn since the night of the feast. They met only at the table now where, he noted with wry amusement, she limited her drinking to ale and that in small quantities. Her manner towards him was unfailingly courteous, but it was also professionally distant. No mention was ever made of that previous brief intimacy; indeed, it might never have happened. Moreover, he was fairly certain that she had been avoiding him. Initially it had the merit of novelty, but he found that fast wearing off. What made it worse was the growing suspicion that it was no mere feminine wile to increase his interest: she meant it. Once or twice, during the morning training sessions, he caught a glimpse of her, usually with the child, but she never even glanced his way. Refreshments were supplied to him and his men, but it was a servant who brought them. She had effectively thrown up a defensive barrier and intended to remain behind it.

In this supposition he was quite correct. Anwyn had sedulously avoided his company where possible, taking care to busy herself with domestic matters during the day. There were also Eyvind's needs to look after as well, so it wasn't particularly difficult. Yet in spite of her best intentions she found herself looking forward to the evenings when she knew she would meet Wulfgar again. On the surface of it the conversation flowed smoothly: she would ask him what progress he had made with the men and he would tell her how he had spent his day. She listened attentively, asking questions at intervals, thoughtful and pertinent questions that revealed a sharp mind and excellent grasp of what he was trying to achieve.

'You would have made an able commander,' he said, as they lingered over the remains of the meal one evening.

Anwyn shook her head. 'An able commander needs to be able to acquit himself well in battle. I fear that my skills stop far short of that.'

'It is not hard to learn the rudiments of sword play. What is much more difficult is to master fighting strategy.'

'Is it?'

'Beyond doubt, and yet you always know what I'm talking about.' The tone was casual enough but it warmed her nevertheless.

'I pay attention.'

'I know.' He leaned back in his chair, regarding her steadily. 'Another unusual quality in a woman.'

Anwyn returned the look. 'Was that remark intended to be provocative?'

'That's right. Did it succeed?'

It drew a reluctant laugh. 'Yes, it did, you rogue.'

His cup paused in mid-air. 'Am I a rogue?

'Yourself best knows.'

'Hmm. Unpromising territory, I admit. Let's talk about something else.'

'Now *that's* an unusual quality in a man.'

His eyes gleamed. 'How so?'

'In my experience they like to talk about themselves—at length.'

'Are we so tedious?'

'How truthful would you like me to be?'

'I would wish you always to be truthful with me.' The words were quietly spoken, but they bore the ring of sincerity.

It wasn't what Anwyn had been expecting and for a moment it threw her off balance. So did the look in his eyes. 'I will try to be,' she replied.

'Good. A successful business arrangement depends upon it.'

'Yes, of course.' She was relieved and grateful that he had brought the conversation back to business. It was much safer ground, as he must have realised.

'Speaking of business,' he continued, 'I need to familiarise myself with Drakensburgh as a whole. To that end I wondered whether you would ride out with me tomorrow.'

Anwyn's heart gave a little leap. Suddenly the footing was distinctly shaky again. 'Well, I don't…I mean, I'm not sure…'

'It would be very useful to me—enable me to see the whole picture, as it were.'

'Would it?'

'Most certainly.' His blue eyes were earnest. 'I already have a sound grasp of the inner defences, but I don't want to leave anything to chance.'

'Oh, I see.'

'It's a matter of strategic importance for the safety of all concerned.' He paused. 'Of course, if you're too busy...'

'No...yes...I mean I am busy, but not so much that I couldn't spare a little time.'

'Thank you. I'd appreciate it.' He looked thoughtful. 'Perhaps Eyvind might like to come along—with Ina, naturally.'

Anwyn smiled. 'I'm sure he would like that.'

'That's settled, then.'

She bade him goodnight a short time later and, watching her go, Wulfgar let out a long breath. Hermund regarded him askance.

'Well, I reckon I've heard it all now,' he said, in accents suggestive of grudging admiration. 'Strategic importance, eh?'

'All right, I exaggerated. I admit it.'

'Exaggerated? I never heard a more desperate ploy in my life.'

Wulfgar raised an eyebrow. 'Desperate? Hardly.'

'Well, you had me fooled.'

The reply was short, pithy and rude. Hermund guffawed.

The riders set out early next day, in a group of a dozen strong. Wulfgar really did want to familiarise himself with the Drakensburgh lands, information that would be useful to his men as well, but he didn't want to be caught napping. Ingvar had sent a force across the boundary once before. Now that relations were less than cordial there was no telling what he might do in future, and Wulfgar had no intention of putting Anwyn and the boy in danger.

The child was bright-eyed with excitement at the treat in prospect, but also a little overawed by the company. Wulfgar smiled, watching as Ina lifted the child on to the waiting pony. Then he turned to Anwyn.

'Ready?'

'Of course.'

The words sounded natural enough, giving no clue to the

chaos of thoughts in her mind. She had lain awake for much of
the previous night, wondering if she had done the right thing
in agreeing to this. However, the escort offered reassurance
and made the excursion perfectly respectable. It occurred to
her then that he must have known that when he organised it.
They wouldn't be alone together. Unwanted memories resurfaced. How was it with her when the very thought of him was
enough to set her pulse racing? He was a temptation she could
not afford.

He held her horse's bridle while she mounted, and waited
until she was settled comfortably. Then he went to his own
mount, a mettlesome chestnut that had formerly belonged to
Torstein. He swung easily into the saddle and then brought the
horse alongside hers.

'Shall we go?'

They rode in silence for a while, keeping to a steady pace
in consequence of Eyvind's presence. At first Anwyn kept
her gaze firmly between the horse's ears, reluctant even to
look at her companion. Instead she let her thoughts dwell on
the scenery around her. As they rode inland rough heath and
stunted vegetation gave way to a softer landscape. Spring was
well advanced now. Fresh new green graced every tree and
bush, and wild flowers adorned the pastures where sheep and
cattle grazed. New crops sprouted in the ploughed strips of
arable land. The effect was of quiet and fertile prosperity.

'A fair domain,' said Wulfgar. 'I can understand why Ingvar
covets it.'

Anwyn threw him a swift sideways glance. 'He will never
take it while I live.'

'He'd be a fool to try now.'

'Ironic, isn't it? I hated Drakensburgh when first I came
here. I used to dream of escape.' She smiled wryly. 'Now I am
fighting to keep it.'

He surveyed her with curiosity. 'Was it really Drakensburgh
that you hated?'

'I hated anything that was connected to Torstein.'

'Except for your son.'

The words elicited another look, this time longer. 'Except for him,' she agreed. 'It is for him that I must hold Drakensburgh.'

'You will have your work cut out for you.'

'I know it. I can only hope that Ingvar will see the futility of his ambitions and seek another wife.'

'He will not give up,' replied Wulfgar. 'In his place neither would I.'

Anwyn's heart skipped a beat. Uncertain how to interpret that remark, she eyed him quizzically. 'An adventurer does not seek lands or the responsibilities of a wife and child.'

The muscles tensed along his jaw. 'I was not always an adventurer. I, too, had land once, and a wife and son.'

She stared at him. 'What happened to them?'

'They died of fever. There was an epidemic that summer. It took hundreds.'

'I'm so sorry.'

He sighed. 'It was long ago and life moves on.' For a brief instant his eyes expressed something very much like pain. Then it was gone. 'We make shift as best we can, in my case to the life of an adventurer.'

'What became of your home?'

'I couldn't bear the sight of it after they died so I burned it to the ground.'

'I see.'

'It served as a fitting funeral pyre.'

Anwyn struggled to assimilate the knowledge. It revealed an entirely different view of this man, one she could never have suspected.

'How old was he, your boy?'

'Three.'

She swallowed hard. That anything similar might happen to Eyvind was too awful to be contemplated.

'What was his name?'

'Toki.'

'And your wife?'

'Freya.'

'Was she beautiful?'

'Very beautiful.'

Once again the succinct replies suggested that she had ventured into a private place, and she was immediately remorseful.

'Forgive me, I did not mean to open old wounds.'

'It's all right,' he replied. 'The wounds are closed.'

'Closed, but not perfectly healed, I think.'

The observation caught him completely unawares. It was gently spoken, but the effect was like a blow to the solar plexus. Feeling that sudden tension in his rider, the chestnut plunged forwards. It took a moment or two to bring it back under control, by which time Wulfgar had mastery of himself as well.

'Everything all right, my lord?' asked Thrand.

'No problem. Just a horsefly, I expect.'

Thrand nodded. 'Evil little blighters those and no mistake. I remember one time...'

The conversation moved on to other topics then. Anwyn let the men's voices flow around her, barely listening, for her thoughts were otherwise occupied. She had little thought to learn so much or that her words might have so pronounced an effect. The loss of a child could not but leave lasting scars, but when combined with the loss of the wife... She must have been a remarkable woman, this Freya, to have won his heart so completely. Even in death she clearly retained it still. Anwyn smiled sadly. It was the kind of love she had once dreamed of finding. Now she never would. More than ever before she was glad she had followed her instincts and avoided the pitfall that Wulfgar represented.

They were on the point of returning home when one of the men behind called out, 'Smoke, my lord!'

At once the whole group reined in, turning to look in the

direction he had indicated. Sure enough a thick, dark pall was rising from behind a stand of trees in the distance.

Wulfgar wheeled the chestnut round and addressed the men. 'It may not be sinister in origin, but keep your eyes open all the same. Look to the woman and the boy.'

The men closed up at once and suddenly Anwyn was no longer at the front of the group, but at its centre with Eyvind. He looked up with mingled excitement and anxiety.

'What is it, Mother? What's happening?'

'I'm not sure,' she replied. 'It looks like a large fire.'

As they approached, the smell of burning drifted towards them on the light wind, and they could hear the roar of the flames. The source of the fire was a large barn, now ablaze from end to end. Men from the nearby fields had left their work and formed a human chain betwixt the fire and the stream, passing relays of buckets. Anwyn surveyed the scene in dismay.

'It's hopeless. They'll never save it now.'

Wulfgar glanced across at her. 'No. It's fortunate the place wasn't near any of the other buildings or the lot might have gone up.'

'I pray no one was hurt.'

Leaving Eyvind with Ina, she and Wulfgar urged their mounts towards the line of fire-fighters.

'What happened here?' she demanded.

In response to the question a man stepped forward. Although he was equally grim faced, he looked different from his fellows. His clothing was of better quality and his manner more confident. Wulfgar guessed him to be one of the geneatas, a tenant farmer who paid rent to his overlord. Likely it was his barn they saw burning.

The man shook his head. 'I don't know, my lady. We didn't notice anything amiss at first, not till we glimpsed the smoke. By then it was too late.'

'Was anyone hurt?' asked Wulfgar.

'No, lord, but they will be. That barn held the last of the village's grain. There'll be no more now till harvest.'

Wulfgar glanced at Anwyn. They both knew the man had not exaggerated. The coming summer months were always the leanest, even in a good year.

'I will ensure that you get enough to see you through,' she replied.

The man blinked in surprise, but was quick to offer his thanks. Anwyn turned to Wulfgar.

'Will you take charge of this matter, my lord?'

'Gladly,' he replied. 'I'll get my men on it at once. The problem can be resolved by the morrow.'

The farmer regarded him curiously but, she noted, with guarded approval. Then he rejoined his fellows who now stood in silent impotence, watching the conflagration.

'You have made a generous gesture,' said Wulfgar.

'I could do no less,' she replied. 'This is a disaster for these people.'

'Could have been an accident,' said Thrand, who had come to join them.

Wulfgar glanced his way and then back at the fire. 'Maybe.'

'No one saw anything after all. Surely they would have if the blaze was set deliberately.'

'Not necessarily. There's plenty of cover hereabouts after all. Take a couple of men and have a look around, especially in those trees over there.'

Thrand nodded and summoned two of his companions. Anwyn turned to Wulfgar.

'Do you really think this might have been deliberate?'

'I don't know yet,' he replied.

She felt suddenly uneasy and her gaze went to Eyvind, who was watching the proceedings a little way off. She saw him say something to Ina, but the words were lost in the sound of the fire. To the child this was merely a spectacle whose implications he could not guess at. Heaven send it turned out to be misfortune only.

They hadn't long to wait for the answer: ten minutes later Thrand and the others returned.

'There was someone in the trees, my lord. Two men. We found footprints and flattened grass.' Thrand jerked his thumb over his shoulder. 'The trail leads north-east. Do you want us to follow?'

'No. The culprits will be long gone. Besides, I think we can guess where it leads.'

'To Beranhold,' murmured Anwyn.

Thrand frowned. 'But why would Ingvar send men to burn down a peasant's barn?'

'To act as a warning,' said Wulfgar.

They rode back in silence for the most part. Anwyn was disinclined for speech, being much disturbed by the ramifications of what had occurred. One look at her troubled face was enough to tell Wulfgar all he needed to know. Thus he bided his time. When at length they reached the confines of the pale and the horses had been led away, he took her aside.

'Don't be afraid. We will send out more patrols from now on. He won't catch us unawares again.'

'I thought that the attack would be here when it came,' she replied.

'This is the strongest point. Ingvar will seek softer targets.'

'It was just a barn this time. Will he kill men next?'

Wulfgar regarded her with a level gaze. 'When you start something like this there's no knowing what will happen, save that it is likely to be unpleasant.'

She sighed. 'This is what you warned me about, isn't it?'

'Aye. For the time being you are best to remain within the pale.'

The green eyes grew stormy. 'For five long years I was

constrained by Torstein. I will not allow Ingvar to limit my freedom thus.'

Wulfgar paused, choosing his next words with care. 'Then if you do go abroad, my lady, you should take an armed escort.'

Anwyn turned away, trying to contain the emotion that threatened to explode. Wulfgar's eyes narrowed a little.

'My lady?'

'Yes, I heard you.' She made a vague gesture with her hands. 'Odd, isn't it? When Torstein died I thought I was free at last, but nothing much has changed after all.'

'It is no part of my plan to play the gaoler. What I say is for your protection only.'

'I know.'

'Then will you do as I ask?'

She nodded. 'Very well.'

He relaxed a little. For a moment he had thought she might refuse point blank. If so, he wasn't quite sure what he would have done. He had the power to make her obey but, if he did, it would alienate her completely, and he had no wish to do that.

'Thank you.' He squeezed her arm gently. 'It is for the best, believe me.'

She did believe him, that was the problem. If he had issued commands, she would have known how to react, but this was harder to deal with—like the pressure of his hand on her sleeve and the way he was looking at her now. In that moment she wanted to draw closer, to feel his arms around her, to rest her head against his breast and forget everything else. However, that was not an option. He was a reassuring presence, but he was just doing the job she paid him to do. Essentially she was as alone now as she had ever been.

She took a step away and his hand fell from her sleeve. 'Excuse me, but I must go if any of us are to eat this evening.'

It wasn't an original excuse, but at least it had the merit of being partly true. More importantly it served its turn, and they both knew it.

Chapter Nine

Anwyn made a hasty *toilette* to repair the effects of the morning's ride, and then went to see about arrangements for the meal. With so many extra men to feed it required close attention. The demand for meat was huge. She could see the possibility of having to send out a hunting party before too long.

Her thoughts preoccupied with the possibility of wild boar, she left the hall. The clash of weapons rang in the warm air. Startled for a moment, she looked up and realised that the men were engaged in combat practice. On the edge of the area she could see Eyvind, his whole attention claimed by the scene. However, Ina was nearby speaking to Wulfgar so the child was unlikely to come to any harm. She smiled to herself and continued on her way.

The practice drew to a close and, having sheathed their weapons, the men gathered in small groups to talk. Eyvind looked up at Wulfgar.

'I want to learn how to fight. Ina says he'll teach me one day.'

His large companion nodded. 'A man must learn the skills of a warrior.'

The boy examined the sheathed blades at Wulfgar's side. 'What do you call them?'

'The sword is Skull-Biter, the dagger Serpent Sting.'

'May I look at them?'

'All right.' Wulfgar drew the dagger and held it across his palm. 'Careful. The edge is sharp.'

Eyvind nodded, eyeing it respectfully. Then, unable to resist, his fingers closed on the hilt. He lifted the blade carefully, grasping it like a sword, which in terms of their relative sizes it might have been. He turned it this way and that to catch the light and then essayed a few thrusting stokes at an imaginary foe.

'I will have a dagger like this one day.'

'I'm sure you will.'

His trial complete, Eyvind reluctantly handed the weapon back. Wulfgar sheathed it again and then drew out the sword.

'May I hold that, too?'

'Very well, but hold it firm. It's heavy.'

Eyvind gripped the hilt with both hands. Even so, the weight of the blade took him by surprise. However, Wulfgar had anticipated it and, reaching out, cupped his hand under the child's, arresting its downwards progress. Looking somewhat crestfallen, Eyvind sighed. His companion smiled.

'One day you'll be strong enough to wield such a blade.'

'Ina says you have to start with a wooden sword.'

'He's right.'

'But a wooden sword won't cut anything,' said Eyvind.

'No, it won't, but it will teach you how to use the real thing.'

'Did you have a wooden sword?'

'Aye, I did.'

'Did your father give you Skull-Biter?'

'No, I had the sword specially made.'

'My father's sword is buried with him, but he didn't die in battle.'

'Oh?' Wulfgar was genuinely taken aback. 'What happened to him?'

'He had a cheezer…no, I mean a sheezer…'

'A seizure,' said a voice from behind them. They looked round to see Ina. His gaze met Wulfgar's. 'He collapsed at meat one night. It was all over in moments.'

'I'm not going to die at meat,' said Eyvind. 'I'm going to die in battle.'

'It is an honourable tradition,' replied Ina.

Together they began to walk back towards the hall.

'I did not know that the Earl had met his end thus,' said Wulfgar. 'I assumed it had been in combat.'

'A fair assumption,' said Ina. 'And it might have been; he was no slouch with a sword.'

'He knew how to pick fighting men, too.'

'That he did.'

'Did you serve him long?'

'Long enough.' Ina grimaced. 'The man had a foul temper.'

'A difficult person to be around, then.'

'He was, but grown men can take what falls to them. 'Twas the woman and boy I felt sorry for—particularly her.' Ina shook his head. 'He kept her a virtual prisoner.'

Wulfgar frowned, recalling an earlier conversation with Anwyn. 'Did he ever use violence towards her?'

'Many a time, but for all that, he never succeeded in crushing her spirit. She stood up to him, anyway.'

Wulfgar now had a very clear picture of Earl Torstein's character; he'd met the type many times. The thought that any man might use his strength that way against a woman filled him with contempt. When that woman was Anwyn… Contempt turned to cold anger. The conversation also shed light on her reluctance to remarry. So many of the things she had said now made perfect sense.

'She deserves better,' Ina went on. 'The boy deserves better.'

'Aye, they do.'

'Well, the right man will come along eventually—a man who will protect her and treat her well.' The old man paused. 'A man she might learn to love.'

Wulfgar frowned. 'That's as may be, but right now the role of protector falls to me.'

'So it does, my lord.'

'You need have no fear that I shall fail in my duty.'

'Oh, I do not fear that.'

With this cryptic remark Ina took his leave and followed the child indoors. Wulfgar watched him go, feeling unaccountably disquieted. *A man she might learn to love?* What man? It couldn't be Ingvar. Was there another local admirer he didn't know about? His frown deepened.

However, there were other matters requiring his attention now. To begin with there was the question of the extra patrols. He went to find Hermund and told him his mind on the matter.

'It's a good idea. I'll organise it, my lord.'

'Patrols will go out day and night, effective immediately. I've been caught napping once, but it's the last time.'

'You could not have foreseen such a trick.'

'Well, Ingvar's given sufficient warning now so I reckon we can expect more such tricks,' said Wulfgar. 'All the same, we can make it difficult for him.'

'That we can. The men will enjoy it; give them more to do.' Hermund paused. 'And if we catch anyone?'

'Send his head back to Ingvar.'

'Right. This underhand connivance is unworthy of warriors. Let him bring his force and face us man to man.'

'It is my thought he will not do it. He will try to achieve his ends by other means.'

Hermund nodded. 'When you consider the prize it's clear he won't give up easily.'

'No, he won't,' said Wulfgar.

* * *

At table that evening he told Anwyn about the arrangements he had made earlier. She listened with quiet approval.

'When will these new patrols begin?'

'They already have.'

'You don't let the grass grow under your feet, do you?'

'If I'd done that, I'd have been dead long since.'

She smiled. 'A mercenary's life requires vigilance, then?'

'Of course.'

'And yet you enjoy the life.'

'It has its advantages.'

'And its disadvantages, too,' she replied. 'Each fight may be your last.'

'It is a risk one takes.'

'Does the thought not disturb you?'

'No, why should it? The thread of a man's life is cut as the Nornir decide—what use to worry when?'

'No use at all, but it might be wiser not to tempt them.'

'I have tempted them often,' he said, 'but they have shown no interest. On the contrary, I have had great luck; much more than I have deserved.'

She heard the note of bitterness in his voice and guessed its origin. 'If you have been thus favoured, then it was not your time to die. Perhaps there is more for you to do in this world before you go to the next.'

'A purpose for which I was intended?' He shook his head. 'There is no purpose, Anwyn. We are born, we fight and then we die.'

'Is fighting the be all and end all?'

'If a man fights, he suffers less than those who do not. That is the way of the world.'

She raised an eyebrow. 'That is a sombre view of life.'

'It is an accurate view of life.'

'Yet you did not always think so.'

'No, but I've learned better now. I will fight whatever battles come, and one day I will meet the warrior whose sword arm is stronger than mine.'

'Your death will not change the past, Wulfgar.'

Her words were softly spoken, but they caught him unawares and their accuracy pierced like a honed blade. His hand tightened round his cup and all trace of former ironic detachment vanished along with the gentleness in his eyes. What replaced it was bleakness and anger, the latter directed towards himself. The odds he chose to fight should have killed him fifty times over; instead he grew rich and his fame spread. He could almost hear the gods laughing.

Seeing the look in his eyes just then, Anwyn felt an inner tremor, glimpsing the mercenary in those icy-blue depths. However, he made no reply and for a little while they lapsed into silence. She threw him a swift sideways glance and decided it was time to change the subject.

'Do your men care to hunt, my lord?'

'Of course. Why?'

'It's just that we could do with some fresh meat and there are boars aplenty in the woods.'

'I'll see to it.'

Anwyn hesitated, regarding him speculatively. 'I wondered if I might go along.'

'Certainly not.' As soon as he'd said it, Wulfgar could have kicked himself. Even to his ears it had sounded arrogant and high-handed. Nor did he miss the way she suddenly stiffened or the expression of resentment on her face. He drew a deep breath and, having hastily re-established the connection between his brain and his mouth, he hurried on. 'Forgive me. That was not the arbitrary decision it may have seemed. What I meant was that it's too dangerous at present. The woods do not only conceal boar, as we have recent proof. You would be an easy target there.'

Some of her resentment faded and was replaced by disappointment. 'Oh, yes, I see.'

Wulfgar seized his chance. 'But perhaps you might care to go hawking instead. Out in open country an enemy can be seen from afar, and thus easily dealt with. And you could enjoy some fresh air and some decent sport.'

The green eyes lightened. 'I'd like that.'

'So be it. We'll go tomorrow if you wish.'

'Oh, yes. That would be wonderful.'

In that moment all her customary reserve fell away and her face lit with a smile that caused his heartbeat to accelerate dangerously. It occurred to him again that she had the most kissable mouth he had ever seen. The memory immediately aroused desire. With an effort he controlled it.

'Of course, I'll have to beg the loan of a falcon,' he said.

'My late husband had many. I am sure we can find something to please you, my lord.'

Wulfgar was quite sure of it. Having already discovered the mews in his exploration of Drakensburgh, he could only applaud Torstein's taste in that as well. However, he wasn't about to lose the advantage now, and steered the conversation to the safe haven of falconry. Anwyn proved surprisingly knowledgeable and, having relaxed, opened up again, speaking without reserve, listening, asking questions.

'Where did you learn all this?' he asked.

'My father and brothers were enthusiasts and taught me much. Torstein, too, was accomplished in the sport.' She paused. 'Of course, he did not invite me to accompany him very often.'

Wulfgar could well believe it, but forbore to make the comment that came instantly to mind. Torstein might have known a lot about hawks, but in other ways the man was an idiot. And only another idiot would make the same mistakes. Thus he kept the conversation away from the personal, drawing her out on other subjects.

The hour grew late but for once Anwyn seemed not to notice. Nor did she seem inclined to leave. Wulfgar didn't dare to hope she was softening towards him, although tonight she seemed to be enjoying his company more. It was a start at least. He had never worked as hard to win a woman in his life, but then she provided the kind of challenge that a man rarely encountered. Circumstances dictated that theirs could only ever be a brief liaison; but for all that he wanted her more than any woman he had ever met.

The following day dawned fair and they set out early, accompanied by half-a-dozen men. Out in the open air, Anwyn's spirit lifted and she found herself smiling for no apparent reason. It felt good just to be alive on such a day. All thoughts of Ingvar receded. Today she was in the company she would most have sought.

Involuntarily her gaze went to Wulfgar, currently stroking the breast feathers of a magnificent gyrfalcon. His hand was firm and strong, but infinitely gentle. He would touch a woman like that, she thought. It brought back the memory she had tried so hard to bury and sent a wave of painful longing through her entire being. As though sensing himself watched, he glanced up and met her eye. She saw him smile, the familiar easy smile that caused her heart to miss a beat.

One of the men called out and she glanced up, following the line of his pointing finger, and saw the pigeon. Sensing danger, it beat hard, winging fast towards the cover of distant trees. Wulfgar removed the hood from the gyrfalcon's eyes and loosed the jesses. Then he spoke softly and cast her off. The raptor climbed, her powerful wings gaining her height with every beat while her golden eyes located their prey. As she mounted, her wingtips felt the edges of a warm air current and she glided effortlessly, her gaze locked on the quarry below. Then she stooped, arrowing downwards in deadly free fall. Anwyn held her breath. A sharp cry and a puff of feather announced the strike. Great talons bore the prey back to earth. Wulfgar whistled and swung the lure, summoning the gyrfalcon back to his wrist, leaving one of the accompanying retainers to retrieve the pigeon.

'A fine kill,' said Anwyn.

'Aye, it was.' He smiled at her. 'However, the next bird we flush is yours.'

By the end of the morning the bag was impressive. They tethered the horses then and, moving a little apart from their companions, spread their cloaks on the grass before settling down to eat an improvised meal of bread and cheese and cold meat. Anwyn ate hungrily for the fresh air and exercise had given her an appetite. It had also brought colour into her cheeks and put a sparkle in her eyes. Strands of hair had escaped her braid and formed an artless halo round her face. The effect was unwittingly seductive.

Wulfgar eyed the ribbon that fastened the rest. He was sorely tempted to pull it loose and free the glorious wilful mass it bound. His imagination ran ahead of him. If he did, what would be her response? He smiled ruefully to himself. Had they been alone… Unfortunately they were not. It was probably just as well, he decided. He wasn't at all sure he could have stopped at just unfastening her hair.

Unaware of his train of thought, Anwyn finished her food and brushed the crumbs from her skirt. Then she got to her feet.

'There's a stream over yonder. I'm going to get a drink.'

'Not on your own, you're not,' he replied.

She looked around, but the landscape was quiet, drowsing beneath the warm spring sunshine. 'There's no danger near.'

'Even so.'

It was a tone she had come to recognise and it signified that he wasn't going to be deflected from his purpose. This insistence on staying close should have annoyed her, but it didn't. She schooled her face into what she hoped was an expression of unconcern.

'As you will.'

They strolled together across the grass. Neither one spoke and, although the silence was companionable, it was also highly charged. With every pace she was more aware of the tall, lithe figure beside her, of his quiet strength and the aura of power he wore so effortlessly.

It was no more than fifty yards to the stream, a bright clear freshet that flowed towards the distant woods. Anwyn bent and scooped a handful of water. It was cold and delicious. For a moment he watched her, then followed suit. His profile was towards her now and she drank in every detail, memorising every line of him, relearning what was already known so well.

Apparently unaware of her scrutiny, he slaked his thirst and then straightened slowly. For a moment he surveyed her in silence, then extended a hand. After a brief hesitation she took it. His fingers closed over hers and he drew her gently to her feet. He should have let go then. Instead he lifted her hand to his lips and, turning it over gently, pressed a soft kiss on the palm. It burned like a brand, sending a delicious shiver through her entire being and stirring other, more dangerous recollections.

Wulfgar smiled at her. 'Come. We should rejoin the others.'

Anwyn let out the breath she had unconsciously been holding, her mind registering both relief and something else, too, a feeling that didn't bear closer inspection.

They rode back after that, keeping the horses to a leisurely pace, enjoying the sunshine. The men of the escort laughed and joked and talked among themselves about hunting. Anwyn listened and smiled to herself. Wulfgar regarded her keenly.

'Did you enjoy yourself today?' he asked.

She nodded. 'In truth I cannot remember when I last enjoyed myself as much.'

'Good.' He smiled. 'We must arrange another such outing, and soon.'

'I'd like that.'

It probably wasn't wise, but she didn't care. Rather she felt as a person might who, having languished for years in a dark place, is suddenly released into the sunlight.

Chapter Ten

As they rode in through the gateway Anwyn's smile faded and, seeing it, Wulfgar immediately followed the line of her gaze to the hall where stood several horses. From the sweat marks on their necks and flanks they had all been ridden hard. A group of men stood nearby. Their clothing identified them immediately as a nobleman and his escort. For a moment he thought Ingvar was back but, hearing the approaching horses, the men turned round and he found himself looking at complete strangers. However, it immediately became clear that Anwyn recognised them.

'Osric,' she murmured.

Wulfgar threw her a quizzical glance. 'Osric?'

'My elder brother.'

Privately he owned to surprise, but then her expression indicated much the same thing. Along with it he detected a suggestion of uneasiness. His curiosity stirred. They pulled up and dismounted and he watched as Anwyn moved forwards to greet the new arrivals. Foremost among them was a man in his mid-twenties. He was of average height and a slender, wiry build. Facially he bore a resemblance to Anwyn in the high cheekbones and the shape of the mouth, but the likeness stopped there. His hair was a gingery brown shade and his eyes pale blue. These were now subjecting her to a quiet appraisal. However, if she noticed it wasn't apparent.

'Osric! This is a surprise.'

She embraced him, saluting him on both cheeks. It was sisterly and correct in every way, but Wulfgar could not see any sign of mutual warmth. Intrigued now, he listened carefully.

'You look very well, Sister. Still in great beauty, I see.'

'What are you doing here?'

'Passing through, on my way north.'

Wulfgar's eyebrow lifted a little. If the man was going north he had come a considerable distance out of his way. Either he had a mighty poor sense of direction or he was being disingenuous.

'It is good of you to call upon us,' replied Anwyn.

'I told you I'd be back.'

'Yes, so you did.'

He smiled rather awkwardly. 'I trust that Drakensburgh prospers, Sister.'

'It prospers.'

'These past months must have been hard for you.'

'I have managed well enough,' she replied. 'I have good men to help me.'

'Ah.'

'You haven't met Lord Wulfgar, have you?'

'No.' For the first time, Osric became aware of the other man's presence and surveyed him now with a critical eye.

'Lord Wulfgar is in charge of Drakensburgh's defensive force,' Anwyn went on.

'Indeed.' He favoured Wulfgar with a nod. 'I'm sure you're doing a good job.'

Wulfgar ignored the patronising tone and returned the nod. 'That is what I am paid for.'

For a moment Osric seemed taken aback and he threw a quizzical look at Anwyn. She ignored it.

'Well, you must be tired after your long ride, Brother. Perhaps you and your companions would care for some refreshment.'

'Thank you, yes.'

She looked at Wulfgar. 'Will you excuse us, please? My brother and I need to talk.'

He inclined his head in acquiescence and with that she led Osric and his companions within doors. Wulfgar surveyed them thoughtfully. The tension between brother and sister had been almost palpable.

'Not much love lost there, my lord,' said a voice at his shoulder.

He glanced round to see Asulf, who had approached unnoticed. 'Apparently not.'

'Might not be a barrel of laughs at table tonight, then.'

'I seriously doubt it.'

Having provided her guests with ale, Anwyn took her brother aside. 'Now, tell me what you're really doing here, Osric.'

'I told you. We're just—'

'Passing through? Hardly.'

He eyed her curiously. 'You've changed since I saw you last, Anwyn. You've become…'

'Older?'

'That, of course, but also more…poised, more self-assured.'

'More like a grown woman, in fact.'

'Yes.'

'Oh, I grew up quickly, Osric, believe me.'

'We all grow up, Sister.'

'What was it you came to say?'

'I bring news from home,' he replied.

Anwyn tensed, waiting. 'The family are all well?'

'Our brothers and sisters are quite well.'

'That's good to hear.'

'Mother sends her warmest greetings.'

'And Father?' she asked.

'Ah, yes, Father.'

The knot in her stomach tightened. Now they would come to it.

'He has been unwell these last months.'

'I am grieved to hear it.'

'In consequence, I have undertaken many of the responsibilities that fell to him in the past.'

'I am sure that he is grateful for the assistance.'

'It is no more than my duty.' Osric paused. 'Speaking of which, have you thought further upon the matter we touched on when last I visited?'

'The wealthy northern earl?'

'Just so.'

'Of course.'

Misreading her response, he nodded. 'Such an alliance would increase our family's standing greatly, to say nothing of wealth.'

'I have no doubt it would,' she replied. 'There's only one problem.'

'What's that?'

'It isn't going to happen.'

His jaw dropped. 'You can't be serious.'

'I was never more serious in my life.'

'Look, Anwyn, I know that your first marriage was not happy, but...'

'My first marriage was a living hell—a hell that you were instrumental in making.'

'I meant it for the best. Torstein—'

'Torstein was a brute and you knew it, yet still you sided with Father.' Her gaze raked him. 'I begged you, Osric, but you ignored me.'

'Father would have insisted on the match anyway. My intervention would have made no difference,' he replied. 'Besides, it's water under the bridge now. We cannot change the past.'

'True, but we can shape the future. I am not a child any more, and I will not be treated like a chattel. If I marry again it will be to a man of my choosing, not yours.'

'Don't be a fool, Anwyn. This is a wonderful chance. You can't just throw it away.'

'Watch me.'

For a moment he was silent, regarding her resentfully. 'You really mean it, don't you?'

'Don't be in any doubt about that.'

'Father won't like it.'

'I'm sorry. I'll just have to live with that.'

'He will compel your obedience.'

'No, he won't and neither will you, even if I have to barricade myself into Drakensburgh with an army.'

Wulfgar sent the game bag to the kitchens and then went to the carpenter's shop. The new yard was almost ready. The repair to the rudder was complete. Had it not been for their current agreement he and his crew would have been on their way tomorrow. His men seemed content enough: the living was easy here. Apart from the promise of gold, they had good food to eat and slept dry. It sufficed, for now. In the end, though, it could never compete with the call of the sea or the feel of the ship beneath their feet. They would do what they had promised here, but eventually the *Sea Wolf* would reclaim her own.

'So who was that with Lady Anwyn?' asked Hermund.

Wulfgar returned abruptly to dry land. 'Her brother, one Osric.'

'Brother, eh? What does he want here?'

'A social call,' replied Wulfgar. 'Says he's on his way north.'

'North? He's well out of his road then, isn't he?'

'My thought exactly. It's more than just a visit with family.'

'Has to be.'

'I expect we'll find out soon enough.'

'Aye, no doubt we—' Hermund broke off, his attention on something beyond his companion's shoulder.

Instinctively Wulfgar turned round, just in time to see Anwyn astride a horse and heading out of the gates.

'She oughtn't to go out alone,' said Hermund. 'It's not safe.'

'I told her that.'

'Ah. Well, I expect she's got a good reason for disregarding the advice.'

Wulfgar's brows drew together. 'She'd better have.'

Leaving his companion, he sprinted to the stables. Minutes later he was astride a horse and heading off in pursuit of the fugitive.

Anwyn had no clear idea of where she was going, only of the need to get out of Drakensburgh for a while. Her brain burned with the memory of that recent conversation with her brother, fuelling anger and resentment. Was she never to be free of the men who sought to control her life? Did they really imagine that she would bend meekly to their will once again? If so, they had another thing coming. Rage spilled over into tears. Damn Osric! Damn all of them! Leaning forwards she gave the horse its head, letting it out to a gallop.

The thudding hooves pounded like the blood in her veins, the pace bordering on reckless, but just then she didn't care. The horse was fresh and keen, the wind in her face exhilarating, giving back a sensation of freedom. They sped on for more than a mile before she slowed a little, reining in to let the animal breathe. Only then did she hear the muffled thud of hoofbeats on turf and looked up sharply to see the advancing horseman. For a moment she tensed, but, realising he was alone, her anxiety faded a little. It wasn't until he was within a hundred yards that she recognised the rider.

'Wulfgar,' she murmured.

Surprise mingled with vague unease as she watched the

other horse pull up. Then she saw the expression on the rider's face.

'Is something wrong, my lord?'

The blue eyes were glacial. 'Just what do you think you're doing?'

The autocratic tone brought all her former ire bubbling to the surface. 'What does it look like I'm doing?'

'What it looks like is a total disregard for common sense. You little fool. Don't you know better than to go off alone like that?'

Anwyn's chin lifted. 'I'll go where I please.'

'Not while I'm responsible for protecting you, you won't.'

'I am the one who gives the orders at Drakensburgh, not you.'

'That isn't the point at issue here.'

'Isn't it?'

He brought his horse alongside hers. 'We had an agreement, remember? If you refuse to honour it, then we can call off the whole arrangement right now.'

Anwyn stared at him. 'Call it off?'

'You heard me. Do you think I'm going to waste my time creating a defensive force only to have my work undermined by a wilful, heedless little idiot who changes the rules to suit herself?'

Her cheeks burned. 'I wasn't changing the rules.'

'Oh, really?' He gestured to the vast expanse of heath around them. 'Then what are you doing out here by yourself?'

'I didn't mean any harm. I didn't think…'

'No, you damned well didn't, or you'd have seen the risk.'

It took every ounce of control not to retort in kind. He was high-handed and arrogant and overbearing. The knowledge that he was right and his anger justified did nothing to improve her mood. Nor did the realisation that she needed him a lot more than he needed her. With an effort she swallowed her pride.

'I don't want to end our agreement.'

'Well, you're giving a good impression of it.'

'I didn't mean to.'

'Then what did you mean?'

'I...it was just...'

His gaze raked her. 'Just what?' Then, for the first time, he noticed her tear-stained face and frowned. 'Anwyn?'

To her horror she felt fresh tears welling and looked away. 'Forgive me.' She dashed the water away with the back of her hand.

Had it been any other woman he'd have suspected a play for sympathy, but this distress clearly had earlier origins. He let out a long breath and anger subsided a little.

'Do you want to tell me about it?'

She nodded. Wulfgar dismounted and waited as she followed suit. Then he tethered the horses and led Anwyn to a fallen log that would serve as a makeshift seat. When they had both sat down he turned to face her.

'Now...'

She took a deep breath, collecting herself again. Then she gave him an unvarnished account of what had passed between herself and Osric. He listened without interruption, but as he did so he felt his anger mount again. This time, however, its focus was quite different. Although her actions had been fool-hardy, he could also understand why she had wanted to get away from Drakensburgh for a while. He also regretted his earlier anger, even though it had been born out of concern.

'If this match is repugnant to you, then you are right to refuse it,' he said, when at length the tale was concluded.

She shook her head. 'It isn't as simple as that. My father is powerful...'

'Surely he would not try to compel you to remarry.'

'He is not concerned with my will, only his own. He would not hesitate to try—or to use force if commanding failed. My brother as good as said so before I left.'

Though she tried to conceal it her agitation was evident.

It touched him more deeply than he had anticipated, more so than if she had wept openly. Along with that was a growing sense of her vulnerability.

'He may try, but he would be unlikely to succeed.' He paused. 'Drakensburgh is strong. You will be safe enough.'

'I wonder if I will ever be really safe.'

'I will not allow anyone to remove you by force.'

Some of the tension went out of her. 'Then you won't withdraw from our agreement?'

'No.'

'Thank you.'

'But in return I want your solemn promise that you will obey me in this matter.'

'You have it.' She hesitated. 'I'm sorry that I gave you cause for concern. I won't do it again.'

He smiled wryly. 'See you don't. Even if Ingvar's men aren't lying in wait to carry you off, you'll break your neck riding at that speed.'

'I wouldn't normally. It's just that I was so angry and I wanted to get as far away from Osric as possible.'

'I suppose I should be thankful I didn't have to pursue you the length of the kingdom.'

She shook her head. 'You would have given it up as a bad job long before then.'

'I never give up when I have a goal, my sweet, and I'd have found you eventually. Only then my temper would have been much worse.'

Anwyn shivered inwardly, but not with fear—or not exactly. She couldn't quite identify the emotion that swept her then.

'Your anger would be justified.'

'Aye, it would. Though in truth I think it would be hard to remain angry with you for very long.'

'I would not have you so,' she replied.

'In any case, anger is a waste of energy that could be put to better use.'

The expression in the blue eyes was quite unmistakable and it sent a flush of heat to the region of her loins. Suddenly she was aware that they were alone and the place isolated. There was nothing to stop him pursuing this. And if he did? Shocked by the answer in her own heart, she turned away from him lest he should read it in her face. He was too experienced not to recognise what was there.

'You're trembling. What are you afraid of, Anwyn?' He paused. 'Me?'

'No, of course not.'

That much was true. It wasn't him she was afraid of.

'Then look at me.'

She took a deep breath and forced herself to face him again, to bear that quiet scrutiny.

'I won't hurt you,' he continued. 'Nor will I let anything happen to you.'

'I know.'

The green eyes expressed trust, possibly the last emotion he had expected to see there at that moment. It was more powerful than he could ever have envisaged. It also prevented any further advance down the delightful route of his imagination. He squeezed her hand gently. Then, reluctantly, he got to his feet and drew her up with him.

'We'd better get back before Hermund sends out a search party.'

She nodded, not trusting herself to speak, every part of her alive to him. His touch was warm and strong, reassuring and disturbing in equal measure. She was just glad that he could not see the extent of her thoughts. This man represented the kind of temptation she could never previously have imagined.

They walked together back to the horses, by which time she had regained a little more composure. Under his watchful gaze she gathered the reins and remounted. Having seen her safely in the saddle, he vaulted on to his own horse and brought it alongside. Then they set off, this time at a much gentler pace.

* * *

The gathering at table that evening seemed a strangely unreal affair. Osric made no secret of his displeasure with Anwyn, adopting a manner of frigid courtesy. If he had thought to dismay her or induce feelings of remorse, he was well wide of the mark. Anwyn barely seemed to notice, much less to care. Her mind was elsewhere. Wulfgar, too, seemed more thoughtful than usual this evening, although his face betrayed no hint of what those thoughts might be.

Once or twice she glanced his way, hoping to glean some inkling, but in vain. She was mortified now by the folly of her earlier actions, and by the recollection of his anger. If he pulled out of their agreement she was lost. Future security depended on his goodwill. If he could ensure ongoing protection for Drakensburgh she would be safe, and all those for whom she was responsible. He didn't seem to be the kind of man who would renege on a promise, but nor would he tolerate any infraction of the rules he had laid down. Rules, she now admitted, that were necessary, not arbitrary.

'I shall leave early in the morning, Sister. My companions and I have a long ride ahead of us.'

Osric's voice broke in to her reverie. Anwyn glanced across at him, noting dispassionately that he looked both disapproving and sullen.

'As you will,' she replied. 'I'll have the servants provide you with food for your journey.'

'Thank you.'

'Not at all. It'll be a pleasure.'

His eyes narrowed. 'You're making a serious mistake, Anwyn, you know that? Father will never allow you to get away with this.'

'I think you are Father's mouthpiece now, Osric. Nevertheless, my decision is made. I shall not go back on it.'

'You're a fool, then.'

'I don't think so.'

'Well, on your own head be it.' He leaned closer. 'This isn't the end of the matter. I'll be back, and with a much larger force next time.'

The implied threat did not escape her. Anwyn took another sip of ale and looked away, unwilling to prolong the discussion. As she did so her gaze met Wulfgar's.

'Your brother seems a little out of sorts, my lady.'

'He'll get over it.'

'No doubt.' He lowered his voice. 'But what of you, Anwyn?'

A pink flush rose along her throat. 'I do not fear his displeasure.'

'Neither should you. It cannot harm you now.'

His words carried all manner of implications, which filled her with wildly contrasting emotions. Although she was nominally in charge of affairs here, his power was considerable—in real terms greater than hers. Caught now between two powerful men, her instinct was still to trust him. She could only pray that her instinct was correct, for the people of Drakensburgh and for herself.

She retired early that evening, needing time to think. For all her brave assertions to Wulfgar, she knew full well that she couldn't ignore the danger posed by her father and brother. Osric's words had not been an idle threat. It would not be beyond either of them to use force if the perceived gain outweighed the disadvantages. Her jaw tightened. She would resist them as far as she could, but resistance meant bloodshed. Freedom came only at a price, and one more costly than gold.

That thought engendered others. She had wealth enough to buy the loyalty of the mercenaries for now, but how if the situation escalated into a conflict on two fronts? Increased risk might well mean an increased demand for payment. The gold was not limitless and there was no way of knowing how long such a conflict might last. Anwyn sighed, feeling as though she were caught between hammer and anvil. A woman alone was a hostage to fortune. In truth, it was a man's world. Marry the unknown northern earl or marry Ingvar. The choice was stark affording no third way.

She drew off her gown and, having laid the garment carefully aside, unfastened her hair and reached for the comb. If only she could yoke the mercenary force permanently, her position would be unassailable. The question was how? She drew the comb slowly through a skein of hair. The teeth had slid about halfway down its length when the third way suggested itself. Her hand froze and she was suddenly very still but, deep within, her heart performed something dangerously close to a somersault. Anwyn mentally shook herself.

'That's ridiculous. It's madness,' she murmured. 'Utter madness.'

Her mind immediately followed through with all the reasons for thinking so. Yet what underpinned that lengthy list was a faint glimmer of hope. It *could* be made to work. The glimmer grew brighter. What it illuminated then was the fundamental shift in her thinking that had somehow taken place without her even being aware of it, until now. With trembling fingers she put the comb down. Such a decision should not be reached in haste. She must sleep on it. The trouble was that sleep had never seemed so far away.

Chapter Eleven

Osric and his companions left early next day after a cool leave-taking in which few words were spoken. Anwyn watched them go, her dominant emotion relief. She wasn't naïve enough to think that she had heard the end of the matter, but it would be a little while before either he or her father were in a position to take any kind of action. By the time they did… She swallowed hard. Then, summoning all her courage, she went in search of Wulfgar.

She found him in the carpenter's workshop with Hermund. Both men looked up and smiled, offering a courteous greeting. She returned it, then looked pointedly at Wulfgar.

'I beg you will forgive the intrusion, but I need to talk to you, my lord.'

'Very well.' He glanced at his companion.

Hermund was quick to take the hint. 'Right, I'll leave you to it then.'

Anwyn was barely aware of his going, only of the growing knot in her stomach. The silence stretched out. She could almost hear her own heartbeat. The man before her disposed himself casually on the edge of the workbench, waiting.

'My lady?'

'It concerns the matter we spoke of yesterday.'

'Your brother?'

She nodded. 'I will never be safe, and nor will the people here, unless I can put myself permanently out of his reach and Ingvar's, too.'

'How do you propose to do that?'

Anwyn drew a deep breath. 'I must be married.'

'Forgive me, but didn't you say—'

'Married to a man of my choosing.' She took another deep breath and steeled herself. 'I want *you* to marry me.'

He was genuinely speechless, as though all the air had been driven out of his lungs. Under other circumstances he might have laughed at the sheer absurdity of it.

'A marriage in name only,' she continued, 'that will put everyone concerned beyond their power.'

Wulfgar regained the use of his voice. 'A noble sacrifice.'

'I do not intend to be a victim.'

His lips twitched. 'I'm pleased to hear it. Such a role sits ill on you.'

'I was being serious.'

'So was I.' He paused. 'You seek permanent protection from me—what do you offer in return?'

'The earldom of Drakensburgh.'

'A tempting prize.'

'Of course I would not expect you to stay here all the time,' she continued. 'I know that yours is a roving life. I would only ask that you leave behind a force sufficient to protect the place.'

'Which you would govern in my absence.'

'Yes.'

'No,' he replied.

'Then you…you mean you would stay?'

'I mean that such an idea is madness. Besides, I am not good husband material, my sweet.'

'I would make no demands.'

He stood up, casually crossing the intervening space

between them. 'But how do you know that I would not?' His presence seemed to fill the little room; the very air between them seemed suddenly energised. 'How do you know that, in seeking to escape Ingvar and your northern earl, you would not be putting yourself into a far worse situation?'

'If I had thought so, I would not be speaking to you now.'

'I'm flattered, truly.'

'I do not speak to flatter you.'

He smiled wryly. 'No, forgive me, I should have known better. All the same I am honoured by your trust.'

'Don't mock me, Wulfgar, please.'

'I wasn't.'

Something about his expression then caused her pulse to quicken. 'Then...will you help me?'

'Anwyn, I wish I could, but...'

'I have no one else to turn to.' The green eyes met his in mute appeal. 'No one.'

'Don't cast me in the role of hero.'

'I ask only that you consider it.'

For the space of several heartbeats he was silent, his mind a mass of troubled memories. He was *not* good husband material; over the last six years he had learned to live with that knowledge. Of course, he had been much younger then: wild, undisciplined, unable to curb the restlessness in his nature. There had been plenty of time since to regret the folly of his youth. Learning from past mistakes was an integral part of maturity. Looked at objectively, Drakensburgh was nothing to do with him. He should probably walk away. And if he did walk away, what then? It shouldn't have mattered, but somehow the thought rankled. She had helped him when he needed it. Could he abandon her now their situations were reversed? Could he abandon another woman as he had before? Their situations might be vastly different but the need was still there.

Unable to follow the thoughts behind the impassive face,

Anwyn prayed silently, clenching her hands so tightly that the nails dug into her palms.

'*If* I were to agree to this,' he said at last, 'it would be because you understood the terms on which it would depend.'

Hope leapt. He wasn't turning her down flat. 'Name your terms.'

'I would ensure that Drakensburgh was protected, you'd have my word on that. But I wouldn't stay for ever, Anwyn. I have a duty to my men and my ship, not to mention an arrangement with Rollo.'

'I know.'

'I might be absent for a long time—years, perhaps.'

'I understand that.'

'There's something more.' The blue eyes met and held hers. 'While we *were* together... You're a very beautiful woman and I would be lying if I said I didn't want you to share my bed.'

Her heart leapt towards her throat and coherent thought fled, along with the possibility of speech.

Misreading that silence, he schooled his expression to careful neutrality and continued, 'However, that would be for you to choose. I would not demand anything you were unwilling to give. Nor would I promise you my undying love.'

The words caused an unexpected pang. However, he was at least being honest with her. 'I understand that, too.'

'Very well, then.'

'You mean you'll do it?'

He nodded. 'Under those conditions.'

Relief mingled with emotions less clearly defined. 'I accept your conditions.'

He surveyed her keenly for a moment. 'Then will you seal the bargain with me, Anwyn?'

'My lord?'

Her wits returned in a blood-thumping rush as he drew her against him, looking into her face, his eyes questioning. It might have been wiser to pull away, but she could not. He bent his head, his lips brushing hers, the touch light and tentative at first, then, as he felt her relax against him, more persuasive. The kiss was gentle and lingering, quite unlike that other time, and yet her heart thumped just as hard. At length he drew back and his hold slackened a little, enough to allow breath, but not escape.

'When is this bargain to be met?'

With an effort she gathered her thoughts again. 'The sooner the better.'

'Then on the morrow, if you will.'

It wasn't quite what she had anticipated, but perhaps he was right. If they were to commit themselves thus it might be as well not to have too much time to reconsider. All the same she could not but be keenly aware of how contrary it was to the accepted mode of doing things.

'It will have to be a quiet affair,' she said. 'Will you mind?'

'No. Besides, there will be time enough to let everyone know afterwards.' He smiled faintly. 'I imagine we're going to get some interesting reactions.'

'Yes, I imagine we are.'

'Not all of them will be friendly. Are you prepared for that?

'As prepared as I'll ever be.'

'Well, you have never lacked for courage.'

Again it wasn't what she had been expecting, but the words had sounded sincere. Moreover, they reflected the expression in his eyes.

'I will try to do you honour, my lord.'

'You already have,' he replied.

Some time later, after Anwyn had left, Hermund returned to find Wulfgar deep in thought.

'Is everything all right, my lord?'

'Everything is fine. However, there's something I must tell you…' He related the substance of his recent conversation.

Hermund's jaw dropped. 'Getting married?'

'That's right. Incidentally, that's just for your information at present.'

'I'll be as silent as the tomb.' Hermund shook his head. 'I've got to hand it to you, lord, you're a fast worker. Not that I blame you, of course. She's gorgeous—and rich.'

'This wasn't my idea, it was hers.'

'Do you know, I had a suspicion she liked you. Not that anyone would wonder at that, either. You make a handsome couple.'

Wulfgar eyed him askance. 'For the love of Odin, could you forget about romance and stick to the practicalities?'

'Aye, right. When's the wedding, then?'

'Tomorrow.'

'She *is* keen, isn't she?' Then, as another thought occurred to him, Hermund added, 'What about Rollo?'

'What about him?'

'Well, I imagine the plan has changed now.'

'Not at all.'

For the second time in the space of a minute Hermund was taken aback. 'Oh.'

'This is a marriage of convenience, nothing more. Of course I'll ensure that Drakensburgh is well protected.'

'Aren't you forgetting Ingvar?'

'Who could forget Ingvar?'

'You know what I mean. He isn't going to like it.'

'His opinion is of no interest. All he has to understand is that Drakensburgh is mine and Lady Anwyn, too.'

His companion nodded. 'I'm sure you'll make it clear.'

'I shall, and that right soon.'

'He won't poach on your preserve after that.'

'He'd better not.'

'No man in his right mind would do that.' Hermund hesitated. 'Doesn't it bother you, though, the thought of leaving her alone all that time? I mean, you could be away for years.'

Wulfgar's jaw tightened. 'It was part of the agreement. She knew that at the outset.'

'I see.'

'She will still have Ina. Besides, she's intelligent and competent, perfectly capable of running things in my absence.'

'Of course she is. It's just that…'

'What?'

'Isn't it going to be a bit lonely for her?'

'She will have plenty to occupy her in my absence.'

'Oh, well, that's all right, then.'

Wulfgar eyed him sharply, but his companion's expression was quite bland. All the same, the words left a strangely sour taste.

'So when are you going to tell the lads?'

'Not yet, but as soon as I can.'

Hermund grinned. 'I'll look forward to that. In the meantime, is there anything you need—for tomorrow?'

'I don't think so. No, wait. There is one thing…'

After the conversation with Wulfgar, Anwyn returned to the women's bower, her heart thumping. She was trembling a little, too. Unable to settle, she paced the floor slowly, trying to order her chaotic thoughts. She had just put her future into the hands of a man she had known only a matter of days and yet, underneath anxiety, was still the instinct that he could be trusted to keep his word. Drakensburgh would be secure and the people safe from the depredations of men like Ingvar. She could watch her son grow to manhood without the permanent shadow of threat hanging over him. And she… Anwyn smiled ruefully. Wulfgar had made his position clear on that score. What mattered was that he had agreed to help her. She could expect nothing more from him.

When Jodis came in a little later she told her the whole, or at least as much as she needed to know. Jodis's eyes widened.

'You've actually done it, my lady?'

'Yes, heaven help me. I've done it.'

'I'm glad you have.' Jodis's face lit in a smile. 'I believe Lord Wulfgar to be an honourable man; he will deal fairly with the people here—and with you.'

'I hope you're right. I hope I'm right. My instinct tells me I am and yet I feel as nervous as a cat on a raft.'

'What does your heart tell you?'

'This is not an affair of hearts, Jodis. It is a matter of business.'

The maid lowered her gaze. 'Of course it is, my lady.'

Anwyn crossed the room to the clothes chest and opened the lid. 'Will you help me find something to wear tomorrow?'

For the next hour gowns were examined and rejected and with each one her uncertainty grew. In the end she selected a dark blue, intricately embroidered with gold-coloured thread, to be worn over a fine linen kirtle. A light headrail completed the outfit, held in place with a slender gold fillet. It was a rich and elegant costume, one that she hoped would do honour to the occasion and to her bridegroom.

The word sent a tremor through her. For all that this was to be a marriage of convenience, Wulfgar would still be her husband. Even there he had been honest. It was his legal right to take her if he wished, and yet he left the choice to her. She had not let her imagination dwell on the more intimate aspects of their relationship. Now she was going to have to confront it. *I would be lying if I said I didn't want you to share my bed...* She bit her lip. How would it be to share his bed? She knew enough about him now to guess that he would not use her roughly, but even so, their coupling would mean nothing to him beyond the sating of physical desire. The wife he had loved was dead. Not only that, she had died young; she would always remain like that for him, her beauty undiminished by time.

Anwyn squared her shoulders. It was no use thinking in

those terms. She had chosen this; she would have to live with the consequences—whatever they were. In the interim she needed to speak to Ina.

He heard her in silence, his craggy face impassive. Only when she had finished did he venture to speak.

'I wish you happy, my lady.'

'Thank you.' She paused. 'You do not venture an opinion on the matter, though.'

'It is not my place to venture an opinion. You are doing what you believe to be best for Drakensburgh.'

'Indeed, Ina, I pray I am doing the right thing. I do truly believe that Lord Wulfgar will be open and just in his dealings with the people here.'

'Thus far there has been nothing in his manner to suggest otherwise,' the old warrior replied, 'but only time will tell.'

'Can I still rely on your support?'

'That is a given, my lady. I thought you knew that.'

'Forgive me. It's just that things have become so complicated of late and…well, I wasn't sure you would approve this latest step. The consequences are so far-reaching—for all of us.'

'Aye, they are, my lady. So I'll continue to watch your back.'

Retracing her steps to the women's bower, Anwyn went to find Eyvind. In truth, she had been putting off the moment when she would have to tell him about the great change that was about to happen in his life. He had not been close to his father, had feared him. The thought of having another, and a near stranger to boot, might not be welcome.

Eyvind listened in wide-eyed silence as she explained, as simply as she could, what was about to happen. Anwyn had been half-prepared for tears and protests, but none were forthcoming. The silence drew out.

'Shall you like having Lord Wulfgar as a father?' she asked.

He lowered his eyes and shrugged. It was hardly an expression of rapture, but nor was it outright rejection. Had he been older, she would have said he was reserving judgement.

'Lord Wulfgar won't be here all the time,' she went on. 'He and his men will have business that takes them to different places.'

'On the ship?'

'Yes, on the ship.'

'Will he take me on the ship?'

'One day, perhaps, when you are older.'

He nodded slowly. Anwyn drew him to her and dropped a kiss on his hair. God send that he would grow to manhood in peace and safety. She could do no more to try to ensure it.

Chapter Twelve

The wedding was a small and private ceremony; Jodis had brought Eyvind and they were joined by Ina and Hermund. For a moment bride and groom faced each other in silence. Wulfgar, too, had dressed himself with care for the occasion, clad in the deep blue tunic he had worn once before at the feast that first night. It became him well, she thought—indeed, rather better than well. It was also a perfect complement to her gown. Not that he could have known that, of course. He smiled at Eyvind for a moment. Then the blue gaze returned to meet hers.

'You look wonderful,' he said. 'I had thought your beauty could not be enhanced, but I see now that I was wrong.'

It was doubtless just a courtesy, she thought, but even so his words brought a warm glow to the core of her being. Torstein's assessment of her appearance had only ever been confined to an occasional grunt. How very different it all was from the last time. Then she had been sick with dread. Her stomach was fluttering now, too, but for very different reasons. No matter what the circumstances of this unconventional match, Wulfgar was a dangerously attractive man.

He took her hand. 'Shall we?'

The touch was light, but it set her flesh tingling nevertheless.

No other man had ever made her feel as she did in his presence. It was effortlessly done and he seemed quite unconscious of the reaction he aroused; unless he was playing a much more subtle game, in which case it made things doubly hazardous.

As they went into the small chapel, Anwyn realised that she knew nothing of her future husband's beliefs and had not asked him. Seeing the expression of dismay that flickered across her face, he squeezed her fingers gently.

'When my word is given it is good.'

Relief washed over her and she returned his smile, albeit rather shyly now. Together they walked to meet the waiting priest. Anwyn had removed her ring earlier, a gesture that was symbolic as well as practical. It occurred to her then that Wulfgar might not have considered the need for a replacement; it was unlikely he would have. Or, having thought of it, he might not have been able to find one.

She was mistaken. He not only produced one, it was beautiful. Made of gold, it was wrought in a cunning and intricate design of flowers and leaves. When he slid it on to her finger it was a near-perfect fit. And then the words were spoken; his in a tone that was clear and assured; a marked contrast to her own more halting responses. A short time later they were pronounced man and wife. He drew her close to him then and claimed the kiss that was his due, in a lingering embrace that turned the core of her being to liquid warmth.

Then Jodis and Hermund came forwards to offer their congratulations. Eyvind stood quietly in the background with Ina, looking on. Wulfgar surveyed the child for a moment and then his eyes met Ina's. The old warrior remained impassive, but led the boy forwards. Wulfgar smiled and held out a hand.

'Come, walk with us.'

Rather hesitantly Eyvind moved forwards and, guided by Wulfgar's arm, came to stand between him and his mother. It was a simple gesture, but it was both tactful and kind. Anwyn's heart warmed. She gave Eyvind's shoulder a gentle squeeze and then looked over his head to the man beside him. Whatever happened between them now, she could tolerate much if he would be kind to her son.

Together the little group returned to the sunshine outside. Wulfgar paused, regarding his bride steadily.

'I suppose that now we had best make this matter known.'

'Yes, the sooner the better, I think.'

'I must speak to my men in private,' he said. 'There are things we need to discuss that concern them alone. Hermund, we'll meet at the ship in an hour.'

'Right you are.'

'I'll talk to the rest tonight after meat.'

'Are you hoping they'll all be mellow by then?' asked Anwyn.

'One can always hope.' He looked at Ina. 'Make sure everyone who can be is present at table tonight.'

'As you will, my lord.'

The old warrior departed then and Jodis took Eyvind off to the bower. Wulfgar watched them go for a moment before turning back to Anwyn.

'Will you be all right?'

'Of course.'

'A foolish question.' He gave her a wry smile. 'I regret leaving you like this, but it cannot be avoided.'

'I know. Go and do you what you must. I'll see you later at table.'

'Aye.' He took her hand and lifted it to his lips. 'Until then, Anwyn.'

She watched him walk away, feeling suddenly bereft, the imprint of his kiss burning her hand.

Wulfgar's men heard him in incredulous silence, which evolved into grudging admiration and then amusement.

'I have to say, lord, it's impressive,' said Thrand, 'when you consider how short a time we've been here.'

Asulf nodded. 'Aye, give us a few pointers, my lord. Then we might all find beautiful and wealthy wives.'

'Wouldn't make any difference how many pointers *you* got,' replied Beorn. 'A woman'd have to be blind before she'd agree to wed you.'

A burst of good-natured laughter greeted this.

'So we're still going to join Rollo, then?' said Thrand.

'Aye,' replied Wulfgar. 'But first there is the matter of Ingvar.'

Asulf grinned. 'No worries, my lord. We'll take care of it. Cut his throat, burn his hall…it's quite straightforward.'

'That's right,' said Thrand. 'While we're at it we can take care of Grymar Big Mouth as well.'

A groundswell of agreement followed. Wulfgar held up a hand for quiet.

'Before we do any of those things I want to try peaceful means first.' Seeing their evident disappointment, he went on, 'I have given my word on this.'

'Pity,' said Hermund. 'Still, once you've promised a woman that's it. Never hear the end of it otherwise.'

'I said I'd try,' replied Wulfgar. 'Of course, it may not work.'

'Chances are it won't. I can't see Ingvar losing with good grace.'

'In that case I might have to reconsider.'

His men exchanged wolfish grins. Shortly after this the meeting broke up and they drifted off in smaller groups. Hermund looked at Wulfgar.

'That went off all right.'

'Aye, but it remains to be seen whether the Drakensburgh retainers are quite as accepting.'

'What's next, then?'

'I want their oaths of fealty. Nothing less will do.'

Hermund nodded. 'Most of them have accepted our presence here. Likely the rest will fall into line.'

'Perhaps. At all events keep your wits about you this evening.'

'I will.'

Despite the limited time available Anwyn had managed to arrange a more splendid repast than usual that evening. The thought had occurred to her, too, that men well fed and plied with several cups of ale might be more amenable to what they were about to hear. Unlike them she ate little for, in truth, her stomach felt knotted.

She glanced at Wulfgar, but he seemed quite unperturbed. However, it was habitual with him to conceal his thought and she could rarely tell what he was thinking. He drank but sparingly, she noted. Evidently he meant to keep his wits sharp.

Eventually, when he judged the time was right, he pushed back his chair and got to his feet, thumping the table with his fist. Conversation died and all eyes turned towards him in surprise. Anwyn's hands clenched round the arms of the chair.

The announcement was received in dumbfounded silence and for the space of a few heartbeats the only sound was of crackling flames in the hearth.

'I hope that we may continue to work together in unity and friendship,' he continued. 'Certainly I need good men. Drakensburgh needs good men. As its new lord I will receive oaths of fealty from all those who wish to give them.'

'And what if we don't?' Across the room Thorkil rose unsteadily to his feet.

'Then you are free to leave and go where you will,' said Wulfgar.

'You didn't waste much time, did you, Viking?' Thorkil glared at him. 'But then a wealthy widow is a fine prize, isn't she?'

Sigurd, and one or two others, muttered agreement. Anwyn's eyes sparkled with anger as she stared them down.

'Do not presume to question my decisions, Thorkil. This was my choice, and freely made.'

'Made for a handsome face, more like.'

With an effort she kept a hold of her temper. 'Made because Drakensburgh needs a fair and capable man to govern it.'

'He's a Viking adventurer, no more. Shall such a man be set above us?'

His nearest companions began to mutter again.

'That he shall,' replied Wulfgar, 'when he is the son of an earl. I am the eldest son of Wulfrum Ragnarsson. My birth is the equal of your former master, my skill in battle well proven.' He surveyed them coolly. 'And if you remain at Drakensburgh, you will swear fealty to me.'

A tense silence followed this, but his words had given them pause. Most lowered their eyes. Thorkil looked around uncertainly. Wulfgar's blue gaze fixed on him.

'One last thing: I shall overlook your swinish manners on this occasion, but if you ever speak to Lady Anwyn like that again I will personally remove your tongue.' He glanced at Ina. 'Get the oaf out of here.'

Ina nodded, looking coldly upon Thorkil. 'Aye, my lord. I'll warrant a dunking in the horse trough will help sober him up.' He spoke quietly to the men nearest him. They crossed the hall and, seizing hold of the protesting offender, dragged him from the room. No-one made any attempt to prevent it.

'Now,' said Ina, 'where were we?'

'Tomorrow I shall hear the oaths of those men intending to stay.' Wulfgar smiled faintly. 'In the meantime, let the celebration continue.'

The conversation resumed and men turned again to their cups. Anwyn let out a long breath. It was over and with less dissension than anticipated. She threw a quizzical look at the man beside her.

'Did you mean what you said just now, about removing Thorkil's tongue?'

'I never make empty threats,' he replied.

'I think I would not like to be your enemy.'

'You are not my enemy, Anwyn. You are my wife.'

The word sent a *frisson* down the length of her spine. She had been so preoccupied with breaking the news of her marriage that the other implications hadn't really sunk in—until now.

'You did not tell me that you were the son of an earl.'

'You did not ask,' he replied.

Suddenly it became clear how little she really knew about this man. He aroused her curiosity as no other ever had, but would they be together long enough for her to discover the answers?

As the hour advanced and the noise in the hall grew loud, Anwyn rose to take her leave. Wulfgar rose with her. She turned to say something, but the words never materialised as, without warning, she was seized by the waist and lifted into his arms. He strode with her towards the door to the sound of accompanying laughter and cheers. Good-natured ribaldry followed them out into the night. Anwyn struggled ineffectually, her heart hammering in her breast. All too soon they reached the door of the bower. Having carried her inside, he heeled it shut behind them and, setting his burden down, barred it securely. Then, taking hold of her wrist, he led the way to the chamber he had visited once before. He drew her in with him and then pulled the screening curtain across the entranceway.

For a moment or two husband and wife faced each other in heart-thumping silence. Wulfgar smiled wryly.

'I apologise for the rough-and-ready nature of our departure back there, but I needed to make it convincing.'

Anwyn stared at him. 'Convincing? I think it was certainly that.'

'Good. They would not understand else.'

'Understand what?'

'If I had let you leave alone.'

'No. I suppose not.'

He paused, surveying her steadily. 'It will be necessary for us to share this chamber tonight.'

The fluttering sensation in her stomach intensified. 'Did we not have an agreement?'

'We still do. I'll not take anything that isn't freely given.'

For a moment she wasn't sure she had heard him aright and then, as the meaning filtered through, that he meant it.

'You don't believe me,' he said.

'It is outside my experience that a man should consider my wishes in the matter.'

He smiled rather ruefully. 'Have no fear, Anwyn. Your wishes shall be respected.'

Some of the tension went out of her. Wulfgar looked around and his gaze came to rest on the bed.

'Which side do you like to sleep on?'

The question took her aback. 'I...er, the right.'

He nodded and began to undress. She watched him unfasten his belt and then peel off tunic and shirt to reveal the powerful torso beneath. The lamplight gleamed softly on the silver arm rings that partly concealed the pale lines of old scars. More were visible across his ribs and chest where a line of dark hair led the eye to a tapering waist and long, hard-muscled legs. As he reached for the fastenings of his breeches Anwyn turned away.

A short time later she heard the bed creak beneath his weight and then the faint rustling sound of the coverlet as he settled himself. She drew a sharp breath and began to unfasten her girdle.

Wulfgar propped himself comfortably against the bolster, surveying the proceedings on the other side of the room. He saw her lay the gown carefully across the wooden chest nearby. Moments later it was joined by the undertunic. Then only the linen shift remained. The fabric was fine, suggesting the lines and curves concealed beneath. Shorter than the other garments, it also afforded an agreeable view of lower leg and slender ankle, one that he was unashamedly making the most of. He wondered if she would unfasten her hair, but it seemed that was not her intention. To his intense disappointment she crossed to the lamp and doused the flame. The room was plunged in darkness. Moments later he felt the mattress shift as she slid into bed. There followed a small movement as she turned on her side and drew the covers closer. Then there was silence. Wulfrum smiled wryly.

'Good night, Anwyn.'

'Good night, my lord.'

Anwyn closed her eyes, listening intently, her body tense and waiting. For all his earlier assurances she could not believe that he meant to keep his word. It had all sounded so easy when first the scheme was hatched: a marriage in name only; two people who would inhabit different rooms at night. She had overlooked the obvious, the need to create an effective illusion in the minds of others. Wulfgar had not. Her cheeks grew hot when she thought just how convincing his behaviour had been that evening. None witnessing it could doubt his intention. After all, he was her husband. It was his right to take her whenever he wished. No man there but thought he would prosecute that right. Anwyn grew hot. If he so chose, there would be nothing she could do to prevent it. He was big and frighteningly strong.

Just for a moment her mind went down that route; the result set her flesh tingling. She knew then that if he reached for her she would not try to prevent it; that some part of her wanted him to. She swallowed hard. It was madness to think like that. This was a business arrangement, nothing more. He had already told her that he could not give his heart, that he would not stay for ever. If she let desire rule her head now, the consequences would be dire; her heart already told her that this man had the power to hurt her badly, and in ways that Torstein never could.

More minutes dragged by, but still nothing happened, and presently her straining ears caught the sound of slow, regular breathing. Some of her tension faded. He had meant what he said. She ought to have been relieved, but the feeling now was more akin to sadness.

Chapter Thirteen

When she awoke the following morning it was to see that the space beside her was empty. Automatically she reached out and touched the place where he had lain, but the sheet was cool. He had been gone some time then. Of course, there had been no reason for him to stay. Anwyn sighed. Climbing out of bed, she bathed her face and hands and then began to prepare herself to meet the day.

Having dressed and arranged her hair, she went to check on Eyvind. He was playing with the wooden horse that Ina had carved for him. He looked up and smiled as she entered and then resumed his game. She had a few words with Jodis and then went to the hall to check on the servants. However, cleaning up was well underway by the time she arrived and the trestles neatly stacked along the walls. Anwyn summoned one of the men.

'Do you know where Lord Wulfgar may be found?'

'No, my lady. He rode out this morning with a dozen men. I have not seen him since.'

'No matter.' Anwyn turned away. Wulfgar had said nothing to her of his intentions, but then she had been asleep when he left. Feeling a little discomfited, she put the matter from her mind and turned her attention to the various household tasks awaiting her attention.

Wulfgar signalled to his escort and then reined in before the gates of Ingvar's fortress at Beranhold, his practised eye taking in the details of the ditch and palisade that formed the outer defences. Moments later the guard's challenge rang out.

'Tell your master that Lord Wulfgar desires speech with him. I will await him here.'

As the man disappeared from view Hermund looked at his companion.

'He may refuse to talk.'

'No, he won't,' replied Wulfgar.

'How do you know that?'

'Curiosity will get the better of him.'

It seemed he was right because a short time later the gate swung open to allow egress for a group of horsemen. At their head was Ingvar. He was flanked by Grymar and half-a-dozen others. They rode unhurriedly towards Wulfgar, pulling up close by. For a space the two men surveyed each other in silence before Ingvar spoke.

'My guard said that you desired speech with me.'

'Aye,' replied Wulfgar. 'So I do.'

Ingvar smiled. 'I am intrigued.'

'I'll make this short. Yesterday Lady Anwyn did me the honour of becoming my wife.'

The smile faded and Ingvar's eyes narrowed. 'What treachery is this?'

'No treachery, but a decision taken of her own free will.'

'A likely tale.'

'I speak the truth.'

'Nay, you used your wiles to gain entrance to Drakensburgh and then seized control.'

Wulfgar surveyed him coolly. 'You judge others by your own standards. I used no wiles here. I had no need of them.'

'He speaks true.' Ina nudged his horse forwards. 'Lady Anwyn married of her own free will.'

Ingvar's gold-brown eyes glinted, but it was clear the old warrior's words had struck home. 'Is it so indeed?'

'It is so. Lord Wulfgar is master of Drakensburgh now.'

'You move quickly, my lord,' said Ingvar. 'But then the prize was great.'

'The prize is mine,' replied Wulfgar, 'and I mean to keep it.' His gaze flicked to Grymar. 'Any more un-neighbourly behaviour will find an un-neighbourly response.'

Grymar glared, his hand moving to his sword hilt. Ingvar checked him with one upraised hand.

'I have never sought enmity with Drakensburgh. I do not seek it now.'

Wulfgar nodded. 'Then we understand one another.'

'I believe we do. I only hope that Lady Anwyn does not come to regret her decision.'

'I shall give her no cause to regret it,' said Wulfgar.

Ingvar's lips curled. 'We'll see, won't we?'

With that he turned his horse's head and, barking an order to his escort, rode away. The others watched them go.

'Nasty piece of work,' said Hermund. 'Still, he knows where he stands now.'

'He knows,' replied Wulfgar.

'Did you believe him, about not wanting trouble?'

'No, but the case is altered and he knows it.'

'Then perhaps he'll back off and accept defeat.'

'If he's wise, he will.'

It was perhaps an hour later when they returned. On leaving his men Wulfgar went in search of Anwyn. He found her in the hall, speaking to one of the servants. Hearing his approach, she looked round and he saw her smile. She dismissed the servant and came forwards to meet him.

'Did you enjoy your ride, my lord?'

He returned the smile. 'Not especially, but it was necessary or, believe me, I would not have gone.'

The implication brought a faint tinge of colour to her face. He thought it became her well.

'I went to see Ingvar,' he continued.

'Then he knows now. I will not ask how he took it.'

'Do you care?'

'Only in so far as his anger may affect Drakensburgh,' she replied.

'It will not—now.'

Her eyes widened slightly. 'Wulfgar, you did not—'

'Kill him? No.'

She breathed a sigh of relief. He saw it.

'Would you have cared if I had?'

'Yes, but not for the reason you suppose.' Her hand came to rest on his sleeve. 'I would not have our marriage vows sealed in blood.'

His gaze met and held hers, but found only sincerity there. It warmed him, like the touch of her hand on his arm.

'Then I am glad I resisted the temptation,' he said.

'So, what now, my lord?'

'I will hear the men give their oaths of fealty.' He smiled down at her. 'After that I am at your disposal.'

Having summoned the men to the mead hall, he seated himself in the great carved chair that was the symbol of the lord's power. Anwyn, sitting beside him, thought he looked as if he had been born to the role. His was a commanding figure in every sense of the word, a strong physical presence who carried with him an aura of authority—a man whom other men would follow. A man to draw a woman's eye and hold it. She pulled herself up firmly at that; no woman would ever hold him for long.

When all were gathered he rose and one by one the Drakensburgh warriors came forwards, each one kneeling and placing his hands in those of the new lord, and swearing the oath of loyalty. It was a solemn and binding promise that held both parties while they lived. Anwyn glanced round at the assembled crowd, but could see no sign of Thorkil or his friends. Their absence implied that they had left, a circumstance verified later by Ina.

'Good riddance, too,' he said. 'We're better off without them.'

Anwyn nodded. All things considered matters had gone more smoothly than expected. She glanced across the room where Wulfgar was engaged in conversation with a small group of Drakensburgh men. He must have said something witty because the words were followed by a burst of laughter. It reinforced her earlier impression of his leadership skills. These men would follow him. Ina followed her gaze.

'I think we may look forward to better days, my lady.'

She surveyed him in surprise; coming from him, the words amounted to high praise. 'Indeed, I hope so.'

As though sensing himself watched, Wulfgar glanced round. With a few words he excused himself from the group and came over to join his wife.

'And now, my lady, what would it please you to do?'

'I would like to go out for a ride, but you have already done that.'

'A matter of duty,' he replied. 'This time it will be a pleasure.'

The words and the accompanying look caused her pulse to quicken. Ina looked from one to the other and his lips quirked.

'I'll have the grooms saddle the horses, my lord.'

Wulfgar held the horse's bridle while she mounted. Then, having seen her safely ensconced, he followed suit.

'Are you ready?'

'Ready,' she replied.

'Come then, wife.'

The use of that word brought spots of colour into her cheeks. She glanced around, but the grooms were too far away to have caught what he said. Wulfgar grinned and she realised then that he was enjoying this. She threw him an eloquent look and turned her horse's head towards the gate.

Once they were beyond it she let the animal out to a canter. Moments later his mount drew level. Anwyn grinned. They crossed the heath and pulled up on the edge of the dunes. The horses fell into single file, picking their way through the soft sand and coming at last to the bay beyond. The sea was calm, the waves breaking gently on the strand where the *Sea Wolf* waited.

At the sight of the ship Anwyn's pleasure faded a little for she could hear Wulfgar's voice in her head. *I won't stay for ever...* With an effort she pushed the thought away. He was here now. She would not spoil the day with fears of what the future might bring.

The men on guard called a greeting which Wulfgar returned. 'Is all well here?' he asked, reining to a halt beside Dag.

'Aye, my lord. No sign of anyone hereabouts until you came.'

'Good.'

'I reckon that Grymar oaf got the hint.'

'Let's hope so.'

Wulfgar rejoined Anwyn and they rode on.

'Do you think Ingvar and company really have taken the hint?' she asked.

'Unless they're stupid.'

'I don't know about stupid, but I believe them to be vengeful.'

'They need not concern you now. Forget about them, Anwyn.'

'I confess I don't find them a particularly edifying subject.'

'No more do I.' He nodded in the direction of the strand. 'That's a mighty tempting stretch of firm sand. What say you to a gallop?'

Her face lit in a smile. 'I'd say it sounded like an excellent idea.'

Given their heads the horses leapt forwards, their hooves flying over the packed wet sand, manes streaming in the wind. The swifter pace was exhilarating and Anwyn's spirit soared. Once she glanced sideways and saw Wulfgar grin. They sped on, their mounts neck and neck, pulling up eventually at the far end of the bay. Anwyn laughed, patting the horse's neck enthusiastically.

'That was wonderful.'

'Aye, it was,' he replied. Then, as they walked on, 'You ride well, my lady.'

'So do you.'

'My father taught me. He's a fine horseman.'

'A great warrior, too, I imagine.'

'How do you know?'

'The old saying—like father like son.'

He smiled wryly. 'I'd like to think so, but his are mighty big shoes to step into.'

The words were spoken matter of factly, but they implied much more and she was immediately curious.

'He lives yet?'

'Aye, he does. My mother, too.'

'Which of them do you resemble most?'

'My father, definitely.'

'Wulfrum Ragnarsson—a noble family heritage.'

'He was an adopted son, though apparently Ragnar was like a true father to him. When King Ella captured and executed Ragnar, his sons took their revenge.'

Anwyn nodded. She had heard the tale of the great Viking invasion, although she had not been born then.

'Was your father married before he came to England?'

'No. He took my mother as a prize of war.'

Her eyes widened. 'She was enslaved?'

'Not exactly. Lord Halfdan gave my father the Ravenswood

estate as a reward for loyal service. My mother had held it till then, following the deaths of her father and brother. In that sense she went with it, so my father took her to wife. She had no say in the matter.'

Anwyn shivered a little. 'Then I pity her.'

'It might have been a lot worse.' He surveyed her steadily. 'My father was in love with her, you see.'

'Was he?'

'She was very beautiful in her youth, and strong-willed. She was not easily won, but then my father is not easily deflected from a purpose. He determined to win her and he succeeded. Eventually she came to love him in return.'

'A fortunate circumstance for both of them.'

'Aye, I suppose it was.'

'The marriage was happy in the end, then.'

'Most happy. It still is.'

Anwyn could identify strongly with the young girl forced into marriage with a stranger. Except that her story had had a happy ending. Earl Wulfrum must be a remarkable man. If his son took after him, then he had undoubtedly been handsome, but there had to be a great deal more. Was that the source of Wulfgar's charisma? Certainly the words offered another tantalising glimpse of his past.

'I was never close to my father,' she said. 'His interest was all for his sons. Daughters were useful only as a means of consolidating power.'

'Was that why he married you to Torstein?'

'Yes.' She paused. 'Do you have brothers and sisters living?'

'Two brothers and a sister, all married now.'

'Did you all get on?'

He grinned. 'Most of the time.'

'That must have been pleasant.'

He heard the wistful note in her voice and understood it. Despite the inevitable fights with his brothers, his childhood had been happy enough. He had assumed, back then, that everyone else shared the same experience. It had come as a surprise to find out later that he was wrong.

For a while neither one spoke. Anwyn found it impossible to read the thoughts behind that handsome face, but just then she didn't care. When she was in his company she could shrug off the past; everything else became insignificant somehow, and every fibre of her being was tuned only to him. It seemed likely that they would not have much time together, but perhaps that didn't matter. She had spent almost two thousand days with Torstein; endless dreary days that blended and merged until she could remember little or nothing of them. The days spent with Wulfgar would not be forgotten so easily.

It was perhaps an hour later when they stopped by a stream and dismounted to let the horses drink. Then, by tacit consent, they strolled together a little way. Stands of alder and willow lined the bank while on the margins of the water clumps of yellow iris made splashes of colour. Brilliant blue dragonflies darted among the reeds and a shoal of minnows basked in the shallows.

'A pleasant spot,' said Wulfgar. 'Will it please you to sit a while?'

Having tethered the horses, they took their ease on the grassy bank, surveying the scene. She had not previously considered Drakensburgh to be a beautiful place, but it was. Not that she had been able to explore much of it then and what she had seen was coloured by Torstein's company. It all seemed like a past life now. She glanced at the man beside her and found herself the object of close scrutiny.

'Did you know that you have the most beautiful hair? I thought so the first time I set eyes on you.' He grinned. 'When you rode on to the beach that day I thought at first that one of the Valkyries was come among us.'

Anwyn laughed, albeit ruefully. 'I seem to recall that I was in a rare temper at the time. It goes with the hair, you see.'

'So I've noticed.'

'It is a failing I'm oft reminded of.'

'No failing. Anger suits you, too.'

It was hard to know what to make of this and she suspected that he was teasing her. Before she could pursue the thought he altered his position, moving behind her. She glanced round.

'Sit still.' Wulfgar reached for the ribbon that bound the end of the braid and untied it.

Anwyn felt the slight tug. 'What are you doing?'

'What I've wanted to do from the first.' Slowly and deliberately he began to unfasten her plait, checking her protest with a hand on her shoulder. 'Be still.'

His hands continued their work, moving higher now, casually brushing her back and shoulders. The touch sent a shiver down her spine that had nothing to do with fear or cold. The rest of the plait loosened and came undone. Wulfgar let the glossy ropes of hair trail through his hands for a moment, then shook out each one until the entirety of it hung down her back like a cloak of flame.

He grinned. 'That's better.'

Anwyn regarded him in mock exasperation. 'How am I going to bind it again now?'

'You're not,' he replied.

'Not?'

'No.'

Her eyes widened a little. 'But, Wulfgar, I can't leave it like this. It isn't decent. Someone might see.'

'I am the only one here to see.'

'Yes, but…'

'And as I am your husband it cannot be indecent.'

'I am not sure that necessarily follows,' she replied.

'No more it does.'

Anwyn glanced about her, but there was no one else in evidence. Seeing that, she relaxed a little. It was unseemly for a married woman to wear her hair loose; only very young girls did that. At the same time it was strangely liberating. Torstein would have had a fit. She bit back a gurgle of laughter. Torstein had had a fit. That was why she was sitting here on the bank of a stream with another man and with her hair undone. Unbidden, the laughter swelled in her throat. She tried to suppress it, but it burst out of her anyway. She buried her face against her knees, hugging them close, shoulders shaking.

Wulfgar regarded her curiously. 'What?'

Unable to speak, Anwyn merely shook her head. It was sometime before she regained a measure of self-control, drying her eyes with the sleeve of her gown.

'Forgive me,' she said then. 'I couldn't help it.'

'Won't you share the joke?' he asked.

'I wish I could, but unless you'd met Torstein it wouldn't be nearly as funny.'

'Torstein?'

'Yes. I was visualising the expression on his face if he could see me now.'

Wulfgar grinned. 'Aye, I suppose that would be interesting.'

'You have no idea.'

'Perhaps it's as well he isn't here then, or your brother, either, for that matter.'

'Osric would run you through.'

'He might try.'

Anwyn eyed him speculatively. 'Would you kill him?'

'If I had to, although I'd be loath to earn your enmity.'

She sighed. 'In truth I don't know if you would.'

'I thought when I saw you together that your relationship was not the closest.'

'It wasn't.' She hesitated. 'It was Osric who sided with my father over the marriage to Torstein.'

'I see.'

'I couldn't let him do it a second time.'

'He shouldn't have done it the first time,' said Wulfgar.

'Well, he's gone now and Torstein is dead.'

'So things could be much worse, then.'

Anwyn caught his eye and they both laughed. He thought it suited her very well, like unbound hair. If he had his way, both were going to happen more often. He leaned closer and then laughter faded a little. For a brief second she seemed to hesitate. Then her face tilted towards his and she gave herself up to his kiss. It was soft and lingering and utterly irresistible.

With a major effort of will he drew back, his blood racing. He wanted her, here, now, wanted to possess her entirely. But more than that, he wanted her consent. Anything else would be a violation. Looking into her face now, what he read was uncertainty. It was better than the fear he had seen earlier, but it was still not enough.

He got to his feet and held out his hands, pulling her up after him. 'Come.'

They strolled together along the side of the stream among the trees. He had retained a hold of one hand. His own engulfed it, warm and firm, the palm roughened from long use of sword and axe—a warrior's touch. It sent a tremor the length of her arm.

They paused once to watch a kingfisher dive, a vivid dart of blue and orange against the green. A silver flash announced the captured fish and then the bird flew off. Anwyn smiled, immeasurably gladdened by the sight. She knew the feeling only partly attributable to the kingfisher; most of it was due to the man beside her. Just being in his company was enough to lift her heart and lighten her spirit.

'The bird is wise. This is a good place to fish,' he said then. 'Look there. See the trout?'

Anwyn followed his pointing finger to the centre of the stream where several large fish finned against the current. Without warning he grabbed her waist, pushing her forwards. She shrieked, only to find herself snatched back to safety at the last moment. Outraged, she turned accusingly.

'You beast!'

'I crave your pardon, my lady.'

'If you want my pardon, you must first wipe that smile off your face.'

'I regret that I cannot.'

'We'll see about that.'

She grabbed a clump of willow herb and advanced on him. Wulfgar allowed her to get close, then turned and seized hold of her, lifting her off her feet. Then he strode towards the stream. Anwyn struggled hard.

'Wulfgar, no!'

He held her easily. 'Perhaps the water may cool your fiery temper.'

She clutched his tunic in desperation. 'Do this, and I swear I'll never speak to you again.'

He checked on the margin, grinning. 'In truth, that would be too terrible a fate to contemplate. I must think of another forfeit.'

Heart pounding, Anwyn glared at him. 'You will not!'

'Say you so?'

His expression then was not calculated to reassure. She renewed her struggles, to his evident enjoyment.

'Of course it may take me a while.'

'Wulfgar, put me down!'

'I dare not, for fear of the reprisal.'

'It would serve you right.'

He walked slowly along the bank. His fighting burden seemed to cause him not the least inconvenience, a factor which served only to increase her ire. Wulfgar glanced down.

'Aye, anger suits you. I've always thought so.'

For a moment she was dumbfounded. Then her sense of the ridiculous returned and she gave a reluctant laugh.

'Do you know that you're the most impossible man?'

'You are not the first to say so.'

'I'll wager I'm not, and that they were all women who said it.'

'I can't deny it.'

She surveyed him speculatively. 'I won't ask how many women.'

His lips twitched. 'Are you jealous?'

'Certainly not!'

'Pity. I was really hoping you might be.'

Anwyn tried to restrain welling laughter, but it escaped anyway. He heard it and smiled, regarding her keenly.

'Anger does suit you,' he said, 'but laughter suits you even better.'

She wasn't sure how to respond to that and so said nothing. Something in his look set her heart to beating much faster, and she was suddenly supremely aware of it and him. This enforced nearness was still a cause for ire, only now it was directed at herself for enjoying it.

He carried her back to the waiting horses before he set her down. Acutely conscious of her dishevelled appearance and of the appreciative smile on his lips, Anwyn felt her face grow warm.

'I must redo my hair. I cannot go back looking like this.'

'Like what?'

'Like a wanton.'

'A wanton? What a delicious thought.' The words called forth an indignant glare. The smile became a grin. 'Turn around.'

'Why?'

'Must you always argue?'

Taking her by the shoulders, he turned her firmly round. Moments later she felt the weight of her hair drawn back.

'What are you doing?'

'Ensuring you don't return looking like a wanton,' he replied.

He drew her ribbon from the pocket of his tunic. Then he divided the fiery mass of hair into three sections and began to re-braid it, weaving in the ribbon as he went. He was surprisingly competent.

'Where do you learn to do that?' she asked.

'I've had a lot of practice over the years.'

'Oh? What kind of practice?'

Wulfgar smiled quietly to himself. 'Horses' manes.'

Another gurgle of laughter bubbled up. 'Liar.'

'What a base idea you do have of me.'

'No, a very shrewd idea,' she returned.

'A worrying thought. Am I so easy to read?'

'In truth, no. I hardly ever know what you are thinking.'

'Perhaps that's just as well.'

She made no answer, deciding it would be safer not to probe.

He finished the task and tied the ribbon securely, surveying his handiwork with a critical eye.

'It would have been better if I'd had a comb to hand, but it will serve.'

Anwyn, examining the braid, was quietly impressed. He had done a creditable job.

'Thank you.'

'My pleasure,' he replied.

He watched her remount and then swung astride his own horse, bringing it alongside. They rode in companionable silence for a while and Wulfgar wondered anew what kind of man Torstein must have been. Just a few hours spent in her presence had been enough to reveal the playful side of Anwyn's nature. What man, seeing her laugh, would not want to see it often? What man could fail to enjoy her spirit and quick wits? Never once had he been bored with her companionship. Indeed, the more he had of it the more he wanted. It stimulated on so many levels.

Unwilling to break into his private reverie Anwyn said nothing. It was pleasant just to be with him, to share his company awhile. In truth, she had never thought to enjoy a man's company as she did now, but then he was different from the rest. It was hard to believe that he was her husband, nominally at least. He had proved honourable in so many unexpected ways.

The events of the afternoon had left her in no doubt that he wanted her, or that he could easily have forced her. Would it have been force in the end, when even his kiss weakened her resolution to the point where she hardly recognised herself? She shivered inwardly. If she yielded to this impulse, it could only lead to heartache.

Chapter Fourteen

She did not linger late at table that evening, pleading fatigue. In truth, the day's events had proved unexpectedly draining for all manner of reasons and she wanted nothing more than to seek her chamber and bed. Wulfgar surveyed her critically, seeing at once the tiredness in her eyes.

'Go then, Anwyn, and rest. I'll be along later.'

The words jolted her back to realisation that she would not lie alone this night, either.

'As you will, my lord.'

Having said her goodnights to Ina and Hermund, she left them. Her chamber was a haven of peace after the noise of the hall. Sliding into bed, she left the lamp for Wulfgar. Since he was not yet wholly familiar with the layout of the room, he might not be best pleased at having to stumble around in the dark. Her earlier anxiety about this unwonted intimacy had dissipated now. If he had intended to go back on his word, he'd had every opportunity to do it. She yawned and drew the coverlet higher, letting her body relax. As the bed warmed the feeling of drowsiness increased.

And then she was not alone any more…

Torstein brought his mouth down hard on hers, forcing her

*jaws open, furred tongue thrusting into her mouth. Half-suf-
focated by the stink of carious breath and stale mead, Anwyn
clenched her fists at her sides, forcing herself to endure it,
knowing only too well what the penalty would be for resistance.
He groaned now and the kiss grew deeper, bruising her lips,
his teeth grating against hers. Eventually he came up for air
and smiled, revealing stained teeth.*

'Turn over.'

Her stomach wallowed. 'Please, Torstein, I don't—'

'Perhaps you'd like me to take my belt to you first?'

'No, my lord.'

'Then you'll get on to your hands and knees—now.'

She sat up with a start, panting, heart pounding, eyes staring
into the shadows at the edges of the room.

'Anwyn? What is it?'

The sound of a male voice elicited a gasp of fright.

'It's all right. There's no one here to hurt you, my sweet. It
was just a bad dream.'

Gradually the voice filtered through the mental turmoil and
she lowered herself on the bed again, letting out a long breath.
Not Torstein after all: Wulfgar.

He sat on the side of the bed, looking into her face. 'Why,
you're shaking. What manner of dream was it that could scare
you so?'

'I…I dreamed that Torstein was here. That he—' She broke
off, sickened.

'That he what?'

She shook her head. 'It was just a dream. It doesn't matter.'

He made no attempt to force her confidence. 'A dream
cannot harm you.' Giving her a reassuring smile, he moved
away to the other side of the room and began to undress. Then
he blew out the lamp and climbed into bed.

Anwyn lay still, every muscle taut, heart still thumping
against her ribs. Every thought of sleep had fled now to be
replaced with memories five years deep. Almost all of them

were repellent. She had never spoken about them to anyone save Jodis, and even then had not told all. Yet somehow, lying here now, she felt an overwhelming need to speak. Perhaps the darkness made it easier. She took a deep breath.

'I dreamed that Torstein was back.'

Wulfgar remained very still, waiting. Slowly, haltingly, she told him the substance of her dream. He listened, sickened to the pit of his stomach. He had already gathered that the relationship had been unhappy, but he had never guessed at the extent of it.

'I loathed him,' she went on, 'and he knew it. For that reason it pleased him to prolong our coupling and especially to…to inflict pain. It aroused him, you see.'

Wulfgar did see. With the knowledge came understanding and a feeling of sadness mingled with deep and burning anger. In that moment he would have been glad if Torstein had returned just to have had the pleasure of killing him again.

'In the early days of our marriage I used every ruse possible to avoid my so-called wifely duties. I even tried to refuse him…' She hesitated. 'A taste of his belt soon showed me the folly of doing so. And after he had beaten me he took me anyway. It pleased him to hear me scream.'

'Anwyn, I'm so sorry.'

'Why should you be? It was not your doing.'

There were so many things he might have replied to that question; there were so many reasons to be sorry. Now more than ever he was glad he had not let desire rule his head. The thought of being equated in her mind with Torstein was anathema.

'No, it wasn't,' he agreed, 'but being a man I cannot help but feel ashamed.'

'You have done nothing to be ashamed of. On the contrary, I owe you much.'

Wulfgar's jaw tightened. *Nothing to be ashamed of?* At any

other time he might have laughed. 'You owe me nothing,' he said.

The words came out more harshly than he had intended. Anwyn stirred and he sensed rather than saw her turn towards him.

'And yet if it were not for you I would have fallen prey to Ingvar.'

'For that I am glad.'

'I also.' She reached out and touched his shoulder, a soft and tentative gesture that set every nerve tingling down the length of his body. 'Thank you.'

'Torstein cannot hurt you now,' he said.

'I know it, and yet the memories remain.'

'They will fade in time, and then the dreams will stop.' Very carefully he shifted his weight and brought an arm round her shoulders. At once he felt her tense. 'Don't be afraid. Nothing bad is going to happen; only that I would hold you awhile.'

He dropped a kiss on her hair. Anwyn didn't move, but as the moments passed and nothing bad did happen some of her tension faded. His warmth was comforting, even reassuring. Slowly, cautiously, she leaned her head against his chest, breathing the scent of musk on his skin, listening to the rhythm of his heartbeat. She felt his hand stroking her hair, a soft caress that soothed fear and removed it. She sighed, and closed her eyes. Somehow it felt right to be here like this, right and strangely safe.

When Anwyn woke it was to a feeling of warmth and general well-being. She smiled to herself and glanced across at the man who now shared her bed. He was still asleep, his face peaceful in repose. Carefully, so as not to disturb him, she shifted her weight, propping herself on one elbow, letting her gaze take in the details. The more she looked, the more of an enigma he became. The memory of his gentleness left a feeling of abiding warmth deep inside her. This tenderness was so far removed from her experience; more beguiling and more disturbing than anything she could have anticipated, not least for the feelings it engendered in return. She knew then how easy it would be to love such a man.

She sighed. Wulfgar was charismatic in so many ways, but at heart he remained an adventurer. One day, in the not-too-distant future, he would be gone and, as he had said, perhaps for years. Given the hazardous nature of his profession there was a chance he might never come back at all. She swallowed hard. His was such a commanding presence that already it was difficult to imagine a world where he was not.

Uncomfortable with the direction of her thoughts, Anwyn rose. Reaching for a comb, she sat down and began to draw it through her hair. The narrow teeth found a small tangle and she winced, focusing her attention that way. It took some time to free, but at last it was accomplished and she resumed, absorbed in the task now. She had been working on it for some time when she had the sensation of being observed. Instinctively she looked round. Her gaze met Wulfgar's and she saw him smile.

'Good morning, my lady.'

She returned the greeting and resumed what she had been doing, supremely conscious of that close scrutiny. Somehow, in his presence, even the simplest personal tasks became strangely intimate and gave rise to sensations that were better left unexplored.

He watched for a little while longer, then rose from the bed and reached for his clothes. Anwyn kept her attention resolutely on the task in hand. Wulfgar undressed was an even greater distraction than usual. Possibly out of deference to her sensibilities he donned breeches and hose before venturing across the room to bathe his face. Having done that, he pulled on his shirt and tunic and latched the belt at his waist. Then he reached for his shoes. Within a short time he was ready to face the day.

'Will you excuse me, Anwyn? I need to speak to Hermund and Ina about training practices for the men.'

'Of course.'

'Then I'll see you later.'

With that he was gone. Anwyn let out another long breath.

Wulfgar kept the men busy all morning, taking them through a rigorous routine of military exercises. In this he was aided by Ina. It left Hermund free to organise the patrols for the day. Just because Ingvar had now been informed of the situation pertaining at Drakensburgh, it didn't mean he would abide by it. Accordingly Wulfgar sent out half-a-dozen patrols to cover different areas of the estate, and when they were done others would relieve them. They were his eyes and ears and he could ill afford to be without them.

He had also spoken to Ina about recruiting more fighters for Drakensburgh from among the local population. When the time came to leave he needed to be sure that there was an adequate force to look after the place in his absence.

'I think it will not be hard to find volunteers,' said Ina. 'The problem will be turning the raw material into an effective fighting force.'

Wulfgar nodded. 'We have enough experienced men to pass on the necessary skills. With an intensive period of training we can knock them into shape.'

Eyvind, who had been watching the practices closely, now turned to look up at them, brandishing a small wooden sword. 'I want to fight.'

'One day you will,' replied Wulfgar. 'But first you must learn how.' He moved to stand beside the child. 'You must hold your sword thus…that's it. Good. Now let's try a few basic moves…'

When, some time later, Anwyn came in search of her son, it was to see him practising alongside his large mentor. Both were so involved in what they were doing that they failed to notice her presence, giving her time to watch unobserved. Eyvind imitated Wulfgar's movements exactly, clearly hanging on every word he uttered. Ina stood some yards off, surveying the proceedings with a tolerant eye.

'Isn't Eyvind a little young for this?' she asked.

The old warrior smiled. 'He is keen to learn, my lady.'

'Yes, he is. Ever since you gave him the wooden sword he's talked of little else.'

'It'll do him no harm to learn a few simple manoeuvres.'

'I suppose not.' Anwyn glanced at the fighting pairs all around them, a somewhat dubious look whose import did not escape Ina.

'No harm will come to him, my lady.'

Feeling a little foolish, she smiled. 'No, you're right, of course.'

Just then Wulfgar looked up and, seeing her, smiled. Eyvind, following the line of his gaze, smiled, too, a great beaming smile that lit his face. She thought he had never looked so happy. The sight brought a lump into her throat. It was a forceful reminder of how much things had changed since Wulfgar's coming—changes for the better and in so many unexpected ways. Unwilling to disturb the little scene she remained where she was, continuing to watch from the sidelines.

After ten minutes Wulfgar called a halt. 'That's enough for today. You can practice what I've shown you.'

Eyvind nodded. 'Can we train again tomorrow?'

'Of course.' Wulfgar ruffled the boy's hair. Then the two of them came to join Anwyn and Ina.

As Eyvind launched into animated conversation with the old man, she looked apologetically at Wulfgar.

'I hope Eyvind isn't being a nuisance.'

'Not at all. He's eager and quick to learn. He has only to be told once.'

The words sounded genuine and Anwyn smiled, experiencing a little glow of pleasure. It was always good to hear someone speak in praise of her son, but somehow this man's words meant even more. She had seen the way the new recruits responded to his praise, how his own men sought his approval. If seasoned warriors valued his good opinion, how much more it would mean to a child. His patience and tolerance gladdened her heart as nothing else could.

'He's like a different child these days. I hardly recognise him.'

'And yet I think you are not sorry for it,' he said.

'No. It's as it should be.'

She experienced a momentary pang, knowing that Eyvind would eventually grow away from her, following the warrior path that was his birthright. Childhood was short. It was one of the reasons she was grateful for the influences acting on him now. A boy needed the right role models to follow.

Unable to follow her thoughts, Wulfgar surveyed her curiously. Her affection for her son was very apparent for all that he was Torstein's offspring.

'Did you never have other children?' he asked.

'No.'

With that one word the mood changed and became tense. Wulfgar mentally cursed his tactlessness. Women often lost babies and infants—losses that left deep scars.

'Forgive me. I didn't mean to pry.'

'It's all right.' She turned to face him squarely. 'Eyvind is my only child because I chose that he should be.'

For a moment he regarded her blankly before the implications began to sink in. 'You mean you...'

'...took measures to prevent any more pregnancies, yes.' She paused. 'Does that shock you?'

It did, but he concealed the fact. 'You must have had your reasons.'

'Eyvind's birth was difficult. At the time I thought it would kill me, but he and I survived. Torstein had his heir, and I vowed that I would bear no more children to a man I loathed.'

'How did you—?' He broke off. 'I mean, you did not deny him your bed.'

'No, I had to endure that, but there are ways a woman may avoid conceiving.'

'I see.' Suddenly the full extent of her anger and detestation were made clear. That shocked him, too, even though he understood it. 'You took a serious risk. If he had found out...'

'He would have killed me, though at the time I did not greatly care.'

'And yet you love your son.'

'He was innocent of his making.'

Wulfgar met her gaze. 'Why do you tell me these things?'

'Because you asked and because...'

'Because?'

'I don't want to lie to you.'

He hesitated, framing the next question very carefully. 'Have you resolved never to have more children, then?'

The words were spoken with apparent casualness, but for no good reason they brought a lump to her throat.

'I was resolved never to have more of Torstein's children.'

'Just his?'

'I...I never thought beyond Torstein, never thought I would be free of him.'

'And now?'

'The question is hardly relevant, is it? Under the circumstances.'

Until that moment he had not considered the matter in that light, but now the terms of their agreement returned with cold clarity. A marriage in name only; swords bought for gold and, latterly, an earldom. Recent events had caused him to forget. When he looked at Eyvind it was not so hard to envisage other sons: his sons. When he looked at the woman beside him, the wish that he had kept so deeply buried resurfaced with painful force. He acknowledged it now, mentally calling himself all kinds of fool for letting imagination outstrip common sense. Anwyn had given him a timely reminder of reality. Children would only add another layer of complications to an already complex set of circumstances. He ought to feel relief to be free of that possibility. In any case, he had agreed to her terms and she to his. He cleared his throat.

'No,' he replied. 'I suppose it isn't—under the circumstances.'

Chapter Fifteen

Over the next few days, recruits arrived from across the estate, young men keen to learn the skills of war. What with that and the patrols that daily rode the boundaries, the men were kept busy. Wulfgar delegated work where it was appropriate so that he was free to check on any aspect of the day's business when he wished to. It kept everyone on their toes for no one knew exactly where he would be or when. Moreover, the newly sworn Drakensburgh warriors were keen to prove themselves, and the newest recruits most of all. He surveyed it all closely, liaising with Hermund and Ina where necessary. When he recalled Anwyn's earlier advice he acknowledged that she had been right: Ina's support was invaluable. Despite his years, the old warrior was still remarkably fit and fast—as the trainees discovered to their cost. More than one came away from the practice bouts with a sheepish expression and a more respectful attitude than they'd had when it began. Ina rarely raised his voice in command; usually an eyebrow was enough to bring an individual back into line if it was required. Wulfgar watched it all with quiet approval.

Apart from the beginning and end of each day he had seen little of Anwyn. Of course, she had her own work to do, and servants to oversee. Even so, he found himself looking out at odd moments, hoping to catch a glimpse of her. She tended not to linger in the hall after meat and by the time he came to retire she was asleep. Although she was unfailingly courteous when occasion did bring them together, the small intimacies that they had shared earlier were conspicuous by their absence now. He found it strangely irksome. It was almost as though she were avoiding him.

Eyvind, on the other hand, was more forthcoming. He had taken to heart all the things that he had been taught and practised them diligently. Wulfgar set aside a little time each day to spend with the boy, watching him repeat the things he had been shown, teaching him new ones. The least word of praise was clearly balm, calling forth a flush of shy pleasure. Wulfgar began to wonder if Torstein had ever bothered with the child at all.

'Precious little,' said Ina, in response to his casual enquiry. 'Torstein didn't like children anyway. He had no patience at the best of times and, as I said before, a foul temper to boot.'

'And yet he had a son any man might be proud of.'

'If he was proud of the boy, he hid it well.'

The words gave Wulfgar food for thought for they tallied with what Anwyn had told him. No wonder she had not wanted to give her husband more children. Now that the initial surprise of that disclosure had worn off, he found he could not censure her for it. All the same it was a pity; sons like Eyvind could only be most pleasing to a man. The thought recurred that it would be good to father Anwyn's children. Hard on its heels came the realisation that fatherhood was a sacred responsibility, and he had failed at it already. Toki was three when he died. What manner of man might he have grown to be? Wulfgar sighed. When he told Anwyn he wasn't good husband material he had spoken no more than the truth.

Another practice session with Eyvind served to chase these thoughts from his mind. Nothing loath, the child rained blows upon the iron-bossed shield on Wulfgar's arm, seeking a way past his guard. However, no matter where he directed the sword, the shield always met it. They were perhaps ten minutes into the drill when, out of the corner of his eye, Wulfgar caught a glimpse of a mauve gown. Instinctively he turned to look. However, that moment's inattention allowed Eyvind past his guard and the point of the wooden sword thrust against his ribs.

'A hit!' Eyvind capered, brandishing the sword aloft. 'You're dead!'

Wulfgar groaned loudly, clutching his side. Then he staggered several paces, feigning mortal injury, before collapsing in the dust. The child laughed delightedly.

'Lord Wulfgar is dead! I've killed him!'

Several of the men nearby glanced round, grinning. Eyvind thrust clenched fists into the air in token of his victory. However, as soon as he turned his back, the 'dead body' came suddenly to life and grabbed him. The child yelled in surprise as strong arms lifted him off his feet. Yells became giggles as the same arms turned him upside down and held him there.

'Let that be a lesson to you, boy,' said Ina. 'Make sure your man is slain before you turn your back on him.'

'That's right. Otherwise you'll end up dead yourself.' Wulfgar swung the child the right way up and sat him in the crook of his arm. 'All the same, you broke through my guard and that was very good.'

Eyvind smiled shyly. Then he was looking over his mentor's shoulder and his face lit in a smile.

'Mother.'

Wulfgar felt his heart give an odd lurch as he turned to see Anwyn, surprising an expression on her face that he had never seen before. It was composed of laughter and pride and something harder to identify, and it transformed her.

'Did you see me slay Lord Wulfgar?'

'Yes, I did.'

In fact, Anwyn had watched the entire scene and her heart was full. She would never have supposed that this man might take such pains with a child who was not even his. She watched him set the boy down and then, retrieving the fallen shield, gave it to Ina. With an injunction to Eyvind to continue his practice, he walked apart with Anwyn.

'He's learning fast,' he said.

'He has made more progress than I ever dreamed, and that is due to you.' She paused, looking into his face. 'Thank you.'

Her expression just then caused his pulse to quicken. All her former reserve was gone to reveal the tenderness beneath—tenderness and vulnerability. Over the years she had learned to conceal it, but it was there if a man knew where to look. How much past events had hurt her. Just then he would have liked to take her in his arms and kiss away the hurt, but he restrained the impulse. Likely she would not welcome it and he would not force his attentions on her. In any case, the past could not be kissed away.

'It's a pleasure,' he said, with perfect sincerity. Under other circumstances he might have been doing the same things with Toki. Unexpectedly his throat tightened and he forced that particular thought away.

Anwyn smiled. 'It is a pleasure to Eyvind, too.' She glanced around at the practising combatants. 'Is the training going on as you would wish?'

'Aye, it is. Ina has been invaluable. You were right about him.'

'He has been like a rock since Torstein died.'

'I can well believe it,' he replied.

'Ina must hold you in esteem or he would not lend his co-operation so readily.'

'Then I am truly honoured.'

Again the words were spoken with perfect sincerity and she heard it. It gladdened her, more than she could have anticipated. Just then it was difficult to express the feelings uppermost in her mind. She was also very conscious that being in this man's company pleased her more than she could ever have anticipated. The attraction she felt was impossible to deny, but still it represented danger. That was why she had tried to distance herself a little in the preceding days. Yet, in spite of her best efforts, she had missed him.

The silence stretched out and she glanced reluctantly towards the bower. She really ought to excuse herself now and leave. Wulfgar intercepted the look and the thought.

'I have to ride out to check the patrols this afternoon. Come with me.'

Taken completely by surprise, Anwyn fumbled for an excuse. 'Well, I…I hadn't planned…'

'Of course you hadn't. I've only just asked you.' He grinned. 'It's called spontaneity.'

'Yes, but I shouldn't…I mean, it's not—' She broke off floundering.

He evinced polite interest. Anwyn felt her face grow hotter. 'Not?' he prompted.

There were many things she might have said in reply, but all of them seemed lame. She shook her head. 'No matter.'

'Good. Then you'll come.' He fixed her with a level stare. 'That wasn't a question, by the way.'

Her chin tilted to a militant angle. 'Have you any idea how overbearing you can be at times?'

'No, but you can tell me this afternoon. The horses will be ready at the end of the practice.' He favoured her with a nod and walked away, leaving her staring after him.

She bit back a smile. 'Impossible man.'

That evening Anwyn was in no hurry to leave the hall after the meal and lingered, listening to the conversation and, where appropriate, contributing. Thus the hour grew late before she eventually announced her intention to retire. She expected Wulfgar to bid her good-night and return to his men, but in this she was mistaken.

'It has been a long day,' he said by way of explanation. 'I'm for bed.'

She nodded. It had been a long day, but far from tedious. They stepped outside and paused a moment. The cressets were lit but, although it was full dark now, the evening was warm and the air sweet with green scents borne on the breeze. It was pleasant after the closeness of the hall. By tacit consent they strolled together towards the bower.

They had not gone a dozen paces when a figure leapt from the shadows and launched itself at Wulfgar. Anwyn saw the raised dagger and cried out a warning. Lightning reflexes saved him. He spun and threw himself aside so that the blade aimed at his heart slashed his arm instead. Enraged, he flung himself on his assailant, seizing his wrist and bearing down hard. The two men crashed to the ground. The flaring cressets revealed glimpses of writhing figures, locked together, the air filled with the sound of laboured breathing. His opponent rolled and the point of the dagger hovered above Wulfgar's throat. He brought a knee up hard and his assailant grunted with pain. The knife wavered and then fell. Seconds later Wulfgar's scrabbling fingers found the hilt and closed on it as a hand tightened round his windpipe. Half-throttled, he lifted the blade and thrust the point into the man's ribs. The grip slackened on Wulfgar's throat and, drawing a ragged breath, he heaved the bulky form aside. Then he staggered to his feet, one hand clutching the injured arm. Blood welled through his fingers.

A moment later Anwyn was beside him. 'Wulfgar, you're hurt!'

'A scratch, that's all.'

The sound of voices and running feet announced the arrival of the men from the hall, swords drawn.

'What happened?' demanded Hermund. Then he saw the still form on the ground. 'Are you all right, my lord?'

Wulfgar nodded. 'Just about.'

'Who was it?'

Ina shouldered his way through the crowd with a torch. Its ruddy light revealed a familiar face.

'Thorkil,' murmured Anwyn. 'What treachery is this?'

Wulfgar frowned. 'Search the place. He may have had accomplices. If you find any bring them to me—alive.' As the men hurried off to do his bidding, he looked at Anwyn. Her face was deathly pale and, seeing it, he felt his heart lurch. 'He has not hurt you, sweet?'

'No. I'm not hurt.'

'Thank the gods for that.' He slid his good arm around her waist. 'Why, you're trembling.'

Anwyn clung to him, taking comfort from his warmth. In the distance they heard shouts and then the unmistakable sounds of struggle.

'They've found someone,' she murmured.

Wulfgar's jaw tightened. 'So it would seem.'

Some minutes later, the men returned, dragging a prisoner with them. His torn clothing and bruised face testified to the fact that he had put up a fight before greater numbers had over-powered him. Hands bound, he was dragged before Wulfgar. Even under the blood and dirt Anwyn recognised the man.

'Sigurd! He was one of Thorkil's companions.'

'We caught him hiding behind the smithy, my lord,' said Hermund.

'Any sign there might be more of them?' asked Wulfgar.

'Not yet, but some of the men are still looking.' Hermund lifted his sword to Sigurd's throat. 'In the meantime this scum can tell us what he knows.'

The prisoner eyed him resentfully. 'I'm a dead man anyway. Why should I tell you anything?'

'That depends on whether you want a quick death or a very, very slow one,' replied Hermund.

Anwyn swallowed hard. The smiling, easygoing men she

had known before were nowhere in evidence now. The faces around her might have been hewn from rock. They were expressionless save for the eyes which were now devoid alike of humour and of pity.

Wulfgar fixed the prisoner with a gimlet stare. 'Well?'

Sigurd darted a glance around and licked dry lips. 'All right.'

'So talk.'

'Thorkil meant to kill you tonight.'

'I gathered that much. Who put him up to it?'

'Ingvar.'

The men around them exchanged glances and there were a few stifled exclamations of anger and disgust.

'What did he offer in return, Dogbreath?' demanded Hermund.

'A place among his warriors and a reward of silver.'

'And what was your role in all this?' asked Wulfgar.

'To help him get into Drakensburgh, and finish the job if he failed.'

More angry muttering greeted this. Anwyn felt cold, thinking of what she had almost lost this night.

'And how *did* you get in?' Wulfgar continued.

'Used a grappling iron and rope to get over the wall. Then we hid and waited for our chance.'

'Well, you missed your chance, you slimy, worm-ridden piece of filth,' growled Hermund. The edge of the sword pressed closer, drawing a faint line of blood along Sigurd's throat.

His eyes glittered. 'You can kill me, but it won't do you any good. Ingvar will slay you anyway and reduce this place to ash.'

Wulfgar lifted one eyebrow. 'And how does he mean to do that?'

'He's planning an attack.'

'When?'

'I don't know.' The sword moved slightly and Sigurd gritted his teeth. 'If I knew I'd tell you.'

Hermund glanced round. 'I'll just dispatch him then, shall I?'

Wulfgar waited but, when no more was forthcoming from the prisoner, said, 'Not yet. Let's give him time to think it over. Chain him in the kennel with the hounds.'

Sigurd swallowed hard. Seeing the beasts in her mind's eye, Anwyn shuddered inwardly. Once they had been Torstein's pride and joy; there were a dozen of them, huge and savage, standing as high as her waist and weighing more than a man. They could bring down a stag or a twenty-stone boar with relative ease.

'It'll be a pleasure,' replied Hermund. 'It's just a shame I fed the animals earlier on. This filth will probably get away with a light mauling now.'

The men heard him in silence, their expressions revealing a combination of mild reproach and disappointment.

Asulf sighed. 'Ah, well, you weren't to know.'

The others nodded slowly, acknowledging the justice of this.

'Besides, the hounds may still be hungry,' said Thrand. 'Let's go and find out, shall we?'

Seizing Sigurd by the arms, the two of them dragged him away, accompanied by half-a-dozen others. For a moment Wulfgar watched them go, before turning back to his remaining companions.

'We'll double the guard from now on and increase the number of patrols.'

'Right you are.' Hermund nodded towards the wounded arm. 'Meanwhile, you'd best get that cut attended to.'

Anwyn stepped forwards. 'He's right, my lord.' She gestured towards the bower. 'Come.'

Wulfgar didn't argue and they went in together. He paused just long enough to bar the door and then followed her to their chamber. Anwyn busied herself fetching water and cloths, glad to have something practical to do. Now that the initial drama was over reaction was setting in. The idea of a hidden threat in their midst was bad enough, but the possible ramifications were infinitely worse. It wasn't until she saw the assassin's knife an inch from Wulfgar's heart that she understood what was in her own.

She set down the basin and cloths and looked at the blood-soaked sleeve of his tunic. How close she had come to losing him.

'You'll need to take that off, my lord.'

He nodded. With his good hand he unlatched his belt and laid it aside. Then, with Anwyn's help, he eased off the tunic and shirt. Now that it was revealed, the wound proved to be a shallow gash, although it had bled copiously.

'It could have been worse,' he said.

'It's bad enough. Sit down here while I cleanse it properly.'

Again he didn't argue, submitting quietly to her ministrations, watching her hands move competently about their task.

'You've done this before,' he observed.

'Once or twice.' She wiped the blood away and cleaned the wound, then gently applied some honey salve. 'This will help prevent infection.'

He grunted, but made no demur. In fact, the touch of her fingers along his skin was pleasurable and turned his thoughts in quite another direction. With an effort he controlled them. Anwyn placed a clean linen pad over the injury and then bound it neatly in place.

'That should stay on for a day or two,' she said, 'but I think the cut will heal well enough now.'

'I'm sure it will. Thank you.'

She regarded him rather anxiously. 'Do you believe what Sigurd said about a planned attack on Drakensburgh?'

'It's entirely possible.'

'Could it succeed?'

'By force, no.'

'But by treachery?'

'Impossible to predict.' Wulfgar surveyed her steadily. 'But we shall be vigilant.'

'Ingvar wants you dead, that much is certain. He must have found Thorkil an easy tool for his purpose.'

'I imagine he did. Thorkil was a hothead with a grudge.'

'The deed was an act of cowardice and he has paid the price for his crime.' She paused. 'Even so, you were lucky tonight, Wulfgar.'

'You were my luck tonight.'

'I thought…I thought he had killed you.'

Her voice shook with delayed reaction and he heard it with some surprise.

'I am not so easy to kill, my sweet.' He hesitated. 'Would it have grieved you then if he had?'

'Of course it would.'

'Gold would buy you another protector.'

'I don't want another protector.'

Her eyes filled with tears. Appalled, she tried to turn away, but he took her shoulders in a gentle clasp and drew her back, looking into her face. What he read there caused his pulse to quicken. Anwyn swayed towards him. Then his mouth was on hers. He felt her arms slide around his neck, her body pressed against his. And then she was kissing him back. His heart seemed to skip several beats. The kiss grew deeper, more intimate. Desire flared.

He removed her gown and let it fall. Then, lifting her braid, he drew it through his fingers until he felt the binding, pulled it free and, reaching behind her, slowly unfastened her hair. It flowed over his hands like silken fire. He breathed its fragrance and almost immediately felt himself grow hard. His arms tightened around her and the kiss became searing. She returned it hungrily, all other thought forgotten as desire flung caution to the wind.

He paused just long enough to carry her to the bed. Never

taking his eyes off her, he finished undressing. Then he came to join her. He gathered the hem of her kirtle and drew it upwards, slowly easing it off. For a moment or two he let his gaze dwell on the beauty of the body beneath before resuming where he had left off, his hands caressing, gentle and assured, bringing her with him and fanning the flame of mutual desire. He took his time, not wanting to do anything that would frighten or disgust her; nothing that might equate him in her mind with what had gone before. The experiences of the past must be expunged, leaving only delight and the wish for more.

His mouth travelled from her lips to her neck and throat and breasts, teasing a nipple erect, feeling the delicious shudder of her response, while his hand travelled lower, sweeping the curves of waist and hip and leg before finding the secret place between her thighs. He stroked gently. Anwyn gasped and he felt the perspiration start along her skin. The scent of her filled his head, spicy and erotic. Resisting the temptation to pursue his own desire, he continued, eliciting a deeper tremor and then another.

When he entered her there was no resistance, only slick and yielding warmth. He moved slowly, restraining his passion, making her wait. Anwyn writhed. He heard her speak his name, her voice pleading. He stroked her hair and smiled.

'Shh. It's all right. You'll get what you want, my sweet.'

He let the rhythm build gradually, the strokes becoming stronger. He felt her shudder, her body arching against him. Her eyes widened a little, their depths darkened to emerald now, her lips swollen from his kisses. Her flesh seemed almost molten, flushed with fire and sweet as summer honey. His own desire flamed and he let go of restraint then, surrendering to his own climax at last with a cry of savage joy so intense he thought his heart might burst with the power of it. Almost light-headed he collapsed onto his forearms, his breathing fast and ragged, every part of him deliciously alive. He had expected to enjoy this, but nothing had prepared him for the sheer soul-lifting delight of the experience.

Anwyn lay beside him, heart thudding against her ribs, her body still resonating with the wonder of it. She had been told a man could make the experience pleasurable for a woman, but never in a thousand years would she have guessed at the heights that pleasure might attain. She understood full well how patient he had been and how considerate. To be treated with such tenderness was so far outside her experience that it brought a lump to her throat. He was her husband now in fact as well as name, and she no longer cared whether it was foolish. All that mattered was to live in the moment.

Wulfgar turned his head and smiled, his hand lightly caressing her cheek. 'That was magnificent.'

She returned his smile. 'Yes, it was.'

'I've wanted to do that from the moment I set eyes on you.'

'It's as well you didn't, considering the number of spectators.'

He grinned. 'Aye, it might have created something of a stir.'

'Ingvar would have had an apoplexy.'

'Ingvar can go and fornicate with Hel for all I care.'

'Mmm. Hel might not be too keen.'

'Then she can give him direct entry to the underworld,' he replied. 'Forget him.'

She lifted one arched brow. 'Are you jealous?'

'Fiercely jealous. I will not suffer you even to spare him a thought.'

'Then he is dismissed.'

'Good.' He reached out and drew her against him. 'I should be forced to drive him out else.'

She looked up at him from beneath her lashes. 'How exactly would you do that, my lord?'

'Don't you know, Anwyn?'

The implications sent a flush of warmth along her skin. 'You are quite shameless.'

He grinned. 'That's right.'

Chapter Sixteen

Anwyn slept soundly and woke just after dawn. She wasn't sure what had woken her at first, until she felt the light pressure of a man's lips on her shoulder. She smiled and stretched lazily, turning to face him. Remembering what had passed between them last night, she smiled.

'Good morrow, wife.'

The use of that term only served to reinforce the memory. 'Good morrow, husband.'

Wulfgar leaned closer, gently nibbling her ear lobe. His tongue probed further, sending a delicious shiver the length of her body.

'Still so lustful, my lord?'

'You have no idea.' He shifted a little and then his mouth was on hers, taking a leisurely kiss while his hands explored elsewhere, sending tingling warmth to her loins. The exploration continued with gentle, unhurried expertise. Hungry for his touch, Anwyn responded eagerly now, wanting to give pleasure in return. She recalled then what had pleased Torstein, but this time there was no fear or loathing, only mounting desire.

Her caresses became more intimate. Wulfgar caught his breath, every part of him alive to her lightest touch. He turned to face her, but she pushed him gently back on to the bed. With delicious anticipation he watched her straddle him, felt himself slide into her and then the slow rocking motion of her hips. His hands reached for her, pulling her deeper. The rocking movement became stronger and he bit back a groan, pleasure setting every nerve alight. Lifting his hips, he thrust into her, moving with her, building the fire anew and letting it consume him in a heart-pounding climax.

Afterwards they rested a while, temporarily sated. Wulfgar watched her drowse, his hand idly stroking her hair. He had always believed her capable of passion, but the extent of her sensuality astonished and delighted him. When he had dreamed of her submission he never imagined it would be like this. He had meant to arouse her, to leave her wanting more. He had not anticipated how much more his own desire would increase. Nor was it only about desire; Anwyn aroused emotions in him that he had not expected to feel again. There had been women over the years, but never any relationship lasting beyond the satisfaction of a physical need. He took what they offered and forgot them. However, no man would forget this woman—unless he was dead.

Unbidden, his thoughts moved ahead to the intended alliance with Rollo and to the adventure that beckoned. It held out the promise of great wealth. Of course, the corollary to that was enhanced risk. The gods might have favoured him with extraordinary luck, but his luck wouldn't hold for ever. He was seven and twenty. How many more years would be permitted him before the Nornir severed the thread of his life? How much of that time would be spent with Anwyn? Precious little in all likelihood. He frowned. That was the reality, but it would not be easy to leave her, especially now. He had wanted her from the first and had been determined to win her; he had expected to enjoy their physical coupling. What he had not foreseen was the extent of his emotional involvement. Feelings he had thought long dead had proved to be only dormant and their slow, insidious growth had crept up and taken him unawares. His weren't the only feelings involved, either. The knowledge only compounded the sensation of guilt.

He sighed, then, taking care not to disturb his slumbering wife, eased himself out of bed and looked around for his clothes. The bandage on his arm was sufficient reminder that there were matters outstanding to be attended to. Shifting the focus of his thoughts to more certain ground, he dressed quickly.

By the time Anwyn woke he was long gone. Rather guiltily she realised that she, too, should have been up and about by now. Hurriedly she bathed and dressed, feeling a certain amount of trepidation. What happened last night had wrought a change so deep, created such happiness, that she was certain everyone would look at her and know it. Her cheeks grew warm at the thought. However, when she looked into the small disc of polished metal that served as a mirror, her face was unchanged. Involuntarily she lifted a hand to her lips. She could still feel Wulfgar's kisses there. Their smooth pinkness gave no hint as to what had occurred although the memory raised a smile.

In fact none of the servants seemed to find anything unusual in her appearance. Only Jodis noticed the new sparkle in her mistress's eyes.

'You look happy today, my lady.'

'I am happy. Is it not a glorious morning?'

The tone reinforced the earlier thought and the maid smiled. 'Indeed it is.'

'Where is Eyvind?'

'He went out earlier with Ina to practise with his sword.'

'He thinks of nothing else now,' said Anwyn. 'Wulfgar encourages him.'

Jodis nodded. 'They are on the way to becoming firm friends.'

Recalling the scene in the exercise yard, Anwyn could only

agree. 'He shows more patience with the child than Torstein ever did.'

'It's a pity Lord Wulfgar won't be around long enough to help Eyvind complete his training.'

The words, though artlessly spoken, sent a little shiver of foreboding through Anwyn. All at once his words returned: *I won't stay for ever...nor will I swear my undying love.* The knowledge took the edge off her earlier happiness. Nevertheless, it was the plain truth and he had not tried to deceive her.

'Are you all right, my lady?'

Anwyn forced a smile. 'Yes, of course.'

She turned her attention to a pile of mending but, although her hands were busy about their task, her mind was at leisure to reflect. What she had shared with Wulfgar had been wonderful beyond belief, but it wasn't going to last. Neither of them had expected this marriage to be more than a business arrangement. The fact that it had become rather more than that did not change things. This brief interlude might be all they would ever have. The knowledge brought a sense of impending emptiness and loss for it was difficult now to imagine a future without him. The days spent with him had made her feel more alive than all the rest of her years put together. His going would hurt more than any pain she had ever known. Yet if it were all to do again she knew she would rather have this than nothing at all.

Wulfgar's first encounter that morning was with Hermund and Thrand. They had conducted a thorough search now, but there was no indication that the would-be assassins had brought more accomplices.

'The story about them coming over the wall is true, my lord. We found the rope and grappling hook,' said Thrand.

'And none of the guards heard anything?'

'No. I questioned them.'

'The traitors chose their moment well—unless they had inside help.'

Hermund nodded. 'That occurred to me, too, but, if they did, it came from among the Drakensburgh men, not our crew.'

'We haven't any proof yet,' replied Wulfgar, 'and I won't create bad feeling on mere speculation. Say nothing at present. Nevertheless, I want a stronger presence on the gate and wall. No one gets in without being searched and their business verified.'

'I'll deal with it, my lord.' Thrand turned to go, then checked as he remembered something else. 'What do you want us to do with Thorkil's body?'

'Send his head back to Ingvar and bury the rest.'

'Right.'

Thrand left them then to expedite Wulfgar's commands.

Hermund smiled grimly. 'I'd like to be a fly on the wall when Ingvar realises his plan has failed, but he won't be slow to hatch another.'

'Which is why we must forestall him.'

'How?'

'I need information about what he's planning and when.'

'Time for another chat with Sigurd, then.'

'Just so,' said Wulfgar.

A night among Torstein's hounds had clearly been a sleepless and unpleasant experience to judge from Sigurd's battered and bedraggled appearance. Nor had his captors handled him gently. In spite of this the prisoner retained a degree of desperate defiance.

'I'm a dead man whether I tell you or not.'

'True,' said Hermund, 'but, like I said, there are many different ways to die.'

A muscle jumped in Sigurd's cheek, but he said nothing. Wulfgar surveyed him in silence a moment and then shrugged.

'Please yourself. Take him back to the kennels.' As the escort moved to obey, he turned to Hermund. 'Only don't feed the hounds today, or tomorrow.'

Sigurd's eyes widened and he darted a glance from one to the other. 'No, please…'

'You have something to tell me?' asked Wulfgar.

The prisoner nodded. 'Ingvar plans to lure you out of Drakensburgh with a ruse.'

'What ruse?'

'He means to divide his force. A small group will fire one of the hamlets and slay the inhabitants. While you and your men deal with that the rest of Ingvar's force will close in. When you are dead he will take Drakensburgh.'

'I see.' Wulfgar's gaze was cold. 'And when was he planning to carry on this scheme?'

'At the dark of the moon.'

Hermund frowned. 'That's just a few days away.'

'What hamlet?' demanded Wulfgar.

'The one nearest the border with Beranhold,' replied Sigurd.

'If you're lying…' Hermund's hand crept to the hilt of his dagger.

'It's the truth, I swear it.'

'It had better be, Toadspawn.'

Wulfgar nodded. 'We'll keep him alive until we've tested the truth of his words. If he speaks false, the hounds can have him. If true, he may have a quick death.'

'What do you want to do with him in the meantime?' asked Hermund.

'Chain him to yonder stake where we can see him.' He nodded to the great post sunk into the ground some yards distant. When it was accomplished he took Hermund aside. 'The time is short, but I mean to be ready for Ingvar.'

'You have a plan, my lord?'

'Not yet, but I will have.'

When he left Hermund, Wulfgar went to watch the practices, turning over various scenarios in his mind. The possibility, however small, of a traitor among the Drakensburgh force was an added complication. However, he couldn't afford to ignore it. Thus far he'd had no cause for complaint. The Drakensburgh retainers had given no trouble. Indeed, there were some good men among them. The new recruits were shaping up well, too. Given time their combined number would be a formidable force to protect the estate. The problem was he no longer had time. His new recruits were about to be tested.

In the interim there were other people who needed to know what was afoot. Ina must be told as soon as might be, and then there was Anwyn. He would have liked to spare her the anxiety, but he had made a bargain with her and it must be met.

A servant came to the bower a short time later with a message requesting Anwyn's presence in the hall.

'Did Lord Wulfgar say what it was about?' she asked.

'No, my lady, only that he wished to speak with you.'

She laid aside the shirt she had been mending. 'I will come directly.'

When she arrived it was to find him already there. He had his back to her, but, on hearing her step, turned to greet her with a smile that made her heart leap. She returned it, waiting.

'Forgive the interruption, Anwyn,' he said then, 'but this is important.'

'Has something happened?

Without preamble he summarised what he had learned from Sigurd. Her face revealed anxiety, but she held her composure.

'What will you do, my lord?'

'Play Ingvar at his own game.'

'I had hoped to avoid bloodshed, but it cannot be avoided, can it?'

'No,' he replied.

'Well, you did warn me.'

'So I did, though in some part of me I also hoped it might not come to this.' He grimaced. 'A forlorn hope when the enemy is a man of Ingvar's stamp. It will not end until one of us is dead.' Then, seeing her face, he added, 'And I do not intend to die.'

She managed a tremulous smile. 'I pray you will not.'

Wulfgar drew her closer. 'My motivation for living is greater than his.'

Anwyn looked up at him, her expression earnest. 'Be extra vigilant, Wulfgar. We have borne witness to the extent of his treachery.'

'He is ruled by jealousy and anger. They will cloud his judgement eventually.'

'I hope you are right.'

'I know I'm right.' He bent and kissed her softly. 'I have what he wants most.'

'He would never have succeeded here,' she replied.

'And yet still I cannot pity the man.'

'Neither should you. He tried to have you killed and I can never forgive him for it.'

He heard the quiet anger in her voice and withal the note of sincerity. It smote him hard. When first this bargain was made, he had not anticipated that she would come to feel so deeply for him, or that he would find an echoing response in himself. It both exhilarated and disturbed. He had no wish to hurt her, and she had always known that one day he would leave. Even so, this growing attraction was an added complication. Yet if he could change things, would he? Would he have missed what they now shared? It took but a moment to find the answer.

'Now I do pity the man,' he replied.

'I was being serious, Wulfgar.'

'So was I.' He lifted her hand to his lips. 'Don't worry for me, my sweet. This matter will be seen through to its conclusion and Drakensburgh will emerge triumphant.'

Long after he left her Anwyn mulled over their conversation. Though he tended to make light of it, it was a serious matter. Ingvar was powerful and he was cunning. He would use any means to achieve his end. He was no different from Torstein, save in external appearance. A handsome face could not conceal a wicked heart.

Wulfgar walked apart awhile, wanting time to think. By the end of the morning he had formulated a plan that he thought might work. He knew the hamlet that Sigurd had identified as the bait in Ingvar's intended trap, but the details of the place and the surrounding countryside were not yet familiar enough. Accordingly he summoned Hermund, Thrand and Asulf and they rode out together.

The hamlet was situated by the side of a stream. A small wood stood hard by, marking the boundary with Beranhold. The rest was open fields and low, rolling hillside. Wulfgar leaned on the saddle pommel, surveying it all keenly.

'It's my guess Ingvar's main force will make use of the wood,' he said. 'He knows that one blazing house will bring our patrols to investigate, and that it will take a little time for them to ride back and report the attack.'

'By which time he will have torched the entire place and slain all the villagers,' replied Hermund.

'We shall arrange for the villagers to be elsewhere. None of them will be harmed. Ingvar's men will likely fire the houses—that part probably can't be avoided.'

'At least it'll provide enough light for us to see them by,' said Thrand.

'We'll bait the trap with part of our own force,' Wulfgar went on, 'and send them in to counter-attack. When Ingvar takes the bait and sends in his main force we'll bring up the rest of our men and surround them.'

Thrand grinned. 'They'll be caught like rats, my lord.'

Wulfgar nodded, pointing to the hill some half a mile distant. 'We'll conceal our force back there. It's far enough to remain unnoticed by the enemy, but near enough to the action to be able to support our own side when we need to.'

Asulf nodded slowly. 'It's a good plan, my lord.'

'Aye, it is,' replied Hermund. 'The men who bait the trap are going to be hard pressed, though, until the main force can get here.'

'That's right,' said Wulfgar. 'So it's going to need a group of seasoned warriors to keep their attention till Ingvar's men are where we want them.'

Thrand's eyes gleamed as he looked at Asulf. 'Sounds like a job for us, doesn't it?'

'I reckon it's got our names on it.' Asulf turned to Wulfgar. 'Let us choose the men, my lord, and we'll hold Ingvar's force as long as you like.'

Hermund's lips quirked. 'Let me think. Your chosen men wouldn't happen to include the likes of Dag or Frodi or Snorri or Beorn, would it?'

'Amongst others,' replied Asulf. 'How did you know?'

'Call it an inspired guess.'

Thrand looked at Wulfgar. 'So what do you say, my lord?'

He inclined his head. 'All right, it's yours. You've got the basis of a good team in those men.'

'All the mad blighters,' said Hermund.

Wulfgar smiled faintly. 'We need mad blighters for this.'

'Then they're your men.'

'Ideal, I'd say,' replied Wulfgar.

Thrand and Asulf grinned.

'One thing,' Wulfgar continued. 'No one outside of our own crewmen is to know anything about this until the time comes. I don't want any hint of it getting back to Ingvar.'

'We won't say a word,' replied Asulf.

'Just get that smile off your face,' said Hermund. 'You look like the cat that swallowed the ruddy cream. It's a dead give-away.'

Wulfgar waited until they were alone in the privacy of their chamber before he spoke to Anwyn of his plans. She listened attentively.

'It's a risk, my lord.'

'A calculated one. We have the element of surprise.'

'Will the new recruits be up to it?'

'They have a good grounding,' he replied. 'Now they need to apply what they've been taught. Besides, they'll learn more during five minutes of battle than they will in six months of drill.

'Their first test has come sooner than expected.'

'They'll have my men alongside them and the seasoned Drakensburgh warriors as well.'

She managed a smile. 'That's true.'

Wulfgar finished undressing and climbed into bed, propping himself on one arm beside her. 'Don't be afraid, my sweet. It will all be well.'

'If anyone can defeat Ingvar, it will be you,' she replied. 'All the same, I cannot help but feel anxious at the thought of a battle.'

'If all goes according to plan, it'll be the last one we ever have to fight, against this particular enemy anyway.'

'Will you slay him, Wulfgar?'

'If I can. He will certainly try to slay me.'

She shivered. 'Don't say such things.'

He reached out and gathered her to him. 'I told you, my reason for coming back is much stronger than his.'

He bent and kissed her, letting his hands explore the soft curves of her body in a leisurely embrace that set every nerve alight. She pressed closer, wanting him, needing the strong reassurance of his touch. He recognised the need and the longing because it found an answering chord in him. It also revived a conflicting sensation of guilt. He knew that she cared for him, and each caress only strengthened the bond of feeling. Severing that bond was going to hurt, something he had never intended, but it was unavoidable now. It would have been wiser never to have begun this shared intimacy and yet he could not regret it. To lie with her was to increase desire and to inflame every sense. Even when she was out of sight her memory remained with him, bright and vivid, seducing his thoughts. Although their time together could not be long, he could at least ensure that what she took from it was positive and memorable—for all the right reasons. Thus he took his time, making love to her and using his skill to give her pleasure. And afterwards he held her in his arms and watched her sleep.

Chapter Seventeen

Wulfgar stood with Hermund on the dark hilltop, listening for any sound that might reveal the presence of the enemy force. No hoofbeats, no jingling harness broke the stillness. The air was cool and the light wind carried with it the mingled smells of wood smoke and cattle and dry grass. Other than that the night was still, as though the earth held its breath. Wulfgar felt the skin prickle along his spine.

'They may not come tonight,' murmured Hermund. 'The new moon won't appear for a day or two yet.'

'They're coming,' replied Wulfgar. 'I can feel it.'

He glanced over his shoulder to where his men lay concealed below the rim of the hill. He could sense their readiness, feel the silent tension all around him.

'There!' said Hermund.

Wulfgar followed the direction of his gaze and saw the glow of a lighted torch. He estimated it must be on the edge of the wood. A few moments later, he saw another and then another, until there were a dozen of them moving in the direction of the hamlet.

'Let's hope the other companies are in position,' his companion continued.

'They will be.'

The torches moved nearer and then a flaming brand was thrown aloft. Wulfgar tracked its trajectory, watched it fall. The brand stopped well short of the ground. Almost at once the small glow flared and became a much larger one.

'They've fired a roof,' said Hermund.

Wulfgar nodded. 'So it begins.'

He turned and raised his sword and whole force moved forwards, guided by the ever-growing beacon ahead of them. Two more roofs blossomed into flame. He gritted his teeth. That was another grievance to be settled with Ingvar when the time came. At least the inhabitants had been evacuated and were now safely within the pale at Drakensburgh. Anwyn would see to their welfare. For a brief instant her image filled his mind. Then it was gone and the night filled with distant shouting and the clash of arms. The team with Thrand and Asulf had sprung their surprise attack.

Wulfgar halted his men some two hundred yards short of the conflict, now backlit by the flames. Darkness thickened and the sky grew murky with towering plumes of acrid smoke that hid the stars. He could see the figures of men, black against the ruddy glow, locked in fierce hand-to-hand fighting. Already bodies littered the ground.

'Thor's bones! Where are the rest of the swine?' demanded Hermund.

Before his companion could reply, the noise of battle was drowned by a roar from fifty throats as the remainder of Ingvar's force broke from the cover of the wood to join the fight. Thrand and his companions formed up in a wedge-shaped shield wall in front of one of the remaining houses. The press around them grew thick, but the available space to attack was small so that, although heavily outnumbered, they were able to inflict much more damage than their foes.

Seeing all attention turn that way, Wulfgar lifted his sword. 'Now!'

His men surged forwards like a tide, racing across the open ground to attack from the rear. At that signal, the other two companies of the Drakensburgh force swept in on either flank. For a short time Ingvar's warriors were unaware of the danger and by the time they realised what was happening they were under attack from all sides. The fighting was close and brutal. Wulfgar carved a path forwards, stepping over the bodies of the slain, his sword smoking red, eyes narrowed against the heat, always seeking one man. And then, through the shimmering haze, he saw him.

'Ingvar!'

The furious, bellowing challenge carried over the din and the warrior turned, looking swiftly about him. Then he saw his foe and checked, eyes glittering with recognition and hatred.

'I have waited for this moment, Viking.'

With that he launched himself into the attack. Wulfgar feinted and the edge of the sword glanced off the rim of his shield. Almost instantaneously he swung his own blade in a slashing cut across the ribs. Saved by his mail shirt, Ingvar reeled back a pace, then recovered and came on. Their swords locked. Ingvar bared his teeth in a smile, his face just inches from his enemy's.

'Did you really think to keep her from me?'

'Your battle is already lost,' growled Wulfgar.

'On the contrary, it's just begun.'

'No matter. I'll keep her safe from you.'

Wulfgar threw his opponent off and there followed a fierce exchange of blows. The heat around them increased and he blinked away sweat, his nostrils filled with the stench of blood and smoke, his arm rising and falling instinctively, blocking his enemy's blade, seeking an opening. Ingvar broke and circled, the smile never leaving his face.

'She'll never be safe from me, Viking. I know how to be patient, you see. And one day you'll grow careless. Then I'll take back what is rightfully mine.'

'She was never yours, nor ever will be.'

He renewed the attack, harrying his opponent hard, but still he could find no way past his enemy's defences. Ingvar laughed.

'Perhaps I won't kill you straight away. Perhaps I'll let you watch while I take her. It'll be the last thing you see before I have your eyes put out.'

Wulfgar's lip curled. 'Hot air, braggart.'

'I'll make good the boast, believe me, and keep her closer than Torstein ever did. One night in my bed and she'll forget she ever knew your name.'

'The very thought of your bed would sicken any woman.'

Ingvar's eyes glinted red in the light of the flames and the blades clashed again in a short, fierce exchange. Then they parted once more.

'She'll come to my bed, Viking, and that right often. My appetites require feeding and they enjoy variety.'

'You will not sate them with her.'

'She'll do whatever I may command. If not, her son will pay a heavy forfeit for his mother's disobedience.'

The words conjured a powerful image of the woman and child in all their terrible vulnerability. Once delivered into Ingvar's clutches their fate would be dire indeed. Wulfgar had no trouble visualising the details and his jaw tightened in anger and disgust. With an effort he controlled both. While he had breath in his body and a sword in his hand, Anwyn and Eyvind would never come to harm.

Fuelled by that knowledge, he renewed the attack, pressing his opponent harder, forcing him on to the back foot beneath a rain of punishing blows. Ingvar parried fast and gave ground. All trace of bravado vanished to be replaced by fury. Around them the number of his force began to dwindle. Noting it, Wulfgar smiled grimly and came on, driving Ingvar backwards, pace by pace. Then his foot slid on a patch of mud and Wulfgar's blade found its opening. Ingvar staggered, cursing and clutching his thigh with one hand. Blood welled through his fingers. Breathing hard, he shot a baleful glance at his opponent and began to retreat. Before Wulfgar could close for the kill, two other fighting men backed into his path. He swore fluently. Hemmed in on every side, he could only watch in impotent wrath as Ingvar turned and fled into the darkness.

Seeing their leader flee and demoralised by their thinning numbers, others of his force broke away from the fighting and followed. Soon the rest were in full retreat, pursued by the Drakensburgh men. The battle continued to the edge of the wood where Wulfgar called a halt.

'Enough! It's blacker in there than the wings of Odin's ravens. I'll not lose men thus.'

'There were precious few of Ingvar's force left in any case,' said Hermund. 'They'll go home to lick their wounds.'

'Unfortunately the one I gave Ingvar wasn't enough to kill him.'

They turned back towards the burning hamlet, now a scene of carnage. The burning huts had collapsed, casting a sullen light on the bodies of the slain and injured. However, almost all of them were Ingvar's men. The Drakensburgh warriors were jubilant. Wulfgar located the group who had baited his trap, clapping Thrand on the shoulder.

'You did well this night. Any losses?'

'No, my lord. The scum couldn't break our shield wall.'

Asulf grinned, his teeth very white in his smoke-blackened face. 'I doubt they'll be back.'

'Not if they know what's good for them,' growled Beorn.

'They know,' said Asulf. 'Didn't you see them run?'

Jeering laughter testified that they had. Wulfgar grinned and turned to Hermund.

'Let's get our injured home. We'll return to bury the dead later.'

'Looks like most of the hamlet has been destroyed.'

'Huts can always be rebuilt,' replied Wulfgar.

* * *

Night was turning into morning before the men returned. Anwyn heard their arrival and hastened to meet them, her gaze desperately searching the crowd for Wulfgar. At last she located him, filthy but indisputably alive, and her spirit soared. His companions laid aside their weapons and began to remove their war gear, then gathered at the trough to wash off the blood and grime of battle. Having given orders for the tending of the wounded, Wulfgar went to join the group of men at the well. He, too, removed his sword and then dragged off the heavy mail shirt in order to strip off the sweat-soaked tunic and shirt beneath. Watching him, Anwyn breathed a heartfelt sigh of relief. The blood she had seen on his mail clearly wasn't his. The hard-muscled torso was unmarked by any fresh wounds. He laved his hands and then sluiced his face and neck and chest, using the shirt to dry himself afterwards. Then, as though sensing himself watched, he looked up. The blue gaze warmed. Then he began to thread his way through the knots of talking men towards her.

Wulfgar's eyes never left her. In the back of his mind he could still hear Ingvar's taunts. The result was fierce, possessive anger and a desire to protect. Underlying that was physical need, the familiar earthy passion that all men knew after combat. Seeing her before him in the flesh did nothing to diminish the sensation.

Several glances came their way, but he was unaware of them, his attention entirely on the woman before him. For a moment neither one spoke. Then he saw her smile and his blood turned to fire. He returned the smile.

'Do I take it that you defeated Ingvar's force?' she asked.

'Soundly.'

'Oh, Wulfgar, I have been so worried these past hours.'

'No cause, my sweet.'

'Sigurd's information was accurate then.'

'Aye, it was.'

'What will you do with him now?'

'Nothing. He can stay where he is until the morrow.'

She paused. 'You must be hungry. There is food and drink ready in the hall.'

'Presently,' he replied.

The blue gaze locked with hers, the expression unfathomable, yet something about it caused her pulse to quicken, like his closeness now. In spite of his recent ablutions she could feel the heat coming off him.

'Is anything amiss, Wulfgar?'

For answer his arm closed round her waist, pulling her hard against him. A moment later his mouth came down on hers in a searing kiss that drove all other thought away. When he drew back from that she had no difficulty in reading his expression. Without another word he bent and scooped her up. Heads turned in their direction and she glimpsed grinning faces. Her cheeks turned pink.

'My lord, your men are watching.'

'Let them.'

He strode towards the bower. Anwyn tried to wriggle free, but he held her easily.

'Wulfgar?' She tried harder, but to no avail. 'Wulfgar!'

'Be still. You're not going anywhere.'

'Put me down.'

'No.'

'You can't…'

On reaching their destination he kicked the door shut behind them and continued on to their chamber. There he spilled her on to the bed, following her down, pinning her there and silencing her protest with another kiss. It grew deeper and more demanding. Protest forgotten now, Anwyn returned it. She could feel his arousal and the answering glow in the core of her body. He smelled of musk and iron and smoke, pungent and dangerous, the scent of the warrior. Her hands slid over the silver arm rings to the hard-muscled flesh between. The inner glow flared and became fire. Her hands fumbled for the fastenings of his clothing, found them, tugged them loose, closing her fingers around him. He drew in a sharp breath, looking into her face, the blue eyes darkened now to violet.

'Odin's blood, I want you, Anwyn, but I fear I cannot be gentle.'

For answer she drew his face down to hers and kissed him, a long and passionate kiss that tasted of honey. Her tongue teased his, seductively probing. Seconds later her skirts were round her waist. What followed was not gentle, but a hot, fierce coupling that made her cry out and sent shock waves of pleasure crashing through the length of her body. Gasping, she arched against him, reaching for him. Wulfgar pushed her down, clamping her wrists to the bed. She writhed beneath him, but he held her fast, riding her hard, until with a cry of triumph he reached his own shuddering climax. Then, chest heaving, he collapsed beside her.

Anwyn turned her head to look at him, temporarily speechless. She had thought that his earlier lovemaking was the sum of all pleasure. Now the error of that assumption was all too apparent. The implications sent a thrill of anticipation through her entire being.

'That was incredible,' she said then.

'It's called post-battle lust.'

'Worth waiting for again,' she replied.

Wulfgar smiled and brushed her lips with his. Then he began to remove her gown. 'It isn't finished yet, my sweet. Not by a long way.'

Chapter Eighteen

⁓⁓⁓

The following morning Wulfgar had the prisoner brought before him. Sigurd darted nervous glances at the warriors gathered around, clearly expecting the worst.

'What do you want us to do with him, my lord?' asked Hermund.

'Fetch a horse,' said Wulfgar, 'and tie him on. Then send him back to Ingvar. I'm sure his master will be pleased to see him. He may wish to question him about the reasons for his recent rout at our hands.'

His men grinned appreciatively. Sigurd's face registered panic and he began to resist the hands dragging him towards the waiting horse.

'I'm only sorry I won't be there to witness that interview,' said Hermund. 'Frodi, you and Dag see he gets safely back.'

'It'll be a pleasure,' replied Frodi.

When Sigurd was securely tied to the horse and the trio was ready to depart, Asulf raised a hand in farewell.

'Be sure to remember us to Ingvar, won't you?'

The response was a brief look of fury and loathing before the horse and prisoner were led away.

* * *

The aftermath of battle had left much work to be done. Wulfgar's next task was to organise a burial detail for the slain who, with the exception of three men, were exclusively Ingvar's warriors.

'If the fight had been out in the fields somewhere, I'd be tempted to leave the bodies to the foxes and the crows,' said Hermund.

'So would I,' replied Wulfgar, 'but as it is we dare not, lest the stink and corruption breed a pestilence.'

'You're right, of course, though the swine are little deserving of the honour.' Hermund glanced at the heap of weapons and mail taken from the bodies of the dead. 'At least their war gear will go to arm our own men now.'

Thrand, who had been examining the corpses closely, gave it up and came to join them, his expression suggestive of disappointment. 'Grymar Big Mouth isn't here, my lord. He must have fled into the wood with the others.'

'More than likely,' replied Wulfgar. 'The man is a survivor if ever I saw one.'

Thrand sighed. 'Ah, well. I'll find the cur one day.'

'In the meantime we've got more important things to think about,' said Hermund. 'Let's start by getting this carrion into the ground.'

'When it's cooled down enough we'll set some men to clearing the fire debris,' said Wulfgar. 'The rebuilding should start as soon as may be. These folk have lost enough.'

'Could have been worse, my lord; could have been the depths of winter.'

'So it could. Even so, with the lean months coming on people can ill afford to lose their homes as well.'

'Looks like we're all going to be busy for a while, then,' said Hermund.

'We'll get as many men on the job as we can. I want this place rebuilt by the full of the next moon.'

* * *

Wulfgar informed Anwyn of his intention later. She wanted to ride out with him at once and inspect the damage for herself, but he would not allow it until the slain had been buried.

'It is not a sight for a woman's eyes.'

'Yet those men died in a woman's cause,' she replied.

'They were warriors. They knew the realities of battle. You do not; nor do I intend that you shall.'

Though the words were quietly spoken, they held an inflexion that she was coming to recognise. He would not be swayed. Anwyn abandoned further argument, reflecting that he probably had a point.

'When the burial is done we will ride out together,' he went on.

She lowered her eyes. 'Yes, my lord.'

Wulfgar's lips twitched. 'This wifely obedience is most pleasing.'

At once her gaze locked with his, flashing emerald fire. He chuckled softly. 'I thought as much.'

For a moment she continued to glare at him but, unable to keep it up, smiled ruefully. 'Would you wish me to be different?'

He put his arms around her and drew her close. 'Not by as much as a hair.'

In fact, Wulfgar was as good as his word and the following day he rode with her to the ruined hamlet. Where people's homes had once stood there now remained only blackened heaps of ash from which drifted wisps of smoke, its acrid stench still strong in the air. Six of the original eight houses had been razed. The sight of that wanton destruction caused Anwyn a sharp pang that was closely followed by anger. Her gaze went from the ruins to the silent knot of villagers standing nearby and her heart went out to them. The best that she could do was to offer assurance that their homes would be rebuilt.

'I'll get the matter in train at once,' said Wulfgar. 'If everyone pulls together it won't take so long.'

The villagers heard his words with evident surprise, but also with the first faint glimmer of optimism. Anwyn saw it and was glad. They had lost much, but not their lives at least.

Although the dead had been removed, large patches of earth were yet stained dark with their blood. Walking around the site now offered her an insight into the ferocity of the fighting, and she understood why Wulfgar had wanted to shield her from it. Just then, however, she would gladly have run Ingvar through herself, and said as much.

'I imagine you would at that,' replied Wulfgar.

'At least the villagers were spared his wrath.'

He nodded. 'Ingvar would have slaughtered them without a qualm.'

'This is what you really meant, isn't it, when you said that things would get dirty?'

'Aye, although in this case we got off lightly. Forewarned is forearmed.'

Anwyn looked around. 'How long will it take to rebuild these dwellings?'

'Not long. We have the materials to hand and plenty of able men for the work.'

'Good.' Involuntarily her gaze went to the wood some hundred yards distant. Its far edge marked the boundary between Drakensburgh and Beranhold lands; a proximity brought forcefully home now.

Wulfgar had little trouble reading her thoughts. 'He won't try it again, unless he's a complete fool.'

'He is no fool, but he is ruthless and vindictive.'

'That is why I must take my men and finish what we began.'

Her eyes widened a little. 'You mean you would go and seek him out?'

'I mean that I would seek him out and slay him, along with the remnant of his war band, and burn his fortress to the ground. Then I would amalgamate the Beranhold lands with those of Drakensburgh.'

'You intend to seize his lands?'

'It is the only certain way to secure the future.'

A knot of dread formed in the pit of her stomach as the real ramifications of the affair sank in. 'This was not part of my plan, Wulfgar. Besides, I would not have more blood spilled.'

'We have come this far and there can be no going back.'

'In this case we did but defend what was ours.'

'If we stop now, it will be taken as weakness,' he replied. 'Ingvar has offered gross provocation. The insult cannot be forgotten or forgiven.'

The blue eyes held no trace of gentleness now, only cold and deadly anger. The expression sent a shudder down her spine. Suddenly she had the sensation of things unravelling, of moving inexorably out of her control into realms beyond imagining.

'You said he would not make the same mistake again.'

'That doesn't mean he won't try something else. The time to strike is now, while he's at his weakest.'

She paled. 'I want peace, Wulfgar.'

'Peace has many forms. Some of them are only found on the far side of war.'

'We had an agreement, you and I.'

'So we did,' he replied. 'I said I would do nothing without telling you of my intention first.'

'Then you are resolved on this?' Anwyn swallowed hard. 'I beg you to reconsider.'

'I am responsible for the security of Drakensburgh and I do not want to be for ever looking over my shoulder.' He paused. 'Make no mistake, Anwyn, that's what we will be doing from now on if Ingvar is allowed to live.'

'How many more men must die with him?'

He met her eye unflinchingly. 'As many as it takes.'

The knot in her stomach tightened. 'You among them, Wulfgar?'

'No. Ingvar isn't good enough.'

'I cannot agree to this.'

'That is unfortunate.'

Her heart thumped against her ribs. 'I *will not* agree, and I am still the Lady of Drakensburgh.'

'But I am its lord—and yours, too, Anwyn.'

Her gaze smouldered. 'Aye, and a fitting successor to Torstein.'

With that she turned on heel. Taken by surprise, Wulfgar called after her. She ignored him, hurrying on, tears of rage running unheeded down her face. She had no idea where she was going. Her only desire was to put distance between them. Beneath anger was a deeper, sharper pain born of confusion. She had trusted him… Too late she saw the extent of his ambition.

Her progress was halted abruptly by a large hand closing round her arm. Wulfgar swung her round to face him, his eyes burning into hers.

'Perhaps you'd care to explain that last remark.'

'I should have thought it self-explanatory,' she retorted.

'I don't care for the imputation.'

'Why? Did it hit a nerve, Wulfgar?'

'You know it did. Is that really your opinion of me?'

'What do you care for my opinion? You'll still be Lord of Drakensburgh and Beranhold, too.'

He paled. 'Is that what you think this is about?'

Anwyn struggled ineffectually to free herself. 'What else is there to think?'

'My concern is not with lordship or with wielding power over you,' he growled. 'It is with your safety and that of your son.' The blue gaze bored into hers. 'Can you get that into your hot little head?'

Her throat tightened and to her horror tears welled and then spilled over. Completely overwrought, she began to sob.

Wulfgar was appalled, his anger evaporating as quickly as

it had risen. He let out a long breath and drew her to his breast. 'Hush, sweet. Don't cry. It's all right.'

It was a little while before the sobs subsided and she regained a measure of control. 'I'm sorry, Wulfgar.' She took a ragged breath, wiping away tears with the sleeve of her gown. 'What I said before, about you and Torstein; I didn't mean it.'

'I know.'

'It was just my wretched temper.'

'Well, it is a fault I share.' He drew back a little, looking into her face. 'Since you so dislike my plan to depose Ingvar I shall relinquish it, albeit against my better judgement.' He paused. 'I have no wish to be the cause of tears from you, Anwyn.'

She managed a rather watery smile. 'I am glad of it, although the tears were not intended as a weapon to dissuade you.'

'If I had thought so, my sweet, they could not have succeeded.'

'I think your heart is not as hard as you pretend.'

'Where my heart is concerned I never pretend.'

'I wish with all of mine that you didn't have to leave Drakensburgh.' Seeing him about to speak, she hurried on. 'Forgive me. I shouldn't have said that. I know that you must. You warned me at the outset, did you not?'

'I also warned you that I wasn't good husband material.'

'I have no complaint to make.'

'And yet I cannot be the husband you want me to be, Anwyn, any more than I was for Freya.'

'What happened to Freya was not your fault.'

His face was suddenly devoid of expression. 'You speak of what you do not know.'

'I know you were not responsible for the fever epidemic. You told me before that it killed hundreds. Your being there would not have changed anything, except perhaps by adding your death to theirs.'

'You don't know how often I have wished for that.'

'It would not bring them back.'

'I'm well aware of it.'

'Then perhaps it's time to forgive yourself, Wulfgar.'

He kept his voice level. 'When I want an opinion on the matter I'll ask for it.'

'I did not mean to be presumptuous.'

'Then don't tell me what I should do.'

'I didn't mean it like that. I only—'

'Leave it, Anwyn. It's over and done with.'

Her gaze locked with his. 'Is it?'

'What's that supposed to mean?'

'Until you face the past you cannot move on.'

'I said leave it.'

There followed a strained silence. Wulfgar took a deep breath, mentally counting to ten. He had spoken more harshly than he'd intended, but then he'd been caught off guard, something that Anwyn was confoundedly good at doing. He didn't want to quarrel, but neither was he going to the place she wanted him to revisit. Even more disturbing was her growing attachment for him. When he had embarked on this relationship he had never anticipated that it would become more than the marriage of convenience she had described. Yet somehow it had happened anyway. Nor was the attachment all on her side. If he stayed longer, it would just make things worse. It was a mess, and that fact only pointed out the truth of what he had told her at the start.

'Have you seen enough here?' he asked.

'Yes.'

'Then I'll escort you home.'

They walked back towards the waiting horses, but neither one spoke. Once she glanced at his face, but its expression was closed to her. Only a few inches separated them, but it seemed to Anwyn that the distance between them had widened to a yawning gap.

Chapter Nineteen

Although he would have liked to forget it, the conversation stayed with Wulfgar in the days that followed. He was not the husband Anwyn needed and deserved, but he could at least provide her with security of another kind. When he left Drakensburgh it would be in the knowledge that she was safe with a strong defensive force at her disposal. The new recruits, having been bloodied in combat, had grown in confidence, and their commitment and determination increased in proportion.

'They're shaping up well,' said Hermund, as he and Wulfgar stood watching the latest training session from the sidelines.

'Aye, they are. They'll be quite capable of defending the place when we leave.'

'Have you decided when that might be? Only some of the men were asking.'

Wulfgar nodded. 'It's a fair question. I'll think on it.'

In truth, there was no reason why the *Sea Wolf* could not sail in the near future. Leaving Anwyn and Eyvind was going to be a wrench, but the longer he stayed the worse it would be. Better for all concerned if he made it sooner rather than later. Besides, he had an obligation to his men, and business with Rollo awaited. He must speak to Anwyn and tell her what was afoot. He owed her that much. All the same it wasn't something he relished doing. Not because he thought she would create a scene, but because he knew that what he had to impart would hurt her. It was becoming a bad habit.

The matter weighed on his mind. For a while work enabled him to forget about it, but in his leisure moments it returned to haunt him. Anwyn was the first to notice his preoccupation. Although he remained attentive and continued to treat her with gentleness, he seemed somehow to have withdrawn from her. At first she wondered whether it had something to do with their earlier disagreement, but he had never adverted to it in any way afterwards. His mood puzzled her, and with that came a feeling of uneasiness. Unwilling to tax him with it, she hoped it was merely a phase that would pass.

On several occasions she rode out with him to inspect the progress of the rebuilding work. It was coming along apace.

'The new dwellings will be ready as planned by the end of the month,' he said.

She nodded and smiled, but those last few words put her in mind of something else—a half-buried hope that she had not given utterance. Her last flux had not come. After Torstein's death she had abandoned the precautions she had taken to avoid conception; she had had no need of them. However, neither had she resumed them following her marriage to Wulfgar. It hadn't been a deliberate decision as such; it was more that the fierce desire to prevent another pregnancy was absent and she had let the matter drift. Indeed, until recently, she had forgotten about it. Had Wulfgar's seed taken root in her? Being unsure as yet she had not mentioned the possibility to him. Now, with this strange mood upon him, she wondered what his reaction might be. Their original business arrangement had become something that neither of them had intended and yet, perversely, both of them had desired. On her part desire had subsequently blossomed into a far stronger emotion. On his part...she did not know. Despite his kindness, he had never actually said that he loved her. The knowledge brought a twinge of sadness.

'Are you all right, Anwyn?'

His voice drew her back to reality with a jolt. 'Forgive me, I was just thinking.'

'You looked totally preoccupied.' He eyed her curiously. 'What's on your mind?'

She forced a smile. 'Many things, but nothing I can identify precisely.'

He didn't pursue it and the conversation turned to other matters. They lingered another half-hour or so and then turned the horses for home. However, they had covered no more than half the distance before Wulfgar turned aside and reined in by the stream. Anwyn looked around and recognised the spot at once; they had visited it together when first he came to Drakensburgh.

'Will you get down and walk with me awhile?' he asked.

'Of course.'

He tethered their mounts and, taking her hand, led her along the bank to the place where they had been before. There he spread his cloak on the grass and sat down to join her. However, his mood was different now with no hint of that former playfulness. The look in his eyes was almost sombre and she felt the first twinge of unease.

'Is something wrong, my lord?'

'Not wrong, but we have to talk, Anwyn.'

Her uneasiness increased. 'You have something to tell me?'

'There is no easy to way to say this so I must be direct.' The blue gaze met hers and held it. 'The defence of Drakensburgh is complete and very soon now my men and I will depart.'

It had come, then. Of course, he had told her this at the outset. It was part of their agreement. Nevertheless, the effect was like a punch under the solar plexus. She drew a sharp breath, fighting the sudden sickness in her stomach.

'I see.' She was surprised to discover how level her voice sounded.

'I gave them my word on this long since. And, of course, there is our arrangement with Rollo.' He paused. 'However, you will be well protected. The men are not only highly trained, they have been tested in battle.'

'Yes.'

'To make doubly certain I will leave a few hand-picked members of my crew as well. You will also have Ina. He's a good man.'

'Yes.'

'He will look after things here in my absence.'

She took another deep breath. 'When must you go?'

'In a few weeks probably, once we have finished the work on the new dwellings and re-provisioned the ship.'

'Will you be gone for long?'

'Long enough, I think. It's impossible to be sure.'

'I shall miss you.'

'And I you. Our time together has been good, has it not?'

Anwyn clasped her knees tightly. 'It has been better than good.' The depth of that understatement only increased the bleakness in her heart.

'I'm glad you think the same.'

'How could I not? With you I have found a happiness I did not know existed.'

'I, too, have been…most happy.'

Summoning all her courage, she forced herself to ask the next question. 'Will I ever see you again, Wulfgar?'

For a fleeting moment his expression registered something like pain. 'If the gods so will it.'

Her knuckles whitened. 'I pray they do.'

'I wish I could make you a promise to return, but war is an uncertain business.' He put his arms about her and drew her to his chest, kissing her bright hair. 'But I shall not forget the time I have shared with you.'

Anwyn held him tightly and closed her eyes, holding the moment and trying to shut out the prospect of all the years ahead without him.

They returned home some time later and while Wulfgar went off to speak with Ina, Anwyn sought the solace of the bower, trying to order the chaos of her thoughts. However, they refused to be ordered. As the full impact of that earlier conversation sank in, it left her reeling. Her stomach churned and a light sheen of sweat broke out on her forehead. The room seemed suddenly stifling. Throwing off her mantle, she hurried to the basin in the corner and vomited repeatedly.

For a little while she thought she might faint but gradually the sensation passed and she found herself able to breathe again. With shaking hands she reached for a cloth, soaked it in the water jar and then used it to bathe her face. The coolness was blessedly restorative.

A footstep in the passage without announced another presence. For a dreadful moment she thought it was Wulfgar returning, but to her intense relief saw Jodis instead. The maid smiled and was about to speak, but one look at Anwyn's deathly pallor caused the words to wither on her lips.

'My lady, you are ill.'

'It's nothing. A momentary sickness is all. I shall be well again presently.'

'Pray, come and lie down awhile until you feel better.'

Anwyn allowed herself to be led across the room and sank down disconsolately on the edge of the bed.

'What brought this on?' the maid continued. 'Something you ate, perhaps?'

'No, it's nothing I've eaten.'

'Some other malady then.'

'One with no cure, I'm afraid.' Seeing the maid's startled expression, she added, 'He's leaving, Jodis.'

The maid didn't pretend to misunderstand. 'Leaving when?'

'Very soon. A matter of weeks, I believe.'

'I am so sorry. I hoped…'

'I think we all hoped.' Anwyn sighed. 'I most of all.'

'But he will come back.'

'One day, perhaps—if he is not slain or imprisoned first.'

Jodis sat down, regarding her with concern. 'He will come back, I'm sure of it.'

'I wish I could say the same.'

'He is Earl of Drakensburgh. He will not forget that. Nor will he forget you.'

'I shall not forget him, that is certain.' The tears she had restrained before now filled Anwyn's eyes. 'I love him, Jodis. I always hoped that one day he might come to feel the same.'

'He cares for you very much, I'd swear to it.'

'Yes, but not enough to stay.'

'He hasn't gone yet. He may change his mind.'

Anwyn shook her head. 'He will not. Besides, I have always known that he would go eventually.' The tears spilled over. 'I just didn't expect it to be so hard.'

'If he knew it, he might reconsider.'

'To do that would be to break his word to his men.'

'What of his word to you?'

'He has never made any promise to me that he was not prepared to fulfil.'

Jodis sighed. 'Why are men such fools? Why can they never see what's right under their noses?'

'We women can be foolish, too, seeing what we'd like to see instead of what is. By the time we do realise, it's too late and there's no going back.'

'Would you wish it undone?'

'No. That's the worst of it.' Anwyn wiped the tears away with the sleeve of her gown. 'I made the bargain and must bear the consequences.'

For a moment Jodis was perfectly still. Then she looked from her mistress to the basin across the room and back again. Her eyes widened.

'Oh, my! You're not…?'

'It's possible. I don't know yet. I won't know for another week or two.'

'Have you said anything to him?'

'There's nothing to say, yet.'

'But…'

Anwyn laid a hand on her arm. 'And you will say nothing, either.'

Any lingering doubts she might have had were banished when her next flux failed to appear. Moreover, the sickness recurred, too. Thus far she had managed to hide it from Wulfgar, but the knowledge of her condition was an additional anxiety. What made it much harder was the realisation of how much she wanted his child. Even the thought of another difficult and protracted labour did not change that. The baby within her was something of his that she could keep and cherish long after he was gone. Mingled with that was the increasing conviction that she ought to tell him. It was just a matter of finding the right time.

Wulfgar sensed her inner preoccupation, though not its cause. He attributed it to the announcement of his imminent departure. The scene was still vivid in his mind. In truth it had been harder than he cared to admit. When he said he would miss her it had not been a mere sop to her feelings. Leaving was going to be a wrench for him, too, more so than he could ever have imagined when he entered into this match. Both of them had always known this was going to happen. He was an adventurer, a mercenary—had never pretended to be other. He also had a duty to his crew. His jaw tightened.

'We're just about done here,' said Hermund, surveying

the men who were finishing the thatch on the last two huts. 'Another day should do it.'

Wulfgar glanced at him; then returned his attention to the thatchers. 'Aye, it will.'

'The Drakensburgh force is ready, too, and at full strength.'

'It is.'

'So, what now?'

'We keep to the agreement we made before. We go to join Rollo.'

'I'll make a start on the ship's provisions, then.'

'Do that. We'll also take her out for a trial run. Make sure everything's as it should be.'

Hermund grinned. 'It'll be good to be at sea again.'

'I am already at sea,' said Wulfgar.

Word of the decision was not slow to spread. When Eyvind heard about the forthcoming sea trial his eyes shone.

'May I come, lord?'

His initial reaction was to refuse, but when he looked down at the boy's eager face Wulfgar relented. 'Why not?' He looked over the child's head at Anwyn. 'It won't be far. Just up the coast a little way and then back. He'll be safe enough.'

She checked the urge to object. Eyvind could not be tied to her apron strings for ever and he had blossomed so much since Wulfgar's coming. He would not let anything happen to the child.

'Very well.'

Eyvind beamed, his cheeks pink with excitement. Together they went out to the courtyard where the crewmen awaited them. Doubting whether the child's short legs would keep up with the longer strides of the men, Wulfgar lifted him on to his shoulders. Then he turned to Anwyn.

'Will you walk with us to the bay?'

'I might slow you down.'

'If I had thought that I would not have suggested it,' he replied.

Something in the quiet tone and the accompanying look caused her pulse to quicken a little.

'I will come.'

Wulfgar let his men move on ahead and matched his stride to hers. They spoke little, but the silence was companionable and she did not mind it. It was enough just for the three of them to be together. Such moments would not come again and she was going to have to live on them a long time. Involuntarily her hand went to the front of her gown and rested there a moment. The knowledge of the baby growing within her was bittersweet. With the certainty came the pressing need to let Wulfgar know of its existence. The thought of him perishing on a foreign shore in ignorance of his child was not to be contemplated. She must speak to him and soon.

By the time they reached the bay the strand was a hive of activity. The tide was in, but, she was relieved to note, there was only a gentle swell and a light wind carrying with it the familiar scent of weed and brine. The blue-green water was touched with gold in the path of the sun. Wulfgar set the child down and they watched him scamper off down the beach towards the men who were readying the ship. Then Wulfgar turned to Anwyn.

'I'll look after him.'

'I know.'

He smiled and bent to kiss her. She swayed towards him, twining her arms about his neck. Then his were around her, and the kiss grew lingering. When at last he drew back it was with an expression of regret.

'I'd like to be able to stay and take that further.'

She glanced towards his crew. 'It might cause a few raised eyebrows if you did.'

'Aye, it might, especially with what I have in mind.'

Her cheeks turned an attractive shade of pink. 'I'm not going to ask.'

'Then I'll just have to tell you later.' He surveyed her keenly. '*Tell* is a figure of speech, by the way.'

'You are incorrigible.'

'Where you are concerned I am.' He took her hand and lifted it to his lips. 'Until later, Anwyn.'

Then he turned and strode away down the beach. She remained where she was, watching as he rejoined the others. A short time later the great ship was sliding down the strand and into the water. Eyvind stood in the prow beside Wulfgar and, seeing her, waved enthusiastically. She forced a smile and waved back. Dimly she heard the spoken commands and saw the long banks of oars rise and dip. Slowly, the *Sea Wolf* turned and then began to head away along the coast. Anwyn watched until it was out of sight.

Wulfgar remained in the prow, his gaze held by the receding figure on the shore. She seemed small and somehow very vulnerable, her loneliness more apparent in that moment than it had ever been. It touched something within him that had been long buried. He wished now that he had brought her along with them; she might have enjoyed it. Certainly her company would have been most congenial to him. She was not yet out of sight, but he missed her already. He did not care to think too deeply about an absence of years.

Chapter Twenty

The men returned in the early evening. Anwyn heard them come and hurried to greet them. As they approached she could see Wulfgar in their midst with Eyvind perched on his shoulders once more. When at length he was set on his feet he ran to meet her. Grubby and dishevelled, he exuded happiness from every pore and began to give her a full account of the day. She listened closely. It soon became clear that he had explored every part of the ship in detail. However, she heard nothing that could give her cause for alarm.

Eventually Eyvind concluded his tale and ran off to find Jodis. Anwyn looked up at Wulfgar.

'Did he behave himself?'

'He was no trouble at all. In fact, I think he'll make a natural sailor one day.'

The words aroused feelings of both pride and pain. 'Thank you for taking him out today. He has obviously enjoyed it.'

'So did I. He's a fine boy.'

'You are very good with him.'

'I happen to like children.'

Her heart leapt. 'Do you?'

'Of course.'

Anwyn glanced around at the milling groups of men. This wasn't the place or the time. She drew a deep breath and smiled. 'Was the sea trial all you expected?'

'Aye, it was. No problems at all.'

'That's good.'

'And now I could eat an ox between two mattresses.'

'As well then that the food is ready,' she replied.

He slid an arm around her waist and they went in together.

The mood in the hall was jovial that evening, the air full of laughter and lively banter. Anwyn let it wash over her, feeling strangely content. Wulfgar's former mood was conspicuous by its absence and he seemed quite at ease, talking and smiling, more relaxed than she had seen him for a while. Anwyn smiled, too. Later perhaps, when they were alone, she would find the words to tell him her news. How would he take it? Would it please him to know she carried his child?

Somewhat to her surprise he did not linger to drink with his men. On the contrary, he seemed keen to retire. Recalling their parting words that morning, she felt her heartbeat quicken. Of course, he might have forgotten that by now. This eagerness to repair to their chamber might be due merely to fatigue.

However, she was swiftly disabused of that notion. As soon as they were alone he undressed her and then himself and took her to bed. It seemed that he had not forgotten their earlier conversation either. His lovemaking was passionate and tender and she surrendered herself completely, wanting to remember every detail, every sensation, storing each one in her heart.

Later, deliciously sated, they lay together in the drowsy darkness. After a little while Anwyn turned towards him, slowly tracing a finger across his chest.

'Wulfgar?'

'Mmm?'

'There was something I wanted to ask you.'

'What is it, sweet?'

'Did you ever wish to have more sons?'

For the space of several heartbeats he was silent, but she sensed that he was looking at her now. Then he spoke. 'The life of a mercenary is hardly conducive to raising children. They are a tie that binds a man.'

She swallowed hard. 'So you would never want children to continue your name and your line?'

'A man's fame lives after him.'

'Is that enough, then?'

'It has been enough for me.'

'I see.'

He glanced down, trying to read her face. 'You need not fear that I would demand sons, Anwyn. You have made your views clear on that subject.'

'I know, but…'

'It's all right. I am not angered that you take good care to prevent the possibility.' He smiled wryly, conscious of an unwonted twinge of sadness. 'It's a complication neither of us needs under the circumstances.'

She closed her eyes, glad of the darkness that hid her face. 'As you say, my lord.'

'In any case you already have a fine son.'

'Yes.'

'Never trouble yourself with such thoughts, Anwyn. I assure you that I don't.' He kissed her cheek. 'Now, my sweet, the hour grows late and we should get some sleep.'

She felt the mattress shift beneath his weight as he turned on to his side, and a short time later the sound of deep and regular breathing. Beside him Anwyn lay awake, staring into the darkness.

Wulfgar woke early and, seeing that Anwyn was still deeply asleep, rose quietly and began to dress. As he did so he pondered their earlier conversation. He had noticed her preoccupied look for some time so clearly the subject must have been weighing on her mind. He had given her the only answer he felt able to make, even if it hadn't been entirely truthful. He would not have her feel guilty. A part of him was honoured that she should even consider the idea of bearing his children, knowing her antipathy for the whole business. Not that he blamed her. Even in a loving marriage it was dangerous. Women often died in childbed. Babies perished, too. For an instant, he saw Toki's face, then Eyvind's. Remorse and wishing didn't change anything.

He looked down at the sleeping form on the bed, conscious of mixed emotions. This brief liaison with Anwyn had brought him happiness, more indeed than he could ever have expected. For that alone he would be for ever in her debt. If he had met her under other circumstances they might well have made a life together, made a family together. It was a beguiling thought. If the gods permitted it he would return one day and then perhaps... He sighed. Bending, he kissed her lightly and then departed.

Now that the new dwellings were finished he could turn his full attention to the forthcoming voyage yet, oddly, the feeling of blood-stirring anticipation that usually preceded a voyage was lacking. Forcing himself to concentrate, he began to make a mental inventory of the things they were going to need. Having done that, he communicated it to Hermund a little later.

'No problem, my lord. We'll find most of it right here—bread, ale, flitches of bacon and the like.'

'We'll have to negotiate elsewhere for smoked herring and eels,' said Wulfgar.

'There's a good place just down the coast a little way. Asulf and I found it one day when we were out on patrol.'

'Tested the quality, did you?'

'Someone had to,' replied Hermund. 'For future reference, of course.'

'Naturally.'

'I could negotiate now for what we need and then arrange for us to collect the goods on our way out. Save having to cart the stuff back here and avoid double handling.'

'True enough. Let's do that.'

'Right you are.'

Hermund went off to oversee the matter and Wulfgar went to the smithy to see Ethelwald for whom he had a small but important commission. After that he went to find Ina.

The old warrior was undertaking some basic sword craft with Eyvind. For a minute or two Wulfgar watched. As he did so he realised how much he was going to miss them both. He had come to respect Ina's quiet wisdom and shrewd mind. Without his support at Drakensburgh things would have been much harder. And Eyvind... He sighed. How old would he be when next they met? Would the boy even remember him? The thought was unwelcome. Suddenly the whole business of departure was becoming fraught with unexpected layers of complexity. Pushing these to the back of his mind, he crossed the intervening space to join them.

Eyvind saw him first and smiled. Ina glanced round. An instant later the wooden sword touched his ribs.

'A hit! A hit!'

'It was a hit, you young rascal,' replied Ina. 'Serves me right, too.'

Wulfgar grinned. 'You shouldn't have fallen for that one, especially after seeing what happened to me before.'

'I know it, my lord.' The old warrior looked proudly at his charge. 'He's going to be good one day.'

'He's pretty good now, I'd say,' replied Wulfgar. 'After all, he's slain the pair of us, has he not?'

Ina chuckled softly, then, giving Eyvind a good-natured pat on the backside, told him to run along. When the child had gone he turned back to Wulfgar, eyeing him shrewdly.

'There is something you wish to speak of, my lord?'

'Aye.' He paused, feeling for the words. 'In a few days from now I shall be gone. There is no way of knowing how long. It would please me to know that you were looking after the boy and his mother.'

The old warrior met his eye and held it. 'I have done so since Earl Torstein died and, in the absence of any other protector, I shall continue to do so.'

Wulfgar heard the implied rebuke and privately acknowledged the justice of it. However, it didn't make him feel any better. 'There will be men enough to protect Drakensburgh.'

'I am sure there will. All the same, a woman and child alone are still vulnerable.'

'They will not be alone.'

'As you say, my lord.' Ina paused. 'The boy has grown fond of you. He will miss you.'

'And I him.'

'Lady Anwyn, too, will feel your absence keenly.'

'As I will hers.'

'Of course. How could you not?'

The words, though quietly spoken, carried a distinct undercurrent. Wulfgar's jaw tightened. 'This decision was not lightly made.'

'I did not think it could have been, my lord.'

Wulfgar made himself meet the other man's eye though it wasn't as easy as it once had been. For some reason he felt increasingly wrong-footed and the more he tried to justify his actions the less convincing he knew they sounded. At the same time he didn't even know why he was trying to justify himself. He was in charge here after all.

'One day I shall return.'

'They must be glad to know that.' The old man's gaze never wavered. 'In the meantime, have no fear. I shall look after them—as you cannot.' With that he made a courteous bow and walked away.

Speechless, Wulfgar watched him go, torn between annoyance and disbelief and another feeling that was uncomfortably like guilt.

Anwyn lay staring at the roof beams, waiting for the queasiness to pass. She was thankful that Wulfgar wasn't there lest he should suspect the truth. If she was careful, he need not find out. Unbidden, two tears trickled slowly down her cheeks. How foolish it had been to think that he might welcome the idea. Although he was kind to Eyvind it did not follow that he would want the kind of encumbrance that children represented. That had never been part of their agreement. *A marriage in name only.* Well, it had turned into rather more than that and she only had herself to blame. He had been honest with her, had never offered his love. And she had led him to believe that there could be no complications arising from their time together.

These thoughts were interrupted by Jodis bringing a horn cup of chamomile tea.

'To help settle your stomach, my lady.'

'Thank you.' Anwyn sat up cautiously. 'I feel a little better now.'

'Good.' Jodis set down the cup and then eyed her quizzically. 'Have you told him yet?'

'I can't.'

'Why ever not?'

Anwyn burst into tears. It was a while before she regained sufficient composure to be able to explain. Jodis heard her in growing concern.

'We made a bargain and I cannot now expect to change it.'

'Like it or not, it has changed,' the maid replied.

'Yes, and I must bear the responsibility for that.'

'It seems to me that he bears half of the responsibility.'

Anwyn shook her head. 'I led him to believe there would be no consequences. He had no idea. If he had, the marriage might well have remained in name only.'

Jodis snorted. 'Yes, and pigs might fly. I've seen the way he looks at you. I've never seen a man more smitten.'

'He won't be if he finds out about this.'

'What man is not pleased to learn that his wife is carrying their child?'

'He said that children bind a man. What if I told him, and then he felt compelled to stay?'

'I thought you wanted him to stay.'

'I do, but not under compulsion, otherwise he would come to hate me for it and the child, too,' said Anwyn. 'I would rather lose him than let that happen.'

With so little time remaining to them any such declaration now was going to seem like a ploy to hold him or, if not, to make him feel guilty about going. She had no wish to do either. Having been largely responsible for this situation, she must be the one to deal with it. Although she had been unable to win his love, she would have his child and keep it safe.

Chapter Twenty-One

The remaining days passed quickly and Anwyn found herself secretly wishing that some unforeseen difficulty might occur to delay the ship's departure, but her hopes proved vain. The preparations for the sailing went without a hitch. Part of her wanted to get Wulfgar alone, to blurt out the truth and beg him to stay. However, she did none of those things. If he must go, then she wanted the last memory of her to be easy on his mind so that, when he did think of her in the months and years to come, it might be with fondness. Then he might also look forward to returning one day.

On the night prior to their departure she organised a feast in honour of the *Sea Wolf*'s crew. She dressed herself with care for the occasion, donning one of her finest gowns. Then she took her place beside him and forced herself to act the part of gracious hostess. It was by far the greatest challenge she had faced.

Wulfgar, alive to every nuance, sensed the tension behind the outwardly smiling manner and understood it. This parting was not going to be easy for either of them and he was grateful that she hadn't made it harder than it already was. She looked beautiful, the sea-green gown a perfect foil for her hair and eyes. It was an apt choice, too. Had that been deliberate? On reflection he thought it probably was. Anwyn was nothing if not acute. Beauty, wit and intelligence were a heady combination. He was going to miss it. Just then he found it hard to visualise a life in which she was absent.

'You look wonderful,' he said. 'As always you do me honour.'

His look summoned up a familiar glow inside her. 'Indeed I wish to, my lord.'

'You could never do other.'

'I thank you for the compliment.'

'I meant it.' He surveyed her steadily. 'How could I not when you embody all that a man could desire?'

'All things to all men?'

'Does the thought not please you?'

She shook her head. 'I had rather be all things to one man.'

'You are particular in your preference, then.'

'I cannot afford to be anything else.'

'In truth, you are more to me than any other woman could be.'

Her pulse quickened a little. Although he did not speak of love his words offered more than she had expected. It hurt to know that she could never have his heart, but she was glad he had not lied. Kindness, gentleness, tenderness were valuable qualities and rare enough. He had offered them freely. She had no cause for complaint; besides, one could only ever have what the other person was prepared to give.

Wulfgar had no inclination to linger in the hall that night. It was their last and he wanted to give that time to her. Leaving the others to talk and drink, he led her away to their chamber. Then he undressed her with slow care and took her to bed. This time he left the lamp burning, wanting to look and remember. In its soft glow he made love to her, tenderly, passionately.

And in return she gave him all of herself, arousing and

sensual, so that she became for him the embodiment of fantasy. Her caresses lingered, hands memorising every part of him, filling her mind with sense impressions, every nerve attuned only to him. The touch and taste and scent of him both fulfilled and created desire and longing. And the night became a cocoon, a world unto itself where nothing else existed and time was suspended.

Later they drowsed awhile, until mutual need brought them together again, this time with a fiercer passion. Again she held nothing back, meeting and matching his desire; feeding it and being fed in return, avid for every shared moment.

The night was far advanced before she slept. Wulfgar watched over her for a while, letting his eyes drink in the details of her face, each line and curve and shadow, and fix each one in his memory. Sleep had softened all traces of strain from her expression. Now she looked peaceful, almost childlike and, withal, strangely vulnerable. He sighed. She would not be vulnerable. He had seen to that. Drakensburgh would be well defended. For some reason the knowledge did not lighten his spirit, or dispel the strange and sombre mood in which he found himself once more. Along with it was the unwelcome sensation of having been here before. The circumstances had been different back then, but the feeling of guilt was just the same—that and the ache in his heart.

Slowly, imperceptibly, grey dawn light filtered through the cracks in the shutters. Anwyn pushed down the sensation of sick dread that lay like lead in her stomach. She had decided to say her farewells at Drakensburgh before Wulfgar and his men left for the ship. Her courage went only so far and she knew she was not equal to watching him sail away. However, when Eyvind had asked she'd told him that he might go with Ina to watch the ship depart. The child had not said much on the subject although he had been rather quieter of late. She knew that he would miss Wulfgar, too, albeit for different reasons, and was glad of Ina's steady and reassuring presence. He would be their rock as he had been before.

They went together to the hall and broke their fast with his men. It was a short, snatched meal with little time for speech. The atmosphere was convivial, but purposeful, too, eagerness bright in the faces of the warriors around them. Although it was not apparent from his expression she guessed that Wulfgar felt it, too. If he concealed it, then perhaps it was to spare her feelings. Adventure beckoned. The sea summoned these men; it was in their blood and it ruled their hearts. She could never compete. The knowledge was bitter.

Presently, when they had eaten, they gathered outside, each man carrying his war gear. A little knot of servants and artisans gathered to watch, among them Ethelwald and Ceadda. The carpenter surveyed the proceedings gloomily.

'Lord Wulfgar will be missed.'

Ethelwald nodded. 'No doubt, and not just by my lady, either. Folk hereabouts have found him a pleasant change from her first husband.'

'So has she, I warrant you.'

'You know it was he who oversaw the rebuilding of the houses that were burned?'

'Aye,' said Ceadda. 'Torstein wouldn't have done it, not in a month of Sundays.'

'No, but then fate doesn't always make the right men lords, does it?'

Wulfgar led Anwyn aside and then, when they were far enough from the rest to not be overheard, turned towards her, taking her shoulders in a gentle clasp.

'It is time.'

'Yes.'

There was so much he wanted to say, but it resolved itself into a simple truth. 'I shall miss you, Anwyn.'

But not enough, she thought. The knowledge caused a flicker of something like resentment. She forced it down.

'And I you, my lord. I will pray for your safe return.'

'I shall return.' He paused. 'My home is here.'

'Is it?'

'Can you doubt it? I little thought when first I came that it would be so hard to leave.'

The words jarred, and with that the hurt she had so long suppressed mutated into something very much like anger.

'How glibly you say that, Wulfgar.'

He stared at her, completely taken aback. 'How is it glib?'

'If this was home, if you truly cared for Eyvind and for me, then you wouldn't leave.'

'You always knew it was going to happen, Anwyn.'

'And so that exonerates you now.'

'I have never deceived you.'

'No, you deceive yourself.'

'What is this about?' he demanded.

'You know full well. All this high-flown talk about your duty to your ship and your crew is no more than the excuse you hide behind.'

'Hide? From what?'

'From commitment.'

'I have met my commitment to Drakensburgh.' He frowned. 'It is ably defended.'

Her gaze locked with his. 'You continue to duck the issue, don't you?'

'What issue?'

'The same one you ducked when you left Freya and Toki.'

Wulfgar paled. 'You know nothing about it.'

'Oh, I think I do,' she retorted. 'What excuses did you fob them off with?'

'Stop this now, Anwyn.'

'Why, Wulfgar? Does the truth hurt?'

'Their loss has never stopped hurting, if that makes you feel any better.'

'What hurts is your guilt,' she accused. 'You avoided the emotional commitment they represented in the name of some dubious adventure.'

'And I have had leisure to repent of it.'

'Yet you're about to do it all again.'

He drew in a sharp breath. 'That's not the reason I have to go.'

'Isn't it? Isn't the real reason that you're terrified of the alternative?' She glared at him. 'Because then you'd have to give all of yourself, not just a few emotional sops now and again to ease your conscience.'

His face went a shade whiter, but before he could reply Hermund called across the intervening space.

'We need to go now, my lord, if we are to catch the tide.'

Wulfgar turned his head. 'I'm coming.'

The men began to move towards the gate. He looked at Anwyn and for the space of several heartbeats neither one spoke. Then she glanced at the others.

'You'd better go. You won't want to miss the tide.'

'I don't wish us to part like this.'

'Just go.'

A muscle jumped in his cheek. 'Farewell then, Anwyn.'

'Goodbye, Wulfgar.'

Sick at heart, she watched him turn away and rejoin his men, mastering the urge to call him back. He would not come in any case. Even if he had not been eager to leave before, her words would have driven him away. She had meant to control her feelings, but in the end all her good intentions had counted for nothing. Now she had alienated him completely. Most likely he would never return and she had only herself to blame.

Once she saw him look back in her direction, but he did not smile and made no sign of acknowledgement. Unbidden, water welled in her eyes. Through blurred vision she watched as the whole contingent moved away towards the gate, joined by the miscellaneous group of spectators who had temporarily abandoned their work to see them off. It was not an everyday occurrence and Anwyn knew that many of them would walk as far as the bay to watch the *Sea Wolf* sail. She ran to the palisade and up the wooden stair to the rampart, watching the long procession file out. Among the crowd she glimpsed Eyvind and Ina. The child looked back and, locating her, waved. She acknowledged it. Then he turned away and the host marched on. Anwyn's gaze found the tall figure at its head and rested there.

'Goodbye, my love,' she murmured. 'May you fare well.'

The host had long disappeared from view before she left the rampart.

Wulfgar had no recollection of the march to the ship, nor did he speak to anyone on the way. His mind was preoccupied with his parting conversation with Anwyn. Her attack had been so sudden and unexpected that it left him feeling strangely shaken. When the initial shock had worn off what replaced it was sadness and then anger. It really wasn't how he had wanted them to part, but he was not to blame there. She had chosen the method.

He watched as his men began to stow their gear aboard the *Sea Wolf* and then turned to Eyvind who, with Ina, had been following the proceedings closely. The child regarded him with solemn eyes.

'Can I come with you?'

'No,' replied Wulfgar. 'I'm sorry.'

'When I'm older can I?'

'When you're older.'

Eyvind swallowed hard. 'You will come back for me?'

'I'll come back. In the meantime I shall expect you to practise your sword craft and listen carefully to what Ina tells you.'

'I will. I promise.'

'Good.' Wulfgar paused. 'Since you have learned more about weapons you are ready to have this.'

He reached into his sleeve and drew out a small knife, a beautifully crafted miniature replica of his own dagger, in a leather sheath. Eyvind stared at the knife and then darted a quizzical glance at the man who held it.

Wulfgar nodded. 'Take it.'

Cautiously, as though afraid it might vanish on the instant, the boy reached out his hand and closed it round the hilt. Then he drew the blade from the sheath and gasped, examining it with shining eyes.

'It's a beauty! Is it really for me?'

'Aye, it is. I had the smith make it for you. The blade is sharp so have a care.'

Eyvind looked up at him, his cheeks pink with pleasure. 'Thank you, Father. It's wonderful.'

Wulfgar stared at him and then glanced over his head at Ina. However, the old warrior's face was expressionless. Apparently unaware of his verbal slip, the child made a couple of experimental passes with the knife, admiring the effect of light on the polished metal. Then he carefully sheathed it.

'Will you help me fasten it on my belt?'

Wulfgar cleared his throat. 'Of course I will.'

He waited while the child removed the little wooden sword and handed it to Ina for safekeeping. Then, going down on one knee so that he was at the child's height, he unlatched the small belt, sliding it through the loops on the back of the sheath and then refastening the buckle. Eyvind squinted down, admiring the effect.

'It looks well.'

Wulfgar nodded. 'It does.'

'I shall wear it always.' Eyvind looked at their companion. 'See, Ina. Isn't it fine?'

'Very fine,' the old warrior agreed. 'It is a generous gift. You are fortunate.'

'Now we can both protect Drakensburgh, can't we?'

'That we can, my boy.'

Eyvind retrieved his wooden sword and offered it, hilt first, to Wulfgar. 'This is for you, so you won't forget your promise to come back.'

Wulfgar took the offering and tucked it into his own belt. Somehow he managed a smile. 'I won't forget.'

Before he could say more a voice hailed him from across the sand.

'We're ready when you are, my lord.'

'Coming.' Wulfgar briefly clasped Eyvind's shoulder, and then nodded to Ina. 'Fare you well.'

Then he turned and strode away down the strand to the waiting ship.

The old man and the boy watched as the crew climbed aboard. Then the oars dipped and rose and the *Sea Wolf* began to turn, heading away down the coast. As she grew smaller the groups of spectators turned away and began to head back towards Drakensburgh. Having taken one last look at the departing ship, Ina and Eyvind set off after them. No one noticed the group of mounted warriors forming up on the far side of the heath.

The first inkling of their presence was the muffled thudding of hoofs on turf. Ina glanced over his shoulder. The riders were closing fast. Sunlight glinted on helmets and mail. He frowned. Then he caught sight of the drawn swords and lowered spear points. A low oath escaped him. Thrusting Eyvind behind him, he called a warning to the rest and drew his blade.

Almost all their companions were unarmed save for small belt knives. Some started to run. Those few that had weapons turned to face the foe. Then the first horses were upon them and the air filled with cries of pain and terror. The slaughter was swift and ruthless and in moments the turf was littered with bodies. Ina accounted for two of the raiders before three more closed in. He fought valiantly, but he was on foot and outnumbered and his defiance was short-lived. The first blow cut deep into his arm, the next into his side. He staggered, glaring at his enemies. Then he recognised their leader.

'I might have guessed.'

Grymar's lip curled. 'You grow careless, old man.'

'Better careless than treacherous, you cowardly dog.'

The smile faded. 'You've just delivered your last insult.'

Grymar spurred forwards, sword upraised. Ina tried to block the downwards blow, but pain and blood loss had weakened him and the deadly blade broke through his defence and found its mark. Eyvind screamed and, heedless of milling horses and slashing weapons, ran to the old man and fell on his knees.

'Ina! Ina!'

The old warrior made no reply. Eyvind sobbed. Then a large hand seized him by the scruff of his tunic and dragged him upright, jerking him off his feet. He kicked and fought. His captor cuffed him hard across the ear. Seconds later he was tossed face down across the pommel of a saddle. Grymar shouted to his companions and, with that, all the horsemen turned their mounts and galloped away.

Chapter Twenty-Two

As the *Sea Wolf* rounded the rocky headland the bay disappeared from view. Wulfgar's jaw tightened and he looked away, his gaze turning back to the coastline now stretching away off their starboard side. It was a fine view and ordinarily he would have enjoyed it, as he'd have enjoyed the salt-sharp tang in the breeze and the movement of the ship beneath his feet. This morning the green water was the colour of Anwyn's eyes. That thought begot others, intimate and sensual, and for a moment he was overwhelmed by a sensation of loss. It was replaced by anger for the memory of their parting was bitter and it smarted like a wound. He took a deep breath, trying to regain his former mental balance, to relocate the focus that had guided him these past five years, but somehow it had vanished like a landmark in fog. The resulting confusion was disquieting and created a feeling that was much like self-disgust.

'A good day for it, my lord.'

He glanced at Hermund, manning the steering oar beside him. 'Good enough.'

'If the weather holds we'll be laughing.'

'No doubt.'

Hermund nodded towards the small cove in the middle distance. 'That's where we pick up the smoked herring, my lord.'

'Right.'

'Man said he'd have it ready and waiting.'

'Good.'

'We can be in and out in half an hour.'

Wulfgar grunted, but vouchsafed no reply. Instead he fixed his gaze on the cove. However, he saw nothing of the coastline. All he could see was the hurt on Anwyn's face as he turned to go. The recollection twisted like a knife and cut more deeply, though not as deeply as her words. *If you truly cared...you wouldn't leave.* Wulfgar shuddered and blinked. The cove reappeared in his line of vision.

Hermund regarded him with mild concern. 'Are you all right, my lord?'

'Of course. Why wouldn't I be?'

'You had an odd look on your face.'

Wulfgar frowned. 'Never mind the look on my face. Just steer the damned ship.'

The words burst out almost before he was aware, but as soon as they were spoken he regretted them. He sighed and let out a long breath.

'Forgive me, Hermund. I'm out of sorts, that's all.'

'Forget it. 'Tis no matter.'

Wulfgar smiled wryly. 'I know of no one else who would put up with my ill humour as you do.'

'It's understandable,' said Hermund. 'It's never easy to leave your woman behind.'

The accuracy of the remark hit hard and Wulfgar had the strange sensation of having been here before. Except that this was different; this time the woman knew who he was; he had warned her from the start what she could expect from him.

'I was just the same,' Hermund continued, 'but a good skirmish would always sort me out.'

Wulfgar's gaze went to the trackless waste of water ahead,

yet try as he might he could not regain the feeling of anticipation it had once inspired. The notion of joining Rollo should have filled him with enthusiasm, but it did not, any more than the thought of dying in someone else's battle. *Your death will not change the past.* Anwyn was right, but his death wish hadn't been about changing the past; it was about losing the present burden of guilt. *Perhaps it's time to forgive yourself...* His throat tightened. It was too late to ask forgiveness of Freya and Toki. *What excuses did you fob them off with?* He grimaced. *What hurts is your guilt.* The scorn in those words was lacerating, but it did not detract from their truth. Nor could he pretend things were different this time; only the excuses were new.

When he entered into marriage with Anwyn had he not already prepared his exit strategy, dressing it in the guise of openness and honesty? *This is what I am prepared to give and no more. Take it or leave it. I am absolved of all other responsibilities.* Yet she had stinted nothing; had given all of herself; had trusted him. Nor was she alone in that trust. His fingers closed on the little wooden sword in his belt. *So you will remember your promise.* The feeling of self-disgust intensified. He was seven and twenty, but in truth no different from the selfish, headstrong youth he had been before; ignoring everything but his own desires; taking the affection of others for granted as if it were somehow his due. He was brave enough in battle, but a coward in all the ways that mattered. *I will not swear my undying love...*because then, as Anwyn had rightly said, he would have had to offer all of himself, unconditionally and for ever, and he had not been man enough to do it. To love was to be vulnerable, to risk hurts far worse than any battle wound, and that was why he feared it. Wulfgar's knuckles whitened. Instead of facing his fear he had abandoned those who needed him most and left other men to shoulder his responsibilities.

The knowledge cut like a blade. Time to forgive himself?

If there was ever to be forgiveness it was going to have to be earned. He looked at Hermund.

'Turn the ship around. I'm going back.'

Anwyn tried to concentrate on the torn sleeve she was mending but her mind refused to co-operate. It was filled instead with thoughts of Wulfgar. Their last words had been spoken in anger, words already bitterly regretted. His absence had left a great void that nothing else could fill. Already she could see the long years of aching emptiness stretching ahead with no possibility of solace, save for Eyvind. He was all that remained to her now.

The entrance of a guard roused her from these sombre reflections. 'My lady, Lord Ingvar is at the gate.'

She stared at him in disbelief. 'Ingvar, here?'

'Aye, my lady.'

Disbelief turned swiftly to unease. 'Has he brought an army?'

'No, a small escort only. Some half-a-dozen men.'

'What does he want?'

'He says he desires to speak with you, my lady. Shall we admit him?'

'Just him. His men remain outside.'

'He may intend you harm, my lady.'

'Then insist he hand over his weapons first.'

The guard bowed and hurried away to the gate. Jodis shook her head.

'After all that has happened, Ingvar will surely not have the gall to ride in here unarmed and alone.'

'He'd be taking a serious risk,' replied Anwyn. 'There must be a good reason for it. I suppose I'd better find out what it is.'

A short time later the gate swung open and a lone horseman rode through. He was unarmed, having clearly anticipated that his weapons would be removed if he wore them. Anwyn stood alone before the hall, watching the rider approach. He held the horse to a walk, apparently quite at his ease, and looking for all the world as though it were a casual social call. Anwyn's unease deepened.

Ingvar reined in a few yards away and for a moment neither of them spoke, each taking the measure of the other. Then he smiled faintly.

'You look well, Anwyn.'

'What do you want, Ingvar? Why have you come here?'

'Direct as always. Well, perhaps you are right. Under the circumstances we can probably dispense with the social niceties.'

'For once we agree.'

He smiled, though the expression stopped well short of his eyes. 'I note that the *Sea Wolf* sailed this morning. In truth, if the Viking had any care for you he would not have gone.'

'Do not presume to judge him.'

'He does not deserve your loyalty.'

'I give my loyalty where I see fit,' she replied coldly.

'He does not deserve you at all—or the farewell party his leaving attracted. Your son was among their number, wasn't he?'

Her stomach wallowed. 'What is your interest in my son?'

'Considerable, I assure you.' He paused. 'He is now under my protection, you see.'

Anwyn blenched. 'Where is he? What have you done with him?'

'Have no fear. He is quite safe.'

'What is it that you want, Ingvar? Tell me.'

'What I have always wanted, Anwyn.'

'Speak plainly. What is your price for Eyvind's life?'

'You are,' he replied.

'My life for his? I will give it gladly.'

'A noble sentiment and one that does you credit. However, that is not what I intend.'

'Then what do you want?'

'You will renounce your marriage to the Viking and you will marry me. Thereafter all Drakensburgh lands will be amalgamated with mine.'

Anwyn felt as though she had been turned to stone. 'And if I refuse?'

'Then you will not see your son alive again.'

'And if I give the order you will not leave here alive.'

Ingvar nodded. 'Quite possibly, but then word of my death will precipitate his.'

She realised she ought to have foreseen it. 'That is why you rode in so confidently.'

'Just so. However, no one need die.'

'Please, Ingvar. I beg you, let him go.'

'You have one hour to decide.' The gold-brown eyes burned into hers. 'You will come alone to Beranhold and present yourself at my gate. If not…'

Anwyn shook her head. 'You could not be so cruel.'

'I am not used to jest, Anwyn. If you do not come I shall send you earnest of my seriousness—one of Eyvind's fingers, or an ear perhaps. His death will not be swift.' He paused, seeing the tears on her cheeks. 'But, if you do as I ask, he shall not be harmed in any way. It's your choice.'

'What choice?'

He gathered his reins. 'One hour, Anwyn. I'll be waiting.'

With that he turned his horse and rode slowly back towards the gate. It swung open and he continued on through. Moments later she heard the sound of hoofbeats as he and his escort rode away.

Wulfgar and his crew were close to shore when first they saw the circling scavenger birds.

'What is it that so interests them?' asked Thrand.

'Dead sheep or cow probably,' replied Asulf.

'Must have died suddenly then.'

'How come?'

Thrand sighed. 'Well, it wasn't there when we left or we'd have noticed the birds then, wouldn't we?'

Wulfgar said nothing, but the feeling of foreboding grew stronger and he waited with mounting impatience for the ship's keel to touch the strand.

'I reckon we'll come with you and investigate,' said Hermund.

Leaving half-a-dozen men to guard the ship, they made their way back through the dunes and reached the heath a short time later. Then they saw the reason for the flocking scavenger birds. The sward was littered with bodies, scattered across a wide area. A swift glance at the first few told its own tale. More disturbingly, it revealed that the faces were familiar.

Beorn frowned. 'These are Drakensburgh folk.'

'They were also unarmed,' replied Hermund. 'Most of their wounds are behind. They were taken by surprise and then cut down as they tried to flee.'

Wulfgar nodded, his expression grim. 'It certainly looks that way.'

They continued their inspection. Then Asulf stopped in his tracks and called to the others.

'Over here!'

His companions hastened to join him and then they, too, stopped and stared at the corpse by their feet.

'It's Ina!' exclaimed Thrand.

The others exchanged incredulous and wrathful glances. Wulfgar's gaze hardened as he stared upon the body, taking in every detail of the savage wounds now encrusted with dried blood and blackened by flies. Close by lay the bodies of two armed men. The old warrior had clearly given a good account of himself before he was cut down. The knowledge filled Wulfgar with cold rage.

'He was a brave and worthy man and he has earned his place in Odin's hall,' he said.

'Which is more than will ever be said of the cowardly earslings who did this,' muttered Asulf, glancing around.

'The perpetrators will pay,' replied Wulfgar.

Thrand nodded. 'You speak true, my lord. Their worst nightmares could not conjure the half of what they will suffer when we find them.'

A loud and growling chorus of agreement greeted his words. Then Beorn looked around.

'If Ina's here, where's the boy?'

His words were greeted with absolute silence, the faces all around him registering angry shock as the implications sank in. Wulfgar's knuckles whitened round the hilt of his sword.

'Eyvind,' he murmured. Then, glancing round, 'Find him. Find my son.'

They resumed the search, fanning out, to cover the remaining ground. Wulfgar joined them, moving swiftly from one body to the next, his heart like lead in his breast. Only once before this had he known a pain so deep. He swallowed hard. Did Anwyn know of this yet? The thought of her grief smote him. She must surely lay the blame at his door, and rightly, too. There could be no forgiveness for this. The knowledge was bitter indeed.

They examined all the bodies of the slain, but the quest proved vain.

'The child is not here, my lord,' said Hermund.

Wulfgar exhaled slowly, and some of the dread he had felt just moments before began to dissipate. 'Are you sure?'

'Quite sure. The rest of the slain are adults.'

'Maybe the lad escaped in the confusion,' said Thrand.

'Aye, maybe,' replied Wulfgar. 'In any event there's only one way to find out. We push on to Drakensburgh.'

They covered the ground at a jog trot and reached the gate a short time later. The guards' expressions revealed blank astonishment, but they were quick to open the gates and admit the returning warriors. Wulfgar paused just long enough to get a brief account of recent events, news which did nothing to improve his mood, and then hurried off to find Anwyn.

However, when he reached the bower it was devoid of company save for Jodis, whose swollen eyelids and tear-stained face spoke more than words could. On hearing his footsteps she looked up, staring as though he were an apparition. Then she began to sob anew. Wulfgar seized her by the shoulders.

'Where is Lady Anwyn?' he demanded. 'Where is Eyvind?'

'G-gone, my lord.'

'Gone where?'

It took some moments before she was calm enough to speak and thus, by slow degrees, he got the story out of her. As he listened his face went white and his heart filled anew with rage and dread.

'When did she leave?'

'Not long ago, my lord.'

Wulfgar left her and ran to the stables. Five minutes later he was mounted and riding in the direction of Beranhold. The horse was fresh and swift and Wulfgar prayed to every god he knew that he might overtake Anwyn before she reached her destination. The thought of her fear and sorrow was like a scourge, and the rage he felt turned inwards and was compounded by self-recrimination. What he had done was unpardonable and that made everything so much worse.

He pushed the horse until it was running flat out, covering the ground in a mile-eating gallop. At the top of the next hill he reined in to get his bearings and scan the countryside. His heart sank as he detected no sign of her. Then, as he was about to give up hope, he spied movement in the distance and he saw the other horse perhaps a quarter of a mile ahead of him. Gritting his teeth, he urged his mount on again. It was not too late. He would catch her.

Anwyn was too deeply sunk in dejection to be aware of pursuit until the other horse was almost upon her. With a start of fear she was jerked out of her gloomy reverie, visualising Ingvar's men. Had he lied? Was this all a ruse? Having lured her out of Drakensburgh, did he mean to have her killed? Leaning forwards she urged her horse on, but the other was bigger and faster and soon drew level. Its rider leaned across and grabbed her reins, pulling both animals to a halt. Only then did she see who the rider was and the resulting flood of emotion almost undid her.

'Wulfgar.'

The sight of her wondering smile cut deeper than tears ever could. 'Anwyn, I'm sorry. I'm so sorry.'

'Ingvar has taken Eyvind.'

'I know. Jodis told me.' He paused, his gaze fixed on her face. 'When she said you had already left I feared I was too late, but the gods have answered my prayers.'

She swallowed hard. 'I thought I would never see you again.'

'Can you ever forgive me for leaving?'

'There is nothing to forgive, Wulfgar. You did what you thought you had to do.'

'I've been a damned fool,' he replied. 'Not for the first time either. I have already lost a wife and child through my own selfish folly. I will not make that mistake again.'

'You once told me that you would not stay for ever.'

'When I said it I did not know how deeply I would come to feel for you,' he replied. 'After what happened before I took care to avoid emotional entanglements. In truth, I feared them. And then you rode into my life and everything changed. I tried to pretend it hadn't but, when I sailed away from you today, I realised I was following my head instead of listening to my heart.'

'I have wished for so long that I might have a place in your heart.'

'You do have a place there, Anwyn—you and Eyvind both.'

'I am glad. The time I spent with you was the happiest of my life. Not only for me—Eyvind also loved you well.'

Her words caused his heart to leap. Perhaps there was hope after all. It took him a moment to realise that she had used the past tense.

'We will get him back, I promise you.'

'There is only way to ensure his safety now,' she said tonelessly.

It was another moment or two before the implications dawned, bringing with them the first icy touch of fear. He stared at her, incredulous. 'You cannot mean to obey Ingvar's behest.'

'He gave me one hour, Wulfgar. The time is almost run.'

'I will not let you go.'

'You must.'

'Never!'

'If I do not arrive Ingvar will maim and kill my son.' Fear and anger warred in her green gaze.

'And if you do?'

'Then Eyvind will live.'

The expression in Wulfgar's eyes became steely. 'And what exactly were the terms of the bargain?'

She drew a deep breath. 'That I renounce my marriage to you and wed him.'

The words dropped into a well of silence. Then, when he could control his voice, he said, 'I see.'

'There is no other choice now.'

'I will not let you do this, Anwyn.'

'It's too late, Wulfgar.'

'It's not too late. I'll find a way.'

'This is the way.'

'I will not lose you to Ingvar.'

'You will never lose me to Ingvar,' she replied, 'but if you care for me at all you will let me go.'

His face grew deathly pale. 'Is that what you want?'

Somehow she found the strength to meet his eye. 'This is

not about what I want, only about what must be done. I must go to Ingvar and you must return to your ship.'

A muscle jumped in his cheek. 'Run away?'

'For my sake and Eyvind's you must go—you and all your crew. Ingvar will spare the rest of the Drakensburgh folk if you do.'

'As he spared Ina?'

Now it was Anwyn who paled. 'What do you mean?'

'He must have been trying to protect Eyvind, but Ingvar's men slew him all the same.'

She blinked back tears. 'They slew that dear, good old man?'

'Aye, along with all the poor, unarmed wretches with him.'

'Then truly there is no mercy left.'

'It is not a quality known to men like Ingvar,' he replied.

'You are right, and that is why I must go. It is the only hope I have of saving Eyvind now.'

The resolution in her voice chilled him to the core and he knew then that he could not dissuade her. As the ramifications became clear, love and fear and dread mingled with admiration for her spirit and her courage. Dredging up the remains of his own, he slackened his hold on her reins and found his voice again. 'Then each of us will do what we must.'

'Goodbye, Wulfgar.' She managed another smile. 'I will never forget that you came back.'

Then, lest her resolution should fail, she touched the horse with her heels and cantered away. He sat motionless, gazing after her until she vanished over the crest of the next slope. Despair swelled like a boil. He threw back his head and a great visceral howl tore from his throat, telling of impotent rage and pain and loss.

Chapter Twenty-Three

∽∾∽∾∽

Anwyn rode slowly towards the fortress of Beranhold, her gaze taking in the guard towers above the entrance and then the great spiked palisade stretching away on either side. Above the gate flew Ingvar's standard: a snarling black bear on a red field, the beast for which the place was named. Her fingers tightened round the reins. Somewhere within that gloomy lair was Eyvind. He was all that mattered now.

She pulled up some twenty yards short of the gate. Men's voices sounded within and moments later the great portal swung open. She took a deep breath. Then, holding her horse to a walk, she rode on through under the eyes of the grinning guards. She ignored them, looking neither to left nor right, her attention focused on the hall ahead. Behind her the gate crashed shut and the heavy locking bar thudded into place. Her jaw tightened. For a moment she was transported back to her arrival at Drakensburgh when she was brought there to be Torstein's bride. Only now the man who stood before the hall was Ingvar instead. He was flanked by Grymar and half-a-dozen others. Anwyn reined to a halt and waited, heart thumping, her eyes seeking a glimpse of Eyvind. There was none.

Ingvar left his cronies and came forwards to meet her. 'Lady

Anwyn, welcome.' The tone was courteous, but was belied by the mocking smile that accompanied it. 'Please, won't you step down?'

Since there was nothing for it she dismounted and came to face him. 'Where is my son?'

'All in good time, my lady.' He gestured towards the hall. 'Shall we?'

As they passed, the group of men nearby watched with appraising eyes and their grins widened. Grymar made her an exaggerated bow. Anwyn lifted her chin and accompanied Ingvar into the hall. Immediately she was hit by the stale smell of roasted meat and soiled rushes that mingled with the stink of dogs and urine and male sweat. Her stomach churned. Two huge hounds started up from their place by the hearth and advanced with low rumbling growls. The growls turned to yelps as Ingvar's boot found their ribs. He rapped out an order and they slunk away again to the hearth. Anwyn swallowed hard, fighting disgust and fear.

Ingvar turned towards her. 'Will you take a cup of wine, my lady?'

'No.'

'Then we will proceed to business.'

With an assurance she was far from feeling she met his eye. 'I will do nothing until I have seen that my son is safe.'

Ingvar was silent, appearing to deliberate, and for a terrible moment she thought he was going to refuse. However, she saw him nod instead.

'Very well. Come.'

Taking a firm grip on her arm, he conducted her through the building and out through a rear door. The fresh air was a blessed relief after the noisome fug of the hall and she breathed it gratefully, hurrying to keep up with her captor's longer stride. He led her, not to another building as she had expected, but to an area of open ground beyond. Out on its own was a large wooden cage, in one corner of which sat a small, forlorn figure. Anwyn's heart missed a beat.

'Eyvind?' In cold fury she turned to face Ingvar. 'How dare you treat my son thus?'

He seemed quite unperturbed. 'The remedy for that lies in you.'

The small figure in the cage looked up and then rose uncertainly to its feet. 'Mother?'

Wrenching herself free of Ingvar's hold, she ran across the intervening space, falling on her knees before the bars. Eyvind flung himself towards her, his hands gripping hers tightly. His face was tear-stained and he was dirty and dishevelled, but otherwise he seemed unhurt.

'Mother, it really is you!'

Anwyn blinked back tears. 'Yes, it's me, my love. Are you all right? Have they hurt you?'

He shook his head. 'They've killed Ina. They cut him down.'

She closed her eyes for a moment, striving to conquer the emotions that threatened to overwhelm her. 'I know, my love. I'm so sorry.'

'Are you come to take me home?'

'Eyvind, I—' She broke off, looking up quickly as Ingvar's shadow fell across them.

'This is your home now, boy.' He looked pointedly at Anwyn. 'How long you continue to live in it depends on your mother.'

With that he leaned down and, regaining his hold on her arm, dragged her to her feet. Her heart thumped in her breast, but fury temporarily conquered fear.

'Free him, Ingvar.'

'When all my conditions are met.'

'You have already named your conditions, and I would not be here if I were not prepared to meet them.'

'There is one more that I didn't mention,' he replied.

'What do you mean?'

'In a little while my servants will prepare you for your wedding. Then, before all my men, you will renounce your present marriage and take me as your husband. This night you will come willingly to my bed and—'

Unable to contain her mounting anger, Anwyn cut in. 'You may take me to your bed, Ingvar, but you will never find me willing.'

He continued, unperturbed, as though she had not spoken. '—and whenever I wish it thereafter.'

'I will resist with every means in my power.'

Ingvar continued to survey her coolly. 'If I detect the least sign of reluctance in you, the boy will be whipped. If I see any further display of defiance in your manner, he will be whipped. If you ever raise your voice or speak disrespectfully to me again, or even look at me in a way that suggests disrespect, he will be whipped. If you think to take your own life, know now that he will die immediately after you do.'

Anwyn's face drained of colour. In that moment she would have given much for a concealed dagger in her sleeve, and the split second of surprise in which to use it. As it was, Ingvar held all the weapons and she dared not antagonise him further.

He paused. 'Am I making myself clear?'

She lowered her eyes lest he should read their expression. 'Very clear, my lord.'

'I hope so.' He glanced at Eyvind. 'So much depends on it, does it not?'

Wulfgar rode slowly back to Drakensburgh, his mind submerged in the emotional chaos of his parting from Anwyn. He had taken wounds in battle, but none of those hurts had ever compared with the pain he felt now. It was as though his heart had been ripped from his breast. Only once before had he ever felt the like. Freya and Toki were lost to him and he could not help them, but while there was breath in his body he would not accept the loss of another wife and child. If he hadn't been such an accursed fool, they would have been with him now. He should have been there. What kind of man had twice to lose what was most precious before he truly understood its value?

In that instant he acknowledged the emotion he had tried so hard to avoid: he knew now that he loved Anwyn beyond all reason, that with her he had found what he never thought to have again. Yet when she needed him most he had failed her. The knowledge burned into his brain. How could this ever be forgiven? How could he even think they might have a future together after this? It wasn't only her he had abandoned. He had failed Eyvind, too. *You will come back for me?* Wulfgar gritted his teeth.

'I'm back,' he murmured, 'and I will come for you, I swear it.'

With that resolution the chaos began to dissolve and give way to more rational thought. Just let him get them both to safety, and he would do whatever Anwyn wanted afterwards. He did not expect her forgiveness, but he would make what amends he might. As he began to lay his plans, grief was gradually overlain by cold deliberation. He knew better than to underestimate Ingvar; there would only be one chance to save Anwyn and Eyvind and it could only be achieved with nerve and a cool head. When that was accomplished there would be time enough to unleash his rage.

On reaching Drakensburgh he summoned all the men to the hall. When everyone was gathered he called for quiet. Having got their attention, he began with an account of those events of which the Drakensburgh men knew nothing. The news was received in a disbelieving and stony silence. Then the man called Rorik spoke up.

'The scum killed Ina?'

'Aye. And now Ingvar has the boy and Lady Anwyn, too.'

'Then we must go and get them back.'

The room erupted in a roar of angry agreement. Wulfgar held up a hand for silence.

'We'll get them back,' he replied, 'but it cannot be done with a show of force. At the very first inkling of trouble Ingvar will kill Eyvind. We have to free the boy and Lady Anwyn before we can deal with Ingvar and the rest.'

'How are we going to do that?'

'I've been thinking about it and I believe it can be done.'

Hermund regarded him shrewdly. 'What have you got in mind?'

Wulfgar began to explain. As they listened the men's eyes brightened.

'And after we've rescued the boy and his mother, my lord?' asked Thrand.

'After that,' replied Wulfgar, 'all insults shall be avenged in blood.'

Anwyn stood motionless while the women servants prepared her, removing her gown and replacing it with another. It was a fine garment of deep-green wool, richly embroidered with gold thread. They combed out her hair and dressed it again in an intricate style around a thin gold fillet, and looped up the heavy locks behind, interweaving them with matching ribbons. They placed a gold torque around her neck and gold bracelets on her wrists. She made no protest, her face impassive, giving no clue to the terror behind. She would do whatever Ingvar commanded now because there was no choice, but she knew full well that whatever she did could only buy a temporary reprieve for Eyvind. Soon enough the child in her belly would become apparent and Ingvar would know it was not his.

Wulfgar's image drifted into her mind, bringing with it the familiar ache in her heart. For the rest of her life she would remember the look in his eyes as she sent him away. It was the hardest thing she had ever done and yet the knowledge that he had cared enough to come back sustained her. It would help her to do what must be done now. It would be the one light in the dark days ahead. She might be forced to share Ingvar's bed, but it would be Wulfgar's face she saw in her dreams.

The servants finished their task and stood back respectfully, holding up a large disc of polished metal for her inspection of their handiwork. Anwyn surveyed it dispassionately. The woman who stared back at her was beautiful, regal in every part of her dress and bearing, but somehow nothing to do with her. She glanced down at the ring on her hand and then reluctantly removed it. If she did not, Ingvar most certainly would. She could easily visualise the pleasure he would take in doing it, and in casting it away. Not only that, he might also take its presence ill and punish Eyvind for her lapse. She couldn't let that happen. However, neither was she prepared to lose this last treasured connection with Wulfgar. Taking a length of ribbon, she threaded it through the ring and fastened the ends about her neck. When it was done she slipped the ring out of sight under the front of her gown. Later she would have to find another hiding place, but it would serve for now.

Footsteps sounded in the passage without and a heavy fist rapped at the door. Then a man's voice spoke.

'It is time.'

Anwyn took a deep breath and moved towards the door. A servant hastened to open it. Four guards waited outside. They fell in on either side, flanking her. Then they escorted her back to the hall where Ingvar waited.

Since the war band would not be leaving until dusk, Wulfgar ordered the servants to bring them food and drink. He knew it would be the last opportunity to eat for a while. However, he limited the liquid refreshment to ale and that in small quantity. There would be a time for drinking later. He joined his men for the meal, but ate sparingly, his mind on the task ahead. The empty chair beside him was sufficient reminder of how much was at stake. He tried not to think about what might be happening to Anwyn right now, but it wasn't easy. He guessed that Ingvar would use the child to control the mother, and the certainty of what he would demand fuelled Wulfgar's rage. What made it worse was knowing that she could not refuse. The idea of any man laying hands on her was unthinkable. That another man should possess her, violate her, was beyond bearing. He could visualise Ingvar's gloating triumph all too well, a triumph made sweeter for knowing that he took an enemy's wife to his bed. Would he compound his victory by hurting her in other ways? Wulfgar's hand clenched round his cup. If Anwyn tried to fight... The thought would not finish itself.

Leaving his men to finish their meal, he got up and went outside for some air to clear his head. The sun was lower in the sky now and the shadows lengthening. He stood awhile, collecting his thoughts. Only a cool mind would accomplish his purpose now.

The voice of the guard on the gate rang out. 'Visitors, my lord. About a hundred men, I reckon.'

Wulfgar's first thought was that it might be Ingvar's force. Then common sense reasserted itself. Ingvar already held too great an advantage to need a show of armed might.

'Do they bear a standard?' he called back.

'Aye, my lord, they do, but I cannot yet make it out.' The guard squinted into the distance. 'Wait! It looks like Lord Osric's banner.'

'Odin's sacred ravens,' muttered Wulfgar. 'Now what?'

He took the steps to the rampart two at a time. A bowshot from the gate the approaching force halted; then a group of six riders detached itself from the vanguard and came on. Wulfgar had no trouble recognising their leader. He frowned. The guard eyed him doubtfully.

'Do we open the gate, my lord?'

'You do.'

He retraced his steps and went to wait before the hall, watching as the riders swept into the compound.

'What in Frigg's name does that little reptile want?' said a voice at his shoulder.

Wulfgar glanced round to see Hermund. 'Good question.'

Osric reined in and dismounted, throwing his reins to a servant. Then he favoured Wulfgar with a curt nod.

'I am come to speak with my sister. Pray go and tell her so.'

'Lady Anwyn is not here.'

'Don't prevaricate with me. Fetch her at once.'

'I said she isn't here.'

'Then where the devil is she?'

He listened in silent and incredulous wrath as Wulfgar gave him the basic substance of what had happened.

'And now you say this Ingvar holds her and my nephew captive?'

'That's right.'

'If she had allowed herself to be guided by me, this could not have happened,' said Osric. 'I would have had her safely married by now, as she should be. I am come to conduct her to her new bridegroom.'

With an effort Wulfgar controlled himself. 'The fault was not Lady Anwyn's; it was mine for not foreseeing the extent of Ingvar's treachery.'

'You are a loyal fellow. My sister is headstrong and I know it all too well. However, whatever her folly, she is still my sister and I will not permit her to be dishonoured by such a lowly marriage as this. It would disgrace our entire family.'

Wulfgar put his hands behind his back where they could do no harm. 'My men and I were about to mount a rescue when you arrived, my lord.'

'You have a plan?'

'Aye.' Wulfgar glanced towards the host outside the gate. 'It would not be hindered by the addition of more men.'

Osric nodded. 'Very well. What do you want us to do?'

Chapter Twenty-Four

A wagon, driven by two men in dirty peasant garb, stopped outside the gate of the fortress of Beranhold. Its arrival was greeted by a ringing challenge from one of the two guards above.

'Identify yourselves.'

'Ethelwine and Elwy, bringing Lord Ingvar's mead and ale from the village,' said the driver.

The guard glanced at the barrels and then at the two men. 'Lord Ingvar never said anything about a delivery.'

'It's for the feast.'

'The feast has already started, Lackwit. You're too late.'

That was undeniably true for the sound of raucous laughter drifted towards them on the quiet air.

'Not our fault,' replied the driver. 'We had to change a wheel.'

His companion nodded. 'That's right.'

'Well, it makes no odds,' said the guard. 'Lord Ingvar doesn't need you or your ale.'

The driver smirked. 'Got enough good cheer, has he?'

'I reckon he has. Anyway, what's that to you?'

'It's nothing to me.'

The guard's lip curled. 'Right, so you can clear off then.'

'Please yourself.' The driver gathered up the reins. 'If they should run out of ale up there, though, you'll let Lord Ingvar know we came?' He paused. 'Only I don't fancy being on the receiving end of his temper, see?'

The guard frowned. Then, as the wagon began to move off, he called out again.

'Wait! Maybe they will need the extra after all.'

The driver sighed. 'Make up your mind, will you? We've got better things to do than sit about here all night.'

'Aye,' growled his companion. 'I'm supposed to be meeting a girl.'

The guard glared at them. 'All right. All right. Bring it through.'

There followed the sounds of heavy footsteps on timber steps and the locking bar being lifted. Then the gate swung slowly open. The wagon drove through and came to a halt on the far side. The driver jerked his head towards the load behind him.

'Where do you want it?'

'Over there, by the storehouse.' The guard looked at his companion. 'Stay here. I'll be back presently.'

The other nodded and turned away. The wagon lurched on again with its lone escort walking alongside. At his command it came to a halt by the building in question. The two men got down.

'Do you want this stuff put inside, or what?' asked the driver.

'No, leave it here. It'll be easier to get at if they need it in the hall.'

'Whatever you say.'

The two men went to the rear of the vehicle and began to lift the barrels down. The guard watched for a while, frowning.

'Come on, you toe rags, hurry it up, will you? I have to get back to my post.'

The driver looked huffy. 'We'd be a sight quicker if you lent a hand.'

His companion nodded. 'Aye. Then I could meet my girl.'

The guard swore softly, but he came to join them nevertheless. As he turned away to reach for a barrel, a large hand closed over his mouth and jerked him backwards. He made a brief muffled choking sound and his eyes widened as Thrand's blade plunged into his side. Asulf leaned closer and murmured confidentially in the dying man's ear, 'You didn't ought to have called him a toe rag.'

Thrand smiled grimly and, catching the body before it could fall, dragged it into the shadow by the wall. Then he pulled the knife free and wiped it carefully on the guard's tunic. Meanwhile, Asulf turned and tapped on the side of the nearest barrel. The lid tilted and was drawn downwards. Wulfgar grabbed the rim of the cask and hauled himself out. Moments later the three of them were joined by Beorn and half-a-dozen others. Wulfgar drew his sword and watched the others follow suit.

'Thrand, Asulf, take the wagon back to the gate and deal with the other guard. Then open for Hermund and the others. The rest of you come with me.'

They moved like ghosts, flitting from shadow to shadow, checking each building that they came to. However, all were in darkness. They saw no one save a few servants scurrying from the kitchen house to the hall from whence the sound of feasting and laughter continued unabated.

'Quiet, isn't it?' murmured Thrand.

'Ingvar thinks us long gone,' replied Wulfgar. 'And while he holds Lady Anwyn and Eyvind he believes that he has a stranglehold on Drakensburgh.'

'I can't wait for the chance to get a stranglehold on Grymar Big Mouth.'

'All in good time. First we must find Eyvind.'

As each successive area of search drew a blank, Wulfgar's concern increased and he began to fear that Ingvar might have

Eyvind in the hall. If so, the chances of getting the boy out alive were minimal. A hand on his arm drew his attention back and he realised that Beorn was pointing towards an area of open ground ahead. Through the deepening twilight he saw the wooden cage. It looked like the kind of structure that might hold a large animal of some sort. At first glance it appeared to be empty, but then he descried the small form in one corner. Hope leapt.

'Eyvind.'

Leaving the others to keep watch, he sprinted across to the cage. The child was asleep, exhausted after the trials of the day. Wulfgar's brow darkened; this was another score to be settled with Ingvar. In the meantime he had to get the boy to safety. However, his heart sank when he reached the door; the latter was fastened with a thick chain and a great iron padlock. Wulfgar tested it, but the hasp didn't budge. He gritted his teeth. It needed no seer to tell him who had the key or that it would require a battle axe to smash that lock. The only other possibility was to try and force the links of the chain, but he had nothing with which to do it. It was a major setback and one he knew he should have envisaged. He sighed, and with a last glance at the sleeping child, returned to his companions to convey the news. They heard him in stony silence. Then Frodi reached for the pouch on his belt and began to rummage through the contents, finally bringing forth the object he had been seeking.

'Don't worry, my lord. We'll have the boy out of there soon enough.'

The others exchanged bemused glances, but no one argued. The two men returned to the cage and, under Wulfgar's curious gaze, his companion turned his attention to the lock. Inserting the thin length of metal into the keyhole, he began to manipulate it. For a little while nothing happened. Then there was an audible click. Frodi grinned and seconds later the hasp was undone. Wulfgar let out the breath he had been holding.

'I owe you one, Frodi,' he murmured.

He sheathed his sword and loosed the chain, dragging the door open. Moments later he was with Eyvind. Feeling the hand over his mouth, the child started awake and began to struggle but, as he recognised the voice in his ear, gradually grew still, his eyes widening in joyful disbelief. Slowly the hand on his mouth withdrew.

'Have no fear, Eyvind.'

'Father?'

'Did I not promise to come back for you?'

'I knew you would.'

Wulfgar held him close, relief flooding his veins. Then he bore Eyvind from the cage and, with Frodi, retraced his steps to join the others. The men grinned to see them.

'Get Eyvind out of here,' said Wulfgar.

The child clung to him. 'I want to stay with you.'

'I'm going to fetch your mother so that we can all go home, but I can't do that unless you go with the others now.' He smiled. 'Will you trust me?'

Eyvind nodded solemnly.

'I'll see you again soon.' With that he handed the boy to Beorn. 'Go.'

It was, thought Anwyn, like being trapped in an evil dream in which she was forced to take part and from which there would be no waking. Her forced renunciation of Wulfgar and the equally forced ceremony that bound her to Ingvar had all the eerie quality of a nightmare. Only thoughts of Eyvind and her unborn child kept her going now. Somehow she must keep both of them safe.

Beside her, Ingvar rose. Then, taking her hand, he led her from the table. All about them his men rose, too, roaring approval. Her heart hammered in her breast. The noisy escort accompanied them to a house nearby. Though smaller than the hall, it was nevertheless the most imposing of the other buildings and she guessed it formed Ingvar's private quarters. He stopped at the door and, no doubt for the benefit of the spectators, took Anwyn in his arms for a lingering kiss. Sickened, she forced herself to endure it. The embrace was greeted with further cheers and lewd jokes. Ingvar took it all in good part and then dismissed his men with the injunction to return to the hall and consume the remaining ale. Then he drew Anwyn with him into the house and shut the door behind them, barring it securely.

'I do not mean to be disturbed tonight.'

Resuming his hold on her arm, he led her through the first room into chamber beyond. The edges of the room remained in shadow, but a small lamp revealed a chair, two wooden chests bound with iron and a large bed covered by a huge bear skin. Ingvar followed her gaze and smiled faintly. Then the catlike eyes returned their attention to her.

Dry-throated she watched him approach, saw him reach for the neck of her gown. She felt a swift downwards jerk and heard fabric part. Ingvar's eyes narrowed and his gaze stopped in the region above her breasts. His brows drew together. Anwyn's hand flew to the ring whose presence she had temporarily forgotten. Ingvar reached out, slid a finger beneath the ribbon, scrutinising the object hanging there. The gold-brown eyes locked with hers and he tutted softly.

'You disappoint me, Anwyn.'

His hand closed round the ring. The other unsheathed the dagger at his side. The cold edge came to rest against her skin. Anwyn shut her eyes, heart thumping so hard she felt sure he must hear it. Would he hurt her? Maim her, perhaps? It seemed that wasn't his intention. The ribbon parted and she felt him pull it free. Risking a glance, she was in time to see him fling the ring aside. It hit the wall and bounced off to land in the rushes across the room. Ingvar's gaze locked with hers once more.

'Don't test me again.'

Her mouth dried. 'Forgive me, lord.'

'That will depend on how well you please me.' He re-sheathed the blade while his gaze travelled the length of her and back. Her belly was still flat; he would not guess her secret yet. Even so her flesh crawled. Without taking his eyes off her, he removed his upper garments. Then he stepped closer and reached down to the fastenings of his breeches where a bulging erection was already evident.

'Kneel, Anwyn.'

As the implication dawned she shook her head, sickened. 'No, please...'

'If you disobey me, I will hand your son over to Grymar tomorrow, and you shall watch while he is thrashed.'

'I think not,' said a voice from across the room.

He swore and spun round to see the tall figure standing in the doorway, sword in hand.

Anwyn's heart missed a beat. 'Wulfgar?' The realisation was followed with relief and joy so intense she felt suddenly faint.

'Aye, my sweet, I'm here.'

'You're a bigger fool than I took you for,' Ingvar sneered. 'You have no business here now.'

'I have come to collect what is mine.'

'Lady Anwyn is no longer yours, Viking. She has renounced you and taken me for her husband.'

Wulfgar's eyes glinted. 'Did you gain her consent for that by the same means I heard you use just now?'

Anwyn's eyes widened. How long had he been there? How much had he heard and seen? Hot colour dyed her neck and face as joy was replaced by an overpowering sense of shame. Hurriedly she drew the edges of the torn gown across her breasts.

'I shall pleasure her all night before your eyes,' taunted Ingvar, 'and then I shall kill you—slowly.'

'Again, I think not.'

Ingvar bent and retrieved his sword, drawing it free of the scabbard. 'Let us make a test of that.'

The two men closed and the blades clashed. Anwyn gasped and scrambled away across the bed, watching in horrified fascination. Then, from somewhere outside, the quiet was split by running feet, a deafening roar of voices and clashing swords.

'I did not return alone,' said Wulfgar.

Ingvar glared and renewed the attack, driving him back a couple of paces and forcing him to parry swiftly. Wulfgar was quick to recover and returned him blow for blow. The noise without intensified, too, the clash of metal interspersed with shouts and curses and the cries of injured men. Ingvar heard it with grim satisfaction.

'You have just sentenced the boy to death.' Hearing Anwyn's stifled cry he smiled. 'Too bad.'

'The boy is quite safe,' replied Wulfgar. 'I freed him a while ago.'

As fast as they had plummeted, Anwyn's spirits rose. Ingvar glowered.

'You lie. Only I have a key to his prison.'

'Ah, his prison. That's something else I wanted to discuss.'

Wulfgar's sword thrust under Ingvar's guard and slashed across his ribs. Ingvar jumped backwards with a snarl, clapping a hand to his side. Blood dripped through his fingers.

'I take his maltreatment much amiss,' continued Wulfgar. 'I also take it much amiss that you should lay hands upon my wife.'

The sword caught Ingvar across the arm. Blood flowed from the cut. Ingvar's eyes blazed with fury and hatred.

'She belongs to me now.'

He flung himself at his foe, pressing him hard, but each time his blade was turned.

'Not only laid hands on her,' Wulfgar continued, 'but suffered her to endure public humiliation and private shame.'

Ingvar's lip curled. 'The shame is yours, Viking. If you

cannot protect a woman, then you shouldn't be surprised if another looks upon her nakedness.'

Wulfgar's gaze became as cold as frosted steel. 'For that alone I will cut out your heart and feed it to the crows.'

Ingvar sensed the tide turning against him and his swordplay grew wilder and more desperate. Darting a glance around, he grabbed a stool and flung it. Wulfgar ducked and the missile sailed past, crashing harmlessly against the wall. Ingvar threw himself sideways and dived across the bed towards Anwyn. With a shriek she turned to flee, only to be brought up short as an arm locked around her neck. The point of his sword checked Wulfgar's furious advance.

'One step more, Viking, and she dies.'

Wulfgar stopped in his tracks. 'Let her go, Ingvar.'

'Did I not tell you she was mine?'

'I will never be yours,' Anwyn ground out.

'We'll see.' Ingvar looked across at Wulfgar. 'Throw down the sword.' Seeing him hesitate, he lifted his own blade to his captive's throat. 'I said throw it down.'

In impotent wrath Wulfgar obeyed. 'This will gain you nothing.'

Ingvar edged towards the door, dragging Anwyn with him. A test of his hold disabused her of the thought that it might weaken. He smiled sardonically and tightened his grip until she gasped.

'I'll hurt you if I must, Anwyn.'

Wulfgar's eyes blazed fury. 'Let her go, coward.'

Anwyn drew a breath and felt Ingvar's hold slacken a little. Without warning she bent her head and sank her teeth into his arm. She heard him swear. His hold loosened and she tore free. Wulfgar dived for the fallen sword, grabbed the hilt and swung the blade at Ingvar's leg. With the full force of his arm behind it the blow would have severed the limb. As it was Ingvar yelled and staggered, blood flowing from the wound in his calf. Wulfgar sprang to his feet and came on, driving his enemy remorselessly back. Forced into a corner, Ingvar had nowhere to go. His face registered fear and he cast aside his weapon.

'I yield. Don't kill me!'

Wulfgar's lip curled in contempt. 'The world will be well rid of you, filth.' He lifted his sword.

'Wulfgar, no!' Anwyn's voice rang out.

Wulfgar checked, the point of his blade hovering over Ingvar's throat. 'What madness is this, Anwyn?'

'He has yielded, Wulfgar. You cannot cut him down. If you do, then you are no better than he is.'

'After what he has done he can expect no mercy.'

'And yet mercy may still be shown.'

'So that the snake can recover and attack again?'

'No. He must swear to leave and never return.'

'You think he will honour such a bargain?'

'I will honour it,' said Ingvar. 'I swear it.' Beads of sweat trickled down his face and he grimaced in pain.

Wulfgar regarded him in disgust, but he lowered the sword a fraction. 'Have your worthless life then, cur, but if ever I see your face again that hour is your last.'

Ingvar nodded and then looked across at Anwyn. 'You are merciful, my lady. I shall not forget it.'

Wulfgar lowered the sword. 'Get out.'

He watched as Ingvar limped towards the door. He paused briefly on the threshold and then moved on towards the far door. Wulfgar turned away and looked at Anwyn. She managed a tremulous smile, her heart full.

'Thank you.'

He sighed. 'You are a bad influence, my sweet.'

'Was it true what you said before? Is Eyvind safe?'

'He is safe.'

Some of the tension went out of her. 'I have been in terror of what might happen.'

'He is unharmed and eager to see you again.'

'As I am to see him. From the bottom of my heart I—' She broke off with a scream. 'Wulfgar, look out!'

He whipped round, lifting his sword instinctively. He had a swift impression of a raised dagger, a snarling face and then a sensation of weight on his arm. Carried by the momentum of his attack Ingvar was unable to check in time to avoid the weapon aimed at his chest. The point plunged deep. He gasped and froze. Wulfgar tugged free his blade and thrust again. Ingvar's snarl became an expression of astonishment and the dagger slipped from his grasp. Then he collapsed beside it in a pool of blood.

For a moment Wulfgar surveyed him in silence, breathing hard. Then he turned to look at Anwyn. The blue eyes smouldered. She swallowed convulsively.

'Wulfgar, forgive me. I had no idea he would—'

There was no time for more because he was across the room in three strides and she was forcibly seized, crushed against him in a fierce embrace. Then his mouth came down over hers, hot, searing, avid. Far from resenting this treatment, she returned the kiss in like manner, oblivious to everything else. For some time they remained thus before eventually he drew back a little to look into her face.

'It is I who should apologise, Anwyn. I've been such an almighty fool, unable to see what was right in front of me.' He paused. 'I love you more than my life. It wasn't until I thought I had lost you that I realised how much.'

A lump formed in her throat and she was unable to speak. Wulfgar sighed.

'I'm not surprised that you should doubt it after the way I've behaved, but I'd gladly spend the rest of my life making it up to you if I thought there was the slightest chance you might forgive—'

The sentence was cut short by a kiss, a gentle and lingering embrace that set his heart thumping and whose implications filled him with painful hope.

'I love you, Wulfgar. I always have.'

'Then you wouldn't mind if I stayed?'

'Mind? It's what I always dreamed of but…Wulfgar, are you sure?'

'I was never more sure of anything in my life.' He drew her to his breast. 'The gods have given me a second chance and I don't mean to throw it away.'

'The gods have given us rather more than that,' she replied.

He glanced down at her. 'How so, my love?'

She took a deep breath. 'In a few months from now there's going to be another addition to the family.'

It took a moment or two before the import of her words sank in. Then he stared at her dumbfounded. 'A child?'

'Our child.'

A slow grin spread across his face. 'That's marvellous!'

'You don't mind?'

'It's wonderful news. Why would I mind?'

'What you said before…about not wanting more sons…I thought maybe the news might not be welcome.'

Wulfgar froze. He had almost forgotten that conversation, but now it returned with terrible clarity and, for the first time, he understood its significance.

'You knew back then.'

'Suspected only.'

'And I let you think that I had no interest in such things.' He was appalled. 'I only said it because I thought you didn't want more children. The circumstances were complicated enough— thanks largely to my high-handedness—and I felt I had no right to make you feel guilty over the matter.' He paused. 'Besides, I believed…you said you had taken precautions.'

'With Torstein. Never with you.'

His throat tightened. 'Then the thought of bearing my sons is not repugnant to you?'

'It never was, Wulfgar.'

The knowledge of what he had so nearly lost was chilling. 'I've been a blind fool. Can you ever—?'

She silenced him with a finger to his lips. 'I love you. I will always love you, but I don't want to try to hold you here if it is your will to be gone. You said from the start that you would not stay for ever.'

'I seem to recall that I said a lot of stupid things back then.' He shook his head. 'The words of a man so fearful of loving that he dared not risk his heart.' He hesitated. 'But my heart is yours, Anwyn—if you want it.'

'Can you doubt it?'

'No, it was my own steadfastness that was in doubt.'

'You have been steadfast, my lord. No man more.'

'I mean to be. You are my home now and I will not leave you again.'

Her heart gave a painful lurch. She took another deep breath, dreading to speak what was on her mind, yet knowing she must. 'I would not have you leave, but you have your men to consider, Wulfgar.'

'They will manage well enough under Hermund's command and, if they ever tire of adventuring, there will always be a place for them at Drakensburgh.'

Anwyn regarded him anxiously. 'Are you quite sure about this?'

'I was never more certain of anything.' He drew her closer. 'I want a future, Anwyn, and I want to share it with you.'

'But what about Rollo?'

'Rollo wants good fighting men and he's going to get them.' He grinned. 'All but one, that is. I can't see him losing any sleep over that.'

They were rudely interrupted by shouting and then the heavy thud of axes against the wooden door without. Wulfgar listened a moment and sighed.

'My men, I imagine.' Reluctantly he relinquished his hold on her. 'I'd better let them know we're here.'

He went into the next room and shouted to the men outside the door. The axe blows ceased. Then he lifted the bar and opened the door. Hermund and half-a-dozen others stepped into the room, looking around.

'Everything all right, my lord?'

Wulfgar grinned. 'Aye, all is well.'

'And Lady Anwyn?'

'Safe.'

'The gods be thanked.' Hermund paused. 'Where's Ingvar?'

'Dead.'

'I'm glad to hear it.'

His companions voiced their agreement.

'What's happened in my absence?' asked Wulfgar.

'Pretty much what we'd planned, my lord. Almost all of the scum were in the hall like we hoped, and most of them half-drunk to boot. By the time they realised what was happening we were on them. To be honest it wasn't much of a fight. Still, you can't have everything.' He glanced over his shoulder at the few remaining combatants outside. 'We're mopping up the remnants now.'

As he finished speaking some more of the *Sea Wolf*'s crew hove into sight. Among them were Asulf and Thrand, the latter carrying a battered helmet on the point of his spear. Wulfgar glanced at it and then at the bearer's grinning face.

'All right, I'm going to ask.'

Thrand glanced up at his prize and beamed. 'I found Grymar Big Mouth.'

Hermund chuckled softly. 'Good lad.'

'It was he who slew Ina,' Thrand continued. 'The boy told us.'

Wulfgar nodded, aware of intense inner satisfaction. 'Then Ina is justly avenged.'

'Most mightily, lord,' said Asulf. 'We've taken no prisoners.'

'And the servants?'

'We let them go, lord, as you commanded. They didn't need

telling twice, either. Seemed only too glad to get out of the place.'

'That's understandable.'

Thrand nodded. 'We liberated Ingvar's stores of grain, too, while we were at it.' He grinned. 'Oddly enough Grymar argued with us over that, but I was able to persuade him in the end. Now there's enough to keep Drakensburgh fed until harvest and beyond.'

'Excellent. Anything else of value?'

'Aye, plenty,' said Thrand. 'The men have liberated that as well.'

'And I declare Beranhold lands annexed to Drakensburgh,' replied Wulfgar. 'All that remains now is to burn this rats' nest to the ground.'

Hermund looked around at his companions. 'You heard him. Get to it.'

Nothing loath, they hurried off to do his bidding. For a moment Wulfgar watched them go. Then he returned to the inner chamber where Anwyn waited.

'Did you hear all that?'

She nodded. 'I am glad. The people hereabouts will sleep easier at night knowing that this robber crew can no longer prey upon their homes and livelihoods.'

'We will rebuild what they have destroyed.' He sighed. 'If I had not left, it mightn't have happened in the first place.'

'If I had not interfered, you would have dealt with the threat long since,' she sighed. 'Forgive me, Wulfgar.'

'You only did what you thought right at the time.'

'I let my heart rule my head.'

'And I once did just the opposite.' He smiled wryly. 'It was a costly mistake, but I shall not repeat it.'

The smell of smoke drifted in through the open doorway. Wulfgar glanced across the compound.

'My men have taken me at my word. We must go.' He

reached out a hand to lead her from the room, but Anwyn checked.

'Wait. There's something else.'

She ran back to the inner chamber. Wulfgar followed, bemused, pausing in the doorway to watch as she scanned the rushes on the floor. Presently he saw her smile and, following her gaze, detected the soft gleam of metal. Anwyn bent down to retrieve it.

'What is it, love?' he asked.

'Something Ingvar threw away.'

She extended her hand and he saw the ring on her open palm. One glance served to identify it and his eyes narrowed. Then he looked at Anwyn. She met his gaze steadily.

'Will you put it back where it belongs, Wulfgar?'

He drew off Ingvar's ring and slid the original onto her finger once more. Then he glanced contemptuously at the body and tossed the unwanted ring across the room to join it. Anwyn shuddered and turned away. Wulfgar squeezed her hand gently.

'It's over, love. He can't hurt you now.'

'He cannot hurt anyone now,' she replied, 'though that is no thanks to me.'

'Forget him. We have more important things to think about.'

'I want to see my son, Wulfgar. I want to be sure he's really safe.'

'He's safe.' Wulfgar grinned. 'Thanks to Frodi. He was the one who picked the lock. Without him I'd have been in real trouble.'

He led her to the outer entrance. Seeing the heavy wooden plank beside it, she threw him a quizzical glance.

'Ingvar barred the door after he brought me here. How did you get in?'

'I was here before you,' he replied. 'Fortunately the shadows in the corners are deep and Ingvar too preoccupied to notice.'

Anwyn's cheeks burned. 'You heard everything then?'

'Aye, I did. It makes killing him even more satisfying.'

They stepped outside. The smell of burning was much stronger now and several buildings were already well alight. Wulfgar grasped her hand.

'Come.'

Wulfgar skirted the battle zone and led her towards the main gate, now standing wide. A group of men stood watching their approach, their faces lit by the flames from the fortress.

'Osric?' she murmured. 'What on earth is he doing here?'

'He arrived in time to play a part in your deliverance,' replied Wulfgar.

'He did?'

Before they could say more her brother strode forwards. For a second or two he surveyed her keenly, his expression cool.

'I am glad to see you safe, Sister, though, frankly, it was your own wilful folly that brought you so close to disaster. Had it not been for Lord Wulfgar…'

She held her temper. 'I know what I owe to Lord Wulfgar.'

'No doubt you do.'

'But I still don't understand how you came to be here in the first place.'

'I told you I'd be back, Anwyn. I am come to escort you into the north country.'

Her eyes glittered. 'Would this be connected with the unknown earl and the splendid match you proposed on your last visit?'

He reddened a little. 'Someone must look to your interests if you will not.'

'My interests or yours?'

'It amounts to the same thing. I will not permit you to throw away this wonderful chance.' He paused. 'If you will not come willingly I regret that I shall have to remove you by force.'

She shot a swift glance at Wulfgar but his expression was indicative only of polite interest. However, the look in his eye was more eloquent, like the hand idly resting on the hilt of his dagger. Quelling a sudden urge to laugh she turned back to her brother.

'By force?'

'He brought an army with him,' said Wulfgar in a confidential tone. 'There must be at least a hundred men.'

Osric eyed him askance. 'Just so.'

'It was quite unnecessary, Brother,' said Anwyn. 'I have thought on your words often since last we met, and have come to the conclusion that you were absolutely right.'

He regarded her with blank astonishment for a moment; then began to look rather more mollified. 'I am glad you are come to your senses at last, Anwyn.'

She sighed. 'I confess it took a while but, on mature reflection, I saw that marriage to an earl was the only course open to me.'

'I told you so.'

'So you did, and I hope you can forgive me for my earlier failure to listen to your advice.'

'Well, I was never one to bear a grudge, as you know. In truth, this is most pleasing to hear, Sister.'

'I was so stricken with remorse after your departure that I vowed there and then to put the matter right.'

'I don't follow.'

'I found an earl and married him at once.'

His eyes narrowed. 'What trickery is this, Anwyn? What earl?'

'The Earl of Drakensburgh and Beranhold.' She smiled and slipped her arm through Wulfgar's. 'But I believe you have already met.'

For a moment Osric could only stare at her in dumbfounded silence. Then he turned his attention to Wulfgar and his expression grew thunderous. 'You mean this Viking adventurer is your husband?'

The Viking's gaze became several degrees cooler but he spoke quietly enough. 'I am Wulfgar, son of Wulfrum Ragnarsson, and descended from an ancient and noble line of Danish earls. My family has wealth and rich estates enough to surpass any lordling in this land.' His gaze locked with Osric's. 'And swords to back his claims if need be.'

There followed a pregnant silence in which his men drew closer around them. Then Osric cleared his throat. 'The, um... noble name of Ragnarsson is, of course, known to me.'

'It is known to many, and with good reason,' replied Wulfgar. 'And you, Lord Osric, are like to hear more of it.' He paused. 'I would prefer it to be in the context of amity.'

'I intended no disrespect, my lord. Of course your family's wealth and status are beyond dispute. My former exclamation was merely...surprise at learning of my sister's unexpected change of fortune.'

Anwyn smiled up at Wulfgar. 'Indeed, I am the most fortunate of women.'

Her brother nodded. 'I can see that now.'

'I hope so,' Wulfgar said evenly, 'because I hold this lady dear and will not relinquish her to any man.'

Osric's expression registered concern. 'Had I known before how the matter stood, my lord, I should never have suggested any such thing. I trust you do not misinterpret my motives.'

'Oh, no. I understand those perfectly.'

'Truly, I am relieved. I would never wish to provoke family discord.'

Wulfgar glanced at Anwyn. 'Our hearts are lighter for knowing that.'

'My men and I shall leave on the morrow,' Osric continued, 'but if you would be so kind as to offer shelter this night...'

'To have you stay would make our joy complete.'

'You are generous, my lord.'

'Not at all.' Wulfgar favoured his brother-in-law with a lupine grin. 'After all, I know it's going to be a long time before we see you again.'

With that he reclaimed his wife's hand and led her away.

Anwyn glanced up at him and he heard a gurgle of laughter. It drew a wry answering smile.

'Blood and sand! I was never more tempted to fillet a man.'

'It's bad form to slay your relatives, Wulfgar.'

'More's the pity.' He shrugged. 'On the plus side, my own family have never appeared in a more advantageous light.'

They continued on through the gateway. As they emerged a small figure detached itself from the waiting group outside and hurtled towards them.

'Mother!'

Anwyn opened her arms to receive her son, hugging him tightly, unable to speak for the lump in her throat. Not knowing whether to laugh or cry, she did both. Wulfgar looked on, his heart full. This time the spinners of fate had been kind. This time he had been given a second chance and he had no intention of throwing it away. The *Sea Wolf* would sail again soon and her crew would join Rollo to seek new adventures and gather loot elsewhere. However, they would do it without him. He'd had his fill of fighting other men's wars. If he fought in future it would be to protect his own. He smiled to himself. Then he bent down and lifted Eyvind, settling the child into the crook of one arm. The other went around his wife, holding her close.

'Come,' he said. 'We're going home.'

Epilogue

⚫⚭⚭⚭⚭⚭⚭⚭⚫

Twelve months later

'Look! They're coming!' From his vantage point on Wulfgar's shoulders Eyvind pointed to the approaching riders.

'So they are.' Wulfgar lifted him down. 'Run and tell Rorik to open the gate.'

'Yes, Father.'

As Eyvind raced off Anwyn took a last swift glance at her gown, smoothing a tiny wrinkle from the blue fabric. The man beside her smiled.

'You look wonderful.'

In truth, she had taken a lot of time and care over her appearance, wanting to do honour to the arriving guests. Even so, she could not help feeling a little nervous.

So much would depend on this meeting and she wanted to be a credit to Wulfgar. Sensing something of her apprehension, he took her hand and squeezed it gently.

'It will all be well. You'll see.'

'I pray it will.'

'Come,' he said.

She took a deep breath and followed him down the steps

from the rampart as the riders passed through the open gateway. She watched as the foremost of them dismounted and moments later he and Wulfgar were locked in a hearty hug. Then the stranger glanced over Wulfgar's shoulder and piercing blue eyes met her gaze.

For a moment she experienced the uncanny sensation of looking at an older version of Wulfgar. The two men were startlingly alike. Like Wulfgar, the newcomer had undeniable presence, but withal he possessed the gravitas that only age and experience could give.

'You must be Anwyn,' he said.

'Earl Wulfrum,' she replied. 'I bid you welcome.'

He smiled and bent to kiss her cheek. 'I always knew my son had good taste, but it seems to have got even better over the years.'

Under that blue gaze Anwyn felt herself blush. The thought occurred that he, too, must have been dangerously attractive in his youth—attractive enough to win the heart of his captive Saxon bride.

Lady Elgiva embraced her son and then came to join them. Advancing years could not hide the vintage beauty she had once been, though they had added silver strands to the gold of her hair. Stunning amber eyes scrutinised Anwyn now from head to toe, then warmed in a smile.

'My husband is right,' she observed.

Wulfgar grinned. 'I take after him in that respect.'

'Well, I'm glad I passed on a grain of good sense at least,' replied Wulfrum. Then his gaze fell on the child who had returned to stand beside Anwyn. 'And who is this?'

Wulfgar laid a gentle hand on the boy's shoulder. 'My stepson, Eyvind.'

'A fine boy. How old are you, Eyvind?'

'Six years and a quarter, my lord.'

Wulfrum's lips twitched. 'Is it so? Have you begun your training yet?'

'Yes, my lord.'

'Then later you shall show me what you have learned.'

Eyvind reddened with pleasure. Anwyn's heart swelled. It was a kind attention that she had not expected.

'Shall we go in?' she suggested. 'You must be tired after your journey.'

'Not so tired that I would wait longer to see my newest grandchild,' said Elgiva.

'Grandchildren,' corrected Wulfgar. Then, as she stared at him, he added, 'Twins.'

'But the messenger said…'

'The messenger told the truth as he knew it. The second baby was born after he'd left. It took us all unawares. Rather than send another man after him, we decided to let the rest come as a surprise.'

Wulfrum laughed. 'Well, by all the gods! Twins, you say?'

'A boy and a girl—Wulfhere and Asta.'

'That's wonderful,' said Elgiva. Then she looked at Anwyn. 'Though no doubt it was hard for you, my dear.'

'Their births were much easier than my first.'

'I'm glad to hear it.' She smiled. 'By and by we shall sit apart and talk.'

Seeing the kindness in her expression, Anwyn's nervousness began to diminish. 'I would like that, my lady.'

Wulfgar gestured towards the hall. 'Let us go in, then.'

The babies had been left in Jodis's care and were currently lying on a rug in front of the fire. They stared at the visitors in blue-eyed wonder. Within moments they were carefully gathered up and became the centre of fawning attention.

'See what a grip the child has!' said Wulfrum as Wulfhere's tiny fist closed round his little finger. 'He's going to be a fine warrior one day and no mistake.'

'And his sister will be a beauty,' said Elgiva. 'Just like her mother.'

Anwyn smiled. 'I hope she won't inherit her mother's faults.'

'Don't worry, my dear. She'll be quite capable of developing her own.' With that, Elgiva began to reminisce about the days when her own children had been young.

Wulfgar smiled and, heart full, let the conversation drift over him, watching the scene with quiet pride. Once, standing amid the ashes of his former life, he had thought himself accursed; now all that he believed lost had been restored in full measure. He had been given a second chance and he meant to seize it: to make Drakensburgh thrive; to watch his children grow up. More than all of that, he had been given a chance to love again. In truth, the gods had been kind. They would not regret such generosity for he had learned how to value their gifts.

* * * * *

HISTORICAL

Where Love is Timeless™

HARLEQUIN® HISTORICAL

COMING NEXT MONTH
AVAILABLE MARCH 27, 2012

A COWBOY WORTH CLAIMING
The Worths of Red Ridge
Charlene Sands
(Western)

MARRIED TO A STRANGER
Danger & Desire
Louise Allen
(Regency)

LADY DRUSILLA'S ROAD TO RUIN
Ladies in Disgrace
Christine Merrill
**Three delectably disgraceful ladies,
breaking every one of society's rules,
each in need of a rake to tame them!**
(Regency)

**TALL, DARK AND
DISREPUTABLE**
Deb Marlowe
(Regency)

You can find more information on upcoming Harlequin®
titles, free excerpts and more at www.Harlequin.com.

HHCNM0312

REQUEST YOUR FREE BOOKS!

 HARLEQUIN® HISTORICAL:
Where love is timeless

2 FREE NOVELS PLUS 2 **FREE GIFTS!**

Taft Bowman knew he'd ruined any chance he'd had
for happiness with Laura Pendleton when he drove her
away years ago...and into the arms of another man,
thousands of miles away. Now she was back, a widow
with two small children...and despite himself, he was
starting to believe in second chances.

Harlequin Special® Edition® presents a new installment
in USA TODAY *bestselling author*
RaeAnne Thayne's miniseries,
THE COWBOYS OF COLD CREEK.

Enjoy a sneak peek of
A COLD CREEK REUNION

Available April 2012 from Harlequin® Special Edition®

A younger woman stood there, and from this distance he
had only a strange impression, as though she was somehow standing on an island of calm amid the chaos of the
scene, the flashing lights of the emergency vehicles, shouts
between his crew members, the excited buzz of the crowd.

And then the woman turned and he just about tripped
over a snaking fire hose somebody shouldn't have left
there.

Laura.

He froze, and for the first time in fifteen years as a fire-
fighter, he forgot about the incident, his mission, just what
the hell he was doing here.

Laura.

Ten years. He hadn't seen her in all that time, since
the week before their wedding when she had given him
back his ring and left town. Not just town. She had left the
whole damn country, as if she couldn't run far enough to

get away from him.

Some part of him desperately wanted to think he had made some kind of mistake. It couldn't be her. That was just some other slender woman with a long sweep of honey-blond hair and big, blue, unforgettable eyes. But no. It was definitely Laura. Sweet and lovely.

Not his.

He was going to have to go over there and talk to her. He didn't want to. He wanted to stand there and pretend he hadn't seen her. But he was the fire chief. He couldn't hide out just because he had a painful history with the daughter of the property owner.

Sometimes he hated his job.

Will Taft and Laura be able to make the years recede...or is the gulf between them too broad to ever cross?

Find out in
A COLD CREEK REUNION
Available April 2012 from Harlequin® Special Edition®
wherever books are sold.

Celebrate the 30th anniversary
of Harlequin® Special Edition® with a bonus story
included in each Special Edition® book in April!